TAKING THE BIT

"How long has it been since someone kissed you?" he asked.

Her eyes widened. "A half hour at the most. You just kissed me right after the ceremony, remember?"

"That wasn't a kiss. That was a . . . well, I don't know what that was. How long has it been since you've had a real kiss?"

"I can't remember exactly, but I'm sure it hasn't been that long." When he gave her a hard look, her chin came up a notch. "Men have kissed me, all right? Dozens of times."

"Dozens?"

"Dozens!"

She was lying, but he didn't know to what extent. "Then you won't mind if I add one more."

She opened her mouth, most likely to protest, when he lowered his head and brushed his lips across hers. Again, it was no more than a borderline peck. Well, maybe it had some punch to it, probably because her mouth had been open. Her breath was warm, her lips soft. And maybe it had punch because she'd made a tiny noise like a sigh.

She looked up at him and swallowed hard. "All right, then. Now I can say I've been kissed dozens of times, plus one."

He shook his head. "No, you can't say that at all. When I've really kissed you, *then* you can say it." He caught on to a handful of flame-red hair and hauled her to him.

Saddled

Delores Fossen

LOVE SPELL ◆ NEW YORK CITY

A LOVE SPELL BOOK®

June 2001

Published by

Dorchester Publishing Co., Inc.
276 Fifth Avenue
New York, NY 10001

Cover art by John Ennis.
www.ennisart.com

ISBN 0-505-52430-9

The name "Love Spell" and its logo are trademarks of Dorchester Publishing Co., Inc.

Printed in the United States of America.

Visit us on the web at www.dorchesterpub.com.

*To my friend and critique partner, Deborah Gafford,
for her daily dose of hey-it'll-happen.*

*And to my editor, Chris Keeslar,
for not making a liar out of her.*

Thanks for the encouragement and support.

Saddled

Chapter One

Abbie Donegan went rail-stiff at the sound of the revolver being cocked. It was probably a Smith & Wesson Schofield .45, but she didn't even get a glimpse of it before the cold, hard gunmetal shoved against her right temple.

"Mind telling me what you're doing?" the gun-pointing man growled.

Hellfire. This wasn't the way she'd planned it at all, and she wasn't exactly in a position to fight back. She was only halfway through the window, her white-gloved hands gripping onto the ledge and her feet dangling. So much for her grand idea. This man would probably shoot her before she could even get the rest of herself inside the saloon.

"Well? Mind telling me what you're doing?" he repeated.

9

"Isn't it obvious? I'm trying to sneak in here without anybody noticing me."

"Stupid."

"Yes, I can see that. *Now.*" The Buffalo Clover Saloon was built on the side of a hill and, because of the steep slope, this particular window was about four feet off the ground. It wasn't ideal for an intended break-in, but she hadn't exactly had a choice.

"I looked in the window and saw you," Abbie said as if that clarified everything. "Will you at least move your gun so I can come inside?"

Neither he, his hand, nor his Smith & Wesson budged an inch. "This is no place for a lady. There's nothing for you here."

Oh, yes, there was. And he was standing in front of her with a gun pointed to her head. Rio McCaine was plenty of something.

Using her elbows, she levered herself higher so she could get her foot onto the sill. She was no doubt showing a liberal amount of ankle, but there was nothing she could do about it. Besides, if she were a betting woman—and she occasionally was—then she would wager Mr. McCaine had seen plenty of women's ankles and a fair amount of everything above them. His sensibilities weren't likely to be shocked over a little female foot flesh.

Abbie made a few unladylike grunts and added a muffled curse that she hoped he didn't hear. The silk fabric on her sleeve tore. It had been expensive, she vaguely recalled. Caught on a raised nail head probably. Again, there was nothing she could do about it. Besides, expensive fabric was replaceable. Rio McCaine wasn't. She finally had him alone and couldn't let him get away.

"You might lend me a hand," she suggested dryly.

"You seem to be doing well enough on your own." He

10

did remove the gun from her head, though, leaned back, and took a lazy puff off his cheroot.

Her knee hit the sill, off-balancing her, and she tumbled into a heap of sky-blue silk and flounced petticoats. The thick pad of fabric helped break her fall, but her bottom made a noisy thump when she crashed to the bare wood floor. She also landed squarely in front of McCaine, his feet between her widespread legs. The toe of his right boot was aligned perfectly with the center seam of her drawers and less than an inch away from touching her. . . .

She looked up, and blinked.

He looked down and grinned. It wasn't an amused grin either. Nor was the look in his suddenly dark eyes. And he had his attention aimed right at her drawers' seam. Or else what was directly behind it.

"You'd better hope I don't get a sudden urge to scratch my toe," he drawled.

Abbie hurriedly tried to right herself. Smoothing down the mounds of fabric, she managed to get to her feet, hoping she looked the pillar of propriety. She seriously doubted that she did, but then she'd never looked proper. All in all, she hadn't considered that a bad thing. Until now, that is. She might need a healthy dose of propriety to get through this.

Thank God he hadn't scratched his toe.

Propriety wouldn't stand a chance against that kind of itch.

"Good evening, Mr. McCaine. Pleased to make your acquaintance." She calmly blew at an escaped copper curl sagging on her forehead and stuck her hand out for him to shake. "Let me introduce myself. I'm Abilene Donegan, but please call me Abbie. I'm visiting my aunt and uncle, Henry and Dorrie Marsh, whom I believe you know. They live here in Fall Creek."

"Miss Donegan." Rio tipped his head in a way that

made a mockery of the otherwise gentlemanly salutation. What he didn't do was shake her hand. "Let me guess. This your first attempt to break into a saloon?"

Abbie shrugged and dropped her hand back to her side. "Most certainly."

A saloon, Rio called it. Well, at least he used the more delicate word. The Buffalo Clover was really a house of ill repute where certain women plied their licentious trade. After watching the place for several hours, Abbie figured out it had earned its reputation because it catered to everyone—including outlaws, half-breeds, and the vaqueros who worked on the nearby ranches. Kitty May O'Reilly, proprietor and resident madame, apparently had a policy of never turning anyone away.

"Well?" Rio asked. "Are you going to tell me why you crawled through a bedroom window of a saloon in the middle of the night?"

Yes, she would, but she needed time to catch her breath. Not easy to do. Like the night air, the room was overly warm and humid. It reeked of cheroot smoke, whiskey, sweat, and flowery perfume. It made her stomach queasy.

The man made her stomach queasy a little, too.

He looked fierce and slightly dangerous. Actually, he looked a lot dangerous. Storm black hair fell wildly against his neck. He had high angled cheekbones, a full mouth, piercing blue eyes . . . not a true blue, either. Winchester blue. The color of her favorite gun.

His Comanche heritage was right there, all over his face. She smiled politely, hoping to soothe those savage features, but her smile didn't soothe a thing. He stared at her mouth a moment, then let his ripe gaze travel the length of her body. By the time his eyes got to her feet, she felt as if he'd undressed her. Twice.

"Abbie." Again, he laced her name with mockery. He

placed his revolver on the night table and stared at her. "You really shouldn't be here."

The door creaked open, and a woman with frizzy black hair scurried into the room. It took Abbie only a glance to know this was one of the Buffalo Clover's employees—employee being a very generous term indeed. The woman wore an indecently cut corset, red, with the bodice so plunged that her rouged nipples peeked over the top. Her thin, snug pantalets left absolutely nothing to the imagination. Abbie wondered where a woman could purchase such garments.

Not that she would want them for herself, naturally.

But she did like that shade of red. . . .

"Sorry, I'm late, sugar. That jackleg preacher from Eagle Pass kept me a while." The last word died on the woman's cherry-painted mouth as she caught sight of Abbie. "Hey, what's she doin' here?"

Rio only shrugged indifferently. "I don't know. She climbed through the window. Evening, Carlotta."

The woman's hands went to her fleshy hips, and she disapprovingly eyed Abbie. She aimed her angry comments, however, at Rio. "I don't go in for that kind of thing with outsiders. If you wanted two women, you shoulda let Kitty know right from the get-go, and I'da brought in Pearl."

Abbie glanced at Rio to see if he intended to say anything. He simply grinned around the cheroot dangling out of his mouth. Abbie frowned. "Mr. McCaine, I realize this is an improper subject for us to discuss, but it's obvious you intend to. . . ." Now, how could she put this? Best not to say anything crude. "It's obvious you intend to know this woman in the Biblical sense. Have you considered the diseases you could come down with—"

"Hey!" the woman protested. "Who do you think you are, sayin' I got diseases? I ain't got no diseases. Besides even if I did, Rio couldn't catch nothin' 'cause he don't want me to do it that way. He only wants me to use my mou—"

"Carlotta," Rio quickly interrupted. "Would you mind waiting outside just a minute?"

The woman stiffened, and her mouth twisted into a tight bud. "If you want that piece of fluff, then I'll be more than happy to let you have her."

"I don't want her."

But the glance he slid in Abbie's direction suggested otherwise. Hmmm. She might not have a lot of experience in this area, but she wasn't so green that she couldn't recognize what was going on behind those Winchester blue eyes. Thank goodness she'd brought along the advertisement for preventatives. She would apparently need it.

Rio placed his hand on Carlotta's back and gently got her moving toward the door. "Just wait outside for a minute or two. I won't be long."

"You better not be." With narrowed cat eyes and without taking her venomous gaze off Abbie, the woman stomped into the hall and slammed the door.

Rio immediately latched onto Abbie's arm. "Do you want to leave the way you came or through the front door?"

"I don't plan to leave at all, sir. I have business I need to discuss with you, and this was the only time I've been able to catch you alone."

"Well now, I wasn't exactly alone, was I?"

Her gaze slipped toward the door and then eased back to him. "No, I suppose not. Just what did Carlotta mean when she said you don't do it *that* way? That you only wanted her to use her—"

His fingers tightened on her arm. "I should tell you, you know. I should describe it in complete detail and watch your lily-white face turn to flame. But I won't. All I want is you out of here so I can enjoy my evening."

She shook off his grip. "And you can do that, just as soon as I've said what I have come to say."

"I don't want to hear what you've got to say, lady, understand? You're alone with me in a bedroom, and I haven't had a woman in almost a year. If you had any sense whatsoever, that fact would make you climb back out that window and run in the other direction."

Abbie had no idea what to do with that information. Was a year a long time for a man to go without a woman? If it was, then Rio McCaine would just have to wait a while before satisfying his manly desires.

"I have no intentions of running anywhere," she said primly.

He gave her another of those long, slow, lingering looks, pausing an especially long time when he got to her breasts. For some reason, her nipples actually tightened. Strange. Other men had gawked at her breasts, and that hadn't happened.

"Then maybe you're willing to do something about my situation, huh?" he asked.

It took a moment for that to sink in. His *situation* would no doubt involve sex. Right here. Right now.

With her.

Abbie tugged at her collar. There was suddenly an enticing scent in the air, and it no doubt emanated from him—something probably intended to stir her female parts into a frenzy. It was potent, all right, but Abbie couldn't let it cloud her mind. She had some fast talking to do. Her female parts would just have to find another way to amuse themselves.

"Give me ten minutes of your time, Mr. McCaine. I assure you it'll be the most profitable ten minutes of your life, certainly better than the time you could spend with Carlotta and her . . . whatever." She motioned toward the bottle of whiskey on the small table next to the bed.

"Would it be possible for me to have a drink? It's hot outside, and my throat's a little dry."

"Yeah, I guess." He paused. "You don't seem the sort of woman who'd drink Rose Bud whiskey."

"Well, looks can be deceiving." And Abbie decided to leave it at that. Maybe looks could deceive a little bit longer.

Rio filled two glasses with the amber liquid and handed one to her. Licking her lips, Abbie took the glass and tossed it back in one gulp. She pinched her eyes shut so they wouldn't water and so she wouldn't make a rough-sounding snort.

"It clears the head," she said by way of explanation. She reminded herself that this plan would fail miserably if Rio found out she could probably drink him under the table. *Remember propriety.*

"It can do that." There was more than a smidgen of suspicion in his voice, and Abbie hoped she hadn't ruined her chances before she even got started.

He motioned toward a scarred Windsor chair, the only other furniture except for the bed and night table. "You've got nine minutes left. Start talking. After that, any activity that takes place in this room will involve clothing removal and that bed. If you don't want to be part of it, then I suggest you get out of here by then."

Oh. All right. It was all the more reason to get on with things. But the image of them on the bed, naked, lingered slightly longer than she wanted.

"I suppose you're wondering why I used the window instead of coming in through the front door?" She didn't wait for him to answer. "Well, I didn't want anyone to know I'd come to see you."

"Understandable. A lady like you shouldn't be within a mile of here." Rio took a gulp of his drink and followed it with another draw off his cheroot. A snaky stripe of smoke streamed in front of his face, and he squinted against it. "Does that mean you walked around the place looking in every window?"

"Not *every* window. Only three."

The corner of his mouth kicked up again into a cocky grin. "Bet you got an eye full."

"In a manner of speaking, yes, I did." That was an understatement. At one window she'd watched for a while, only because she couldn't believe two people could tangle their bodies like that. But again that wasn't something she would mention to him . . . though she intended to give it some thought later. "Aunt Dorrie said your mother was Comanche."

"Yes," he said flatly. He added nothing else.

All right. With that topic apparently exhausted, Abbie glanced around the room. So much for chitchat. "Aunt Dorrie also mentioned that you've worked for the army as a sort of scout and negotiator with the Indians." She'd meant to make the remark sound casual, even spontaneous, but from the slippery rise of his dark eyebrow, Abbie knew she hadn't been successful.

"Your Aunt Dorrie seems to be a wellspring of information, but she's wrong. I didn't work for the army. Until a couple of days ago, I worked for the Office of Indian Affairs, negotiating the surrender of people who would otherwise get *killed* by the army." He propped an elbow on the bedpost and stared down at her.

Blinking several times, Abbie looked up. And up. My God, this man was tall. She hadn't noticed that about him when she first climbed through the window or when she'd followed him around town half the day. He was easily over six feet. And Rio McCaine was big, too. He had wide shoulders that his blue chambray shirt couldn't disguise, and a healthy span of chest, complete with bronze skin.

It wasn't hard to see that skin because he had his shirt completely unbuttoned. Provocatively so. She could see his navel and the whorl of dark hair that spun down from it. It didn't take much imagination to guess where that arrow of hair led. Nope. No imagination whatsoever. His tightly fitted jeans outlined it in more than adequate detail.

"Uh." *Get your mind off his jeans and back to what it needs to be on. Remember all that stuff about propriety.* "Have you heard from your brother yet? Aunt Dorrie said he's flown the coop."

"My *half-brother* hasn't contacted me, and I don't expect him to." He paused. "I understand you've had a difficult time of your own just recently."

"Ah, that." Abbie nodded. She hadn't dared believe he hadn't heard. Fall Creek was a small town, and even though he'd been back less than twenty-four hours, Rio probably knew as much about her as she did about him. Well, maybe not quite as much as she knew about him. "Yes, a couple of weeks ago, I was held captive by the Apaches for two days. I suppose you've heard that I'm ruined?"

Rio choked on his drink. It took him several moments to recover. "Yes, I did hear that," he said finally, sticking his cheroot back in his mouth.

"Well, it couldn't be helped."

"You're lucky to be alive."

She made a sound of superficial agreement and tugged off her gloves. "There is that, I suppose, but the incident was helpful in other ways. There's something quite comfortable about being ruined."

His mouth stilled around his smoke. "How so?"

"You do know I'm a heiress of sorts?"

"I've heard. You're Augustus Donegan's only child and the sole heir to his huge fortune."

"Yes. Well, I'm the only one who's not an outside child anyway. There are others," Abbie said matter of factly. She hoped she hadn't offended him with that remark. Only after she'd said it did she remember that Rio himself was the illegitimate child of Andrew McCaine. Since he did look a little annoyed, she continued. "Anyway, now that I'm ruined, suitors won't be pestering me for my father's money."

"I suppose that was a problem before?"

"Oh, yes. Money can attract the worst sort. Wendell Calverson, for example. He's chased me for years. I thought once I became a spinster, things would change. They didn't. Apparently some men, including Wendell, don't care if I'm seventeen or twenty-seven—as long as I'm well off. I think this thing with the Apaches just might help though. Don't you?"

"Maybe." He took the final sip of his whiskey and placed the glass on the table. "I figure you've only got about five minutes left, and you still haven't said why you're here."

So, he had already moved to the bottom line. Abbie appreciated that in a way. When she wasn't as nervous as a lifetime sinner standing at the Pearly Gates, she was a bottom-line kind of woman. "I have a proposition to make. A business proposition. This is going to sound a little odd. That's why I want you to hear me out before you say no."

He paused again. Nodded.

She squared her shoulders and looked straight into his eyes. "I am in need of a man."

"A man?" He flicked the cheroot ashes into a cigarette tin and grinned. It was *that* grin. The one that reminded her they were only a few feet away from a bed. The bed where he intended activity to take place in the next couple of minutes if she didn't finish her business and get out. "Any particular sort, or will just any man do?"

Abbie cleared her throat, wishing for another shot of

whiskey. She didn't dare ask for one. "I'm desperately in need of a husband, actually, and I think you're just what I'm looking for. So, Mr. McCaine, will you marry me?"

Chapter Two

All right. That got Rio's complete attention.

In fact, she'd managed to dumbfound him, which was not easy to do. In his thirty-two years, he'd seen and heard just about everything. Well, except for this, of course. No woman, sane or otherwise, had ever proposed marriage to him.

He figured this one wasn't anywhere near sane.

Any woman who would crawl through a whorehouse window to propose to a man had to be a few cups minus a full jug.

"Are you about done talkin' to that piece of fluff, Rio?" Carlotta yelled from the other side of the door.

"Not yet," Rio called back. He returned his attention to Abbie. "A husband," he flatly repeated. "And why do you need a husband?"

"Well, partly because of Wendell Calverson, the suitor who just won't leave me alone, but there's a more important reason." She hesitated and licked her lips. "Now, let me see how I can put this delicately. Before my father died three months ago, he enjoyed the company of several women. Camellia is the last and unfortunately the worst of the lot. Anyway, in addition to being a thorn in my already thorn-riddled side, Camellia's nettled that my father didn't leave her one penny in his will. She's taken up residence in my family home of Kingston and refuses to leave."

Yep, Abbie Donegan wasn't all right in the head. But she looked all right in every other place where he wanted a woman to look good, with fiery red hair and eyes like green pine trees. And that expensive southern accent made her sound sane, too, unless he actually listened to what she was saying.

All in all, Rio had a hard time concentrating on her exact words. He thought it might have something to do with that cute little mole just to the right of her bottom lip. There was something about it that appealed to him.

Actually, there was a lot about her that appealed to him. Her mouth. Her breasts. And just about everything else below the waist. Above it, too. But he wasn't about to let her looks and curves aplenty turn his brain to dust.

"You think you need a husband to toss this Camellia out?" he questioned, just so his mouth would do something other than water. "Miss Donegan, all you need is a lawman. The woman's trespassing."

"Abbie," she corrected again. "It's not that easy. My father asked that I allow Camellia to stay at Kingston until such time that she marries." She rolled her dark green eyes in dramatic fashion. "At the rate she's going, that might not happen before I die of old age. A state she's pushing me to rather quickly, I might add."

"And you agreed to your father's request?"

She seemed surprised. "It was his dying wish. How could I not agree?"

"I wouldn't have," he muttered. "But that doesn't matter. You've wasted your time coming here. I have no plans to marry. Not you. Not anyone."

"I can tell you that I felt the same until quite recently, that is. May I speak frankly, Mr. McCaine?"

He cocked his head and stared at her. "I thought you already had." How much more frank could the woman get without tossing him on the bed and having her way with him? Rio had used that bed as a threat, a ploy to get her out of here. It obviously hadn't worked. Well, it hadn't worked other than making him wonder just how pleasurable it might be to spend some time on that mattress with Miss Donegan.

"No, there's more," she assured him.

More? Damn. And Carlotta was still in the hallway probably getting madder by the moment. He didn't think she'd stay around much longer waiting for him to finish talking to a crazy woman—and if she did, it would cost him. "Then, by all means get on with it. You've got three minutes left."

"Three minutes?" It wasn't a ladylike complaint. There was more than a tinge of irritation in her voice. "I don't know how you could possibly keep time when we're trying to discuss a matter as important as this. I'm offering you the chance of a lifetime!"

"You're offering me marriage, and that appeals to me about as much as beddin' down with a scorpion. And speaking of bed—"

"You haven't even heard my terms. Just listen. Please."

It was the please that got him. Again, she hadn't said it ladylike. There was no sweetness or gentleness in her tone. Rio got the impression she didn't say please very often to anyone. Maybe that's why it worked. It had taken a lot for her to get that out. "You have two minutes."

If she clenched her teeth any harder, he figured they'd

crack. "I'm very aware of what's happened recently with your brother, Julian."

"Half-brother," he quickly corrected.

"Yes, half-brother. Each of you owns half of the McCaine ranch. Anyway, I know that Julian . . . Now how should I say this . . . ?"

"He ran the ranch—both his half and mine—into the ground, then disappeared just one step ahead of the creditors."

She nodded. "And those creditors are now hounding you. I also know this morning you went to the bank and asked for a loan so you could pay off the debts. They wouldn't give it to you because, well—"

"Because I'm a half-breed bastard."

"Well, yes." She paused and lowered her voice as if asking him to reveal a secret. "Are you?"

"Am I what?"

"A bastard?"

"In every way humanly possible." Now that surely would send her running to the nearest—

"I appreciate your honesty, Mr. McCaine. I really do. I'm not always easy to live with either."

"Hard to believe."

If she had a reaction to his sarcasm, it didn't show. Abbie Donegan kept right on talking. "But I think I have a solution that just might satisfy both of us. You need money, and I have it. Plenty of it. I'm willing to pay off all your debts, both personal and those related to the McCaine ranch, if you accept all the terms of my very generous proposition."

He didn't say anything for a while. He couldn't. Good God. Rio didn't think she could stun him anymore than she already had. He'd been wrong. Was this woman really offering him the ranch? It sure sounded like it. "And exactly what are the *terms* of this very generous proposition?"

She moistened her lips and took a deep breath before she continued. "That you marry me within the week and accompany me to my family home, Kingston, after we've made a small detour."

"What detour?" Rio asked.

"We need to collect someone."

This didn't sound good. Not good at all. A crazy woman could come up with all kinds of detours to places he wouldn't want to go. "Collect someone?"

"Yes. A woman. She used to live at Kingston, and it's necessary that I take her back to where she belongs."

"And this person wishes to be collected?"

"Very much so. Her name is Harmony, and the Apaches are holding her. By now, she probably wants nothing more than to get away from them."

"The Apaches took another woman?" he asked in disbelief.

She nodded eagerly. "Yes, it's a small group, not connected with Geronimo. They were just awful to me. And to Harmony."

He didn't doubt it. "Any reason the Rangers didn't go in after her too?"

She gave another of her irritating hesitations. "I was afraid the Apaches would hurt her if the Rangers went in there with guns blazing. I'd, uh, managed to get away from them, and that's how the Rangers found me. But the renegades won't release Harmony."

"This group's not led by a man named Gray Wolf, is it?"

"Yes."

"And he's the one who held you captive?"

Another nod, and her right eyebrow winged upward. "By any chance do you know him?"

"I know of him." It was a pity that this Harmony and Abbie had crossed paths with a man like Gray Wolf. But why the heck did Rio care? He had no intentions of marrying a crazy woman, even if she owned every piece of currency in the state of Texas. Did he? Jesus, how could he even consider it?

Because he wanted his father's ranch, that's why.

The ranch had always been out of reach simply because he was born on the other side of the sheets—a fact of life that he hadn't created and was having a damn hard time finding his way around. His father had given him half of the estate in his will, but Julian hadn't left anything for Rio to inherit. Well, except for debts.

"I'm afraid you'll have to talk with this Gray Wolf and secure Harmony's freedom," Abbie continued. "But you can't let anyone around here know that's what you're going to do."

"Why not?"

"Because if anyone else knows, the Rangers or the army might get wind of it. I honestly believe Harmony will get hurt or worse if they go in after her."

Rio could see that side of it. Sort of. Most people wanted the law called in on something like this. Of course, he could say with absolute certainty that Abbie wasn't like most people, and he'd only known her a couple of minutes. "So you haven't told your aunt about this other woman?"

"No, and you won't be able to either. All I want you to do is negotiate with Gray Wolf to secure Harmony's release. I don't think it'll be that difficult, but he won't talk to me, well . . . because I'm a woman."

"You've tried?"

"Heavens yes. I can't get near the man."

Good thing, too. Gray Wolf had a reputation as a cold-blooded killer. No woman should be near him. It made Rio wonder if this Harmony was even still alive. He didn't think her chances were good.

"Mr. McCaine, did you hear my offer?"

"I heard it, but I'm not sure I understand it. Let me

get this straight: You want me to collect this woman and marry you. In exchange, you'll pay off the outstanding debts and loans on my ranch. Anything else?" He waited for the other boot to fall. She'd probably have some godawful condition that no man could ever meet.

"Well, actually there is."

Here it comes.

"I also want you to remain at Kingston until Camellia has moved out," Abbie explained.

"And how long will that be?" Forever, no doubt. Ah, he got it now. He could own the McCaine ranch, but he could never live there. Sort of like Moses and the Promised Land.

"I believe we're looking at a week or two. A month at the most. I'm hoping that your presence will, uh, inspire her to find someplace else to live."

"Inspire?"

"I'm hoping you'll put the fear of almighty God into the horrible woman," Abbie quickly clarified. "You see, the way I've figured it, I made that promise to my father when I didn't have a husband or even any prospects of getting one. So, if my husband objects to Camellia's presence, then she'll have no choice but to leave—and I won't be breaking a deathbed promise."

"You don't want me to beat this woman up, do you?"

For just a second it seemed Abbie considered that notion, but she finally shook her head. "No, I don't think that'll be necessary. If you just tell her she has to leave, I think that will be enough. She's a distant relative of Uncle Henry, so maybe she could even be persuaded to come here to Fall Creek."

He paused, eyeing her expression. Damn it, something else was wrong. Now the other boot would fall. "There's more?"

"Some." She swallowed noticeably hard. "You would have to, uh, give me half of your family's ranch."

It was more proof of her dementia. Total proof. "Right now, the ranch is worthless because of the debts. The bank is only days away from taking it to pay the creditors. You could pay it off, yes, but why don't you just use that money to buy another ranch, maybe even one closer to your home?"

Abbie nodded. "Yes, I can see where that would confuse you. I don't really want a ranch, but what I'm trying to do is work out a deal with you. If you turn the ranch over to the bank to pay for the debts, then they'll assume ownership of it."

Oh, yeah. She had some real drafty spots in that pretty head of hers. "That's exactly what I don't want to happen."

"I know. But it'll work out best if the bank does own it—for a couple of minutes or so anyway."

"How do you figure that?" he asked.

"That way, your brother won't have any claim to his half. For those few minutes, it won't be McCaine property at all. Then, I'll buy it from the bank. I'll sign the ranch over to you as my wedding gift. You'll sign a paper saying that half of it's mine. Then, I'll sign another paper giving the whole place right back to you."

"Any reason why you'd go through all that . . . signing?"

"The ranch will be yours free and clear, not only half yours. Besides, it's the only way I can do this, you see."

He had to go through everything just to see if she'd said what he thought she had. This foolish woman was perhaps the answer to his prayers, but he couldn't get his hopes up yet. She still wasn't making a lot of sense on some important points. "What do you mean by that last part?"

She took a deep breath. "I have to do it this way because it's another deathbed promise I made to my father. He didn't want me to marry any man who wasn't willing to give me half of what he owned. I think he made that condition to prevent some fortune-hunter from marrying me for my money and to stop me from doing what I'm doing now."

"But you're doing it anyway."

"Well, yes, but I think I'm upholding the intent if not the letter of my father's last request. You wouldn't actually be marrying me for my money. I'd give it to you free and clear. Well, almost. You'll have to do those other things I asked."

He paused. "You do know the debts at the ranch come to well over ten thousand dollars?"

She didn't even blink an eye. "That's about what I figured. I consider it a good investment. We both get what we want."

Rio hated that his resolve just took a big slip. He could think of it as an investment. The Donegan money could help him get back on his feet, and when the ranch was solvent again, he could begin to pay her back. Except there was another problem. One this strange demented woman obviously hadn't considered.

"Has it escaped your attention that most people don't react well to white women marrying half-breeds?" he asked.

"I'm aware of that. Is it something that bothers you? Me being white, I mean. I figured since your father raised you for the most part that you wouldn't mind. He was white, after all."

He rolled his eyes and debated having another whiskey. "I wasn't talking about how *I* feel about the color of *your* skin. I was talking about how people will turn against *you* if you marry a half-breed."

"Oh, is that all?" She blew out a short breath of relief. "Your Comanche blood doesn't bother me in the least. And as for what people might think, that's never concerned me before."

"Rio!" Carlotta yelled. "I'm tired of waitin'. If you don't send that woman on her way now, I'm findin' another man."

"How much do you pay her?" Abbie asked impatiently. She reached in her bodice as if to pull out some money, but Rio stopped her by catching her wrist.

"If anybody pays off Carlotta, it'll be me. Got that?" He let go of her and crushed out his cheroot on the whiskey bottle. "Why are you really doing this?"

"Paying her? Because I want to get rid—"

"Not that." He scrubbed his hand over his face. "Why are you offering me this, well, whatever the hell it is?"

"I've told you already. I need a man to negotiate with Gray Wolf for the release of one of his captives. And you can force Wendell Calverson to leave me alone. I also would expect you to encourage Camellia to leave." She reached into her pocket, blushing a little. "Speaking of services, I couldn't help but notice the way you, um, look at me. Well, maybe not me exactly, but my undergarments and such. I suppose that means you'd want to have marital relations with me."

His eyebrow rose, and he hoped it didn't betray his shock. This woman certainly had a way of keeping him on his toes. "If things get that far, then I would say that's quite possible." He'd meant it to sound sarcastic, but Rio heard something else in his voice. Need. Raw need. Yep, it'd been way too long since he'd been with a woman.

She retrieved a small slip of paper from her pocket. Clutching it between her fingers, she thrust it forward.

"It's an advertisement for a male preventative," she explained. She scratched her eyebrow with her index finger and looked at the floor. "These are made of rubber, not pig intestines, and are therefore more, uh, reliable. I have an acquaintance in New Orleans who can get them for you."

"Is that so?"

Her voice lowered slightly. "If you are repulsed by the notion, my acquaintance has mentioned a female preventative for me, even though I will tell you that the idea of using it has me repulsed." Her mouth twisted. "You just can't imagine what I'd have to do with one of those contraptions."

He placed his fingers under her chin and lifted it, forcing her to make eye contact with him. "But the idea of slipping into my bed doesn't repulse you?"

She looked at him as if he'd slapped her. Rio knew how she felt. That's the way he'd been since she'd crawled through the window and fallen at his feet. "Do you have some disease?" she asked earnestly.

"No."

Relief flooded her face. "Well then, everything should work out fine. Which brings me to my next concern. I do not wish to have children, and it is one condition on which I won't compromise."

"Not fond of children?"

"No, it's not that. My mother and grandmother both died in childbirth. I don't want to die any time soon. I apologize if you had your heart set on children, but you can always have them with your next wife."

"My next wife? Are you telling me that you don't wish to stay married to me?"

She ardently shook her head. "Oh, heavens no. I wouldn't think of disrupting your life permanently. No, you're free to divorce me at any time after the conditions are met. It's possible you could even get an annulment if you forego your right to marital relations."

"I don't plan to forego anything until I've decided if I'll go along with this plan of yours."

"And when exactly do you think you'll know if you'll go along with it?"

Rio repeated everything to himself again. Until she'd mentioned the divorce part, he'd been about to refuse her flat out, even if the marriage would mean he could fulfill a lifelong dream. But this latest development put a new light on things. "Can I have some time to think about it, or do you want an answer now?"

"Oh, of course you may think about it. I'm sorry. I should have offered that right from the start."

"Good, then I'll have my answer for you soon."

He took one step toward her. What he intended to do, he didn't know, but it did seem he should do something after her proposal. Shaking hands seemed impersonal considering she'd just offered him the ranch and her body. Besides, this situation called for a kiss. A hot, wet one, right on the mouth.

She had a nice mouth. Her lips were full and soft, slightly damp. Luscious, like some exotic fruit he had never tasted but wanted desperately to sample. They were lips begging to be kissed. His own mouth pleaded with him to do so.

But he wouldn't.

This, if it came to a *this,* was business. She was business. Business he intended to do business with . . . and nothing else. "I've decided to accept your offer."

"You have?"

Using his fingers, he closed her gaping mouth. "I have." Well, he would accept it with a condition—he would pay her back every cent. He would have the ranch on his terms, not hers.

"That's wonderful." She paused and smiled nervously. "What made you decide so quickly?"

"Desperation."

"Ah, yes." She nodded. "Something I understand completely. Well, for whatever reason, I'm glad you accepted."

The moment grew a little awkward. No surprise there. The whole visit had been awkward, but it seemed to Rio that Abbie was waiting for something else to happen.

Maybe he wasn't the only one who'd thought about a kiss.

She rubbed her palms against her skirt and finally offered him her hand. Probably to finalize the deal. Instead, Rio brought it to his mouth and kissed the spot just below her knuckles.

Her breath caught a little, and she smiled. He didn't. Instead, he frowned when he felt the calluses on her hand. They weren't something he expected to find on a wealthy heiress.

Abbie tugged her hand away and gave another of her nervous smiles. "I suppose I should be going." She glanced at the bed. "I know I went well past my ten minutes, but you're not going to hold me to that clothing removal part, are you?"

It took Rio a moment to find his tongue. "Do you want me to?" God help him if she said yes.

She didn't. Instead, she laughed, though the sound was nervous. "Perhaps I should just leave by the window?"

"Worried about your reputation?"

"Not mine, sir. Yours."

"Mine?"

She nodded. "Best to keep our little arrangement a secret until I can speak to Aunt Dorrie and Uncle Henry. Your reputation won't fare well when people hear that you're my fiancé. After all, remember I'm ruined."

"Yes, but as you know, Abbie, the same is true for me."

Chapter Three

"She's quite ruined, you know." Reverend Eugene Waddill said. Tea cake crumbs fell from the minister's wrinkled lips onto his dark brown suit coat.

Rio angled his eyes in Abbie's direction. She was on the other end of the veranda talking with her Aunt Dorrie, and Rio didn't think the women were in the middle of a pleasant conversation. He knew for a fact he wasn't having a pleasant conversation with Reverend Waddill.

He swirled his glass of lemonade, wishing it were something much stronger. Whiskey would do. While he was at it, he wished he didn't have such a keen sense of smell. The reverend reeked of snuff, sweat, and vanilla cake—not a pleasant combination for a muggy summer day when there wasn't even a breeze to blow the odors away.

"Yes, sir. She's as ruined as the sky is blue." The walrus-jowled man took another large bite of tea cake and swallowed noisily before addressing Rio again. "The

34

only child of Augustus Donegan. The poor girl must be as fixed as Solomon. Still, no matter. Abilene's quite ruined. There are just some things that money cannot fix, and that's what you must remember."

Oh, Rio wasn't sure that was true. Money would certainly fix most of his problems. Which didn't mean he trusted the woman who had so generously offered to bail him out and give him the ranch. No, he didn't trust Abbie Donegan anymore than he trusted his worthless, lying half-brother, Julian. However, that didn't mean he would toss aside her offer. As far as he was concerned, Abbie was his gift horse, and he wasn't about to look her in the mouth.

Besides, if he did anything with her mouth, it would involve a heck of lot more than looking.

"As Dorrie and Henry Marsh's minister, I consider it my Christian duty to talk you out of this ridiculous notion," Reverend Waddill continued. "It's hardly fitting."

"Oh?" Hell, he hoped this didn't turn into one of those conversations, one where he had to defend his Comanche blood. In his opinion, there was nothing to defend. His white father had bedded down with his Indian mother. Nine months later, he'd come along. End of story. And he was damn tired of taking the blame for something he'd had no part in starting.

The minister hesitated, giving a long humming sound of contemplation. "Don't get me wrong. I like you. Henry and Dorrie like you. We've all managed to look beyond the color of your skin and can see what a fine young man you've turned out to be."

Uncomfortable with the unexpected compliment, Rio squirmed. "Then what's the problem?"

"The problem is Abilene. And her unconventional upbringing." Eugene started to chew the wad of cake he shoved into his mouth. "Did you know Augustus Donegan?"

"I knew of him. He owned a riverboat company near Brownsville."

"A very successful company that he started before the war, but the man died several months ago. Under mysterious circumstances, I might add." His voice lowered, and he leaned closer to Rio. "Too indelicate to speak of."

"Oh?"

Apparently, that was enough of a suggestion for the man of the cloth to speak of it. "Mysterious circumstances, all right. People say he died while in the arms of a young woman. Unclothed, he was, and I won't even mention what she was wearing." He paused, his mouth tightening. "Like a fairy, she was. White silk wings and little else. People say it was some sort of perversion on Augustus Donegan's part. Perversion, indeed."

Rio gave a soft grunt. He could certainly think of worse ways to die. He wondered how Abbie would look wearing a pair of wings and nothing else. With those full breasts and plentiful curves—damn fine, probably.

The reverend grunted, too, but there was distinct disapproval in his tone. "Augustus barely had time to say good-bye to Abilene, and she had to go into that room knowing the perverse situation that caused her father's death. Dorrie said the woman was still there, too, fairy wings and all."

Well, that certainly put a whole new light on those deathbed requests that Abbie had mentioned. To think she'd made those promises to her father with a naked fairy standing around. No wonder she had agreed. She had probably wanted to get out of there as fast as she could.

"Anyway, Augustus Donegan left his daughter a fortune and made her an orphan at the same moment." The reverend finished off the rest of his tea cake and set its plate aside. "Pity. Her mother died years ago. Birthing, I believe. No brothers or sisters. At least not ones she's likely to know about."

Rio angled himself so he could better see Abbie. All in all, she was reasonably attractive. He preferred black hair, but hers was a pretty shade. She had pulled the springy mass of coppery locks into a knot high on the back of her head, but her hair's natural tendencies fought the rigorous constraints.

"You've been away and probably haven't been privy to the latest," the clergyman continued. "But Abilene's story is a sad one."

"How so?" Rio asked, his attention still on his bride-to-be. She rolled her eyes and huffed at something her aunt said.

"The Apaches had her for two days." Eugene Waddill held out a pair of sausage-like fingers to emphasize his point. "Two days of. . . ." He paused, apparently searching for the right words. "Of God knows what happening to her. You've lived in the civilized world since you were a lad, but you've been around savages enough to know what they're capable of doing to a young white woman. The savages ruined her, that's for sure, but Abilene has to share in that blame. Yes, indeed."

Rio suddenly felt sorry for her. He knew the tortures that captives had to endure to survive. A woman would be especially vulnerable. They had no doubt raped her. "Certainly it wasn't Abbie's fault that she got captured."

"No matter. It's what happened after the abduction. She'd apparently managed to escape, and the Rangers found her wandering around, but she refused to go with them. They had to take her by force. Hog-tie her, I believe. Apparently, she had every intention of returning to her captors. The way she behaved is a sin to Crockett."

Abbie probably hadn't wanted to leave until she secured the other woman's release from Gray Wolf. It also made Rio wonder—did she want him to negotiate Harmony's release or did she want revenge? Rio was sure he'd learn soon enough, but he leaned more toward the idea that she wanted revenge. If a rescue was all she had in mind, then she would have probably asked the Rangers to go back in after her friend.

As if she had read his thoughts, Abbie glanced at him and frowned.

"As I was saying,"—Eugene Waddill cleared his throat, which regained Rio's straying attention—"Abilene didn't want to leave her captors, so naturally the Rangers had to bring her here by force."

"Why here, why not her home?" he asked almost idly. Trying not to be conspicuous, he studied the delicate grip that Abbie had on her silk fan. She certainly didn't look capable of fighting off Indians or Texas Rangers, but he knew she was capable of breaking into a whorehouse so she could talk him into marrying her. Maybe he should feel sorry for the Apaches who'd held her. They'd probably been more than ready to let her go after two days.

"Fall Creek was closer. Of course, her Uncle Henry and I have been friends for years, so naturally he's told me all about his niece. Aberrant, she is. And that coming from Henry's own mouth. He says she's prone to bouts of, well, unladylike behavior. Dorrie and Henry have taken her in. The Christian thing to do, I suppose. Even though I know it must be difficult for them."

"And for Abbie."

Eugene tipped his nose as if to sniff out the true intent of Rio's remark. "Of course, Abilene, too. I wonder if you've considered the possibility of her being with child?"

"I believe Abbie would have told me if she was." And he also didn't think she would insist on preventatives if she were pregnant.

"Perhaps."

Rio's eyes shifted toward the man. "If you know something, you'd best tell me now." Not that it would make any difference to him, but Rio figured if she was pregnant, he'd put off the divorce until she had the baby. He didn't want any woman to go through what his mother had. No child deserved to be born a bastard.

"It seems as if she's not in that way. Henry asked Dorrie to question her gently, and it seems as if Abilene . . . now, how shall I put this? She had her monthly courses right after she arrived here. So, in that respect, she is indeed a lucky woman. But you see the problem," the minister continued. "She's been touched by the Apaches. It wouldn't be proper for any man to bed her after that."

Oh, Rio wasn't so sure of that. If he married her, he most certainly intended to bed her. He'd have to be gentle, of course, because of the ordeal she'd been through. But at least she wasn't a virgin. The thought of bedding a virgin was far more disconcerting than Abbie's travails.

Eugene began to fan himself. "Pity you've recently had your own troubles. Your father must be tossing in his grave to know the affairs of his ranch."

Rio only nodded, wincing. It wasn't so much how his father would have reacted that pained him, but that Rio had been unable to prevent his half-brother's squandering of the estate.

"I heard the bank manager sent you a telegram about the situation?" Reverend Waddill asked.

"He did. If he hadn't done that, I wouldn't have known."

"Well, let's hope your knowledge of it will do some good. I've heard the bank will take possession of the ranch in a day or two." He didn't wait for Rio to answer. "A pity that. The McCaine family has owned good land in Comal County since before the battle at the Alamo. Still, this can't be helped. All because of the poor management of your half-brother. Are you bitter about what he's done—running the ranch into the ground and then sneaking out of town so he wouldn't have to face you and his creditors?"

Rio ignored the question. Besides, the answer was obvious. Of course he was bitter. Julian had behaved irresponsibly even for a McCaine.

Noticing Henry Marsh's arrival on the porch, Rio got to his feet. "If you'll excuse me, Reverend, I'd like to speak with Abbie's uncle."

"By all means."

Rio walked to the much shorter man. Shorter, smaller, and older, Henry Marsh was somewhere in his early sixties and had sugar-white hair and a pink wrinkled face. However, his age and small stature didn't diminish his air of authority.

"Rio McCaine," Henry thundered. He patted his hands on his chest and hooked his thumbs under his suspenders. "Now, what's this nonsense that Dorrie and the minister's been telling me? Do you really plan to marry my niece?"

Reverend Waddill stood, tea cake crumbs falling from his coat to the porch. "Oh, no. Rest assured. I've talked him out of that." He lowered his voice. "Rio knows the whole story now, and there will be no wedding."

"Yes, there will," Rio corrected. "That is, if Abbie will still have me."

Nearby, Abbie gave her head an overly modest nod and piped up. "I would be honored to be your wife, sir."

Her words conveyed the right amount of respect and humbleness. Rio saw none of that in her clear green eyes. There was a hint of the devil in them, though. "I think I can have everything arranged for the day after tomorrow," she said. Then, giving her uncle a look, she pulled Rio aside. "Will that be all right?"

"The sooner the better."

Abbie smiled. "There's just one other thing we didn't discuss. It's about the wedding trip."

Actually, he'd been thinking about the wedding trip, too. Or, more accurately, the wedding night. He had also given fairy wings and Abbie's breasts some thought. "What about it?"

"Instead of taking the train, maybe we could ride the old cattle trails to Kingston? The weather's nice this time of year, and we could camp out under the stars." She gave another smile. Rio noticed this one was slightly tentative.

"The train would be faster," he pointed out.

"But not nearly as . . ." She paused for a very long time. "Well, it wouldn't be as romantic."

Romantic. Yes, it might be that. Abbie and he making love by a campfire. Even without the fairy wings that had a nice feel. His body twitched just thinking about it.

"Besides," she added in an even softer whisper. "It'll be easier for us to collect the woman we discussed. The cattle trails pass right through where I believe Gray Wolf is holding her."

Which was a drawback, to Rio's thinking. He'd be taking his new bride through an area where an Apache raid had occurred. A very recent raid, since Abbie had been snatched from there only a couple of weeks earlier.

"It could be dangerous," he said.

Before she could answer, Henry Marsh muscled in and placed his hand on Rio's shoulder. "You about done talking to Abilene? Because I'm thirsty for something stronger than lemonade. How about you, my boy?"

"Yes, sir."

"Then, come. Let us discuss this so-called wedding. Abilene's a lovely girl. Or at least she can be. She's got a good head on her shoulders. But there are a few things you need to know about her before I'll agree to this marriage."

Abbie stepped closer. She pulled her eyebrows together when she looked at her uncle. "What things?"

Henry's stalwart expression never changed, and he didn't answer her. He led Rio down the hall. "Abilene's just plain pigheaded when she's a mind to be. Unfortunately, she's a mind to be that way quite often."

"Careful with those compliments, Uncle Henry," Abbie called out. "And I'm not pigheaded."

Again, Henry didn't respond. He just kept right on talking to Rio. "I don't believe you know what you're getting yourself into, son. She's my wife's kin, and I'd truly like to see her married off, but I don't think any man should try to take on Abilene."

From behind them, Rio heard Abbie harrumph.

"Besides," Henry continued. "She's ruined, you know. As ruined as a gelding at a stud farm."

"So, I've heard."

And Rio felt sure he would hear it again before they'd finished their man-to-man talk.

Abbie kept her eyes on Rio and Henry until they disappeared into her uncle's library. Apparently, her aunt had done the same thing because Dorrie began to speak the moment the men were out of sight.

"Now what, pray tell, is all of this about?" she gave a frustrated huff. "Why have you let Rio McCaine think you'll marry him?"

Abbie moved closer to the door, hoping to catch some of the conversation Rio was having with her uncle. "I'm not letting him *think* anything that isn't true. I do intend to marry him."

Dorrie caught on to Abbie's arm to keep her from getting any closer to the door. "Oh, hogwash. For years I heard my brother, God rest his eternal soul, complain that you would have no man. The Bryler boy from Atlanta, the one with the fancy English title. One of Sam Houston's own cousins. That doctor from Dallas. You've refused them all, saying you wouldn't let anyone run your life. And now you intend to marry Rio?"

Abbie tried to get around her aunt, but Dorrie kept a firm grip on her arm. "What have you got against him?" Abbie asked.

"Nothing. I like him. I truly do. He's always been respectful, helpful. A far better man than his brother will ever be."

"Then what's the problem?"

"You," Dorrie quickly answered.

"Me?" Abbie rolled her eyes. "God help me. Will this turn into another discussion about how hardheaded and otherwise unreasonable I am? Because if so, it won't do any good. I'm marrying Rio. End of discussion."

"It most certainly is not the end of this discussion." Dorrie released her grip on Abbie and propped her hands on her hips. "Remember, I've got Donegan blood too, and I can be equally hardheaded."

"Some would say that's not possible," Abbie muttered. "Besides, I thought this marriage would be exactly what you want. You'll finally see me settled down."

"If I believed for one minute this would truly settle you down, I'd personally put you on Henry's fastest horse and send you straight to the church. But I know you, and I know it isn't love or the desire for a husband that's prompted this marriage. So, why have you coerced Rio into this?"

Well, Abbie certainly wasn't about to tell her.

"You used your money, didn't you?" Dorrie continued when Abbie didn't say anything. "You bribed him."

So what if she had? "Rio has his reasons for this marriage," Abbie calmly stated. "So do I."

Dorrie tossed her hands in the air. "Oh, I give up. Maybe Henry will have an easier time talking Rio out of this."

Abbie didn't think there was much chance of that, especially since the door to the library opened, and she could hear Rio bidding her uncle farewell. He caught Abbie's gaze and winked at her.

Well, that was one obstacle down.

Apparently Rio would still go through with it, even after listening to what was no doubt Henry's list of her flaws.

She gave her aunt a reassuring pat on the arm. "I think you'll just have to accept that come day after tomorrow I'll be Mrs. Rio McCaine."

"I won't accept anything yet. I'm hoping Sister Victoria can talk some sense into you."

Abbie turned her head so quickly, she heard it pop. "Victoria? Why would Victoria be talking to me about anything?"

"I've wired her to come, and she should be here this evening. Your father used to say that Victoria was the only one who could talk any sense into you."

Lord, she didn't need this—a surprise visit from her best friend, her half-sister by blood, and a real sister in a religious order. "I really wish you hadn't sent for Sister Victoria."

"Well, you left me no choice. I fear, Abilene Elizabeth Donegan, you've lost your mind."

Chapter Four

"You've lost your mind, Abbie." Sister Victoria clucked her tongue and shook her head disapprovingly. "It's completely gone." She ran her fingers over the delicate beads of the rosary and prayed in Spanish.

Abbie ignored the woman's criticism and eyed her wedding dress as if it were a rattlesnake. It had arrived only hours earlier on the train and was the most uncomfortable-looking garment she'd ever seen, with lace, crystal beads, and around the hem, a pleated ribbon that Victoria called ruching that weighed down the garment. The gown would probably have stayed anchored in a full-blown twister. Thankfully, she'd only have to wear it a few hours.

She made it a point to avoid prolonged wear of clothes that made noise.

"Did you hear me?" Victoria snapped.

"Yes, I heard you. So, now I'm ruined and mad." Abbie shoved her arm into the lace-flounced sleeve. "A rather harsh criticism considering my plan is very close to working. I'll soon have Camellia out of the house. Rio will get Harmony from the Apaches, and Wendell will have to find another heiress to pester. I'd say for a ruined, mad woman I'm doing very well for myself."

Obviously disgusted at the way Abbie was treating the expensive silk of her dress, Victoria helped with the other arm. "And you'll get your revenge. I don't suppose you've mentioned *that* to Mr. McCaine?"

"Not yet. And I don't expect you to tell him either. Will you?" The last part wasn't exactly a request. It had come through slightly clenched teeth.

"I should tell him, you know."

"But you won't."

Victoria made a sound to indicate that was true, but she wasn't happy about it. She slapped at Abbie's hand when Abbie roughly tried to adjust her bodice. "Why did you purchase such an expensive dress if you intend to treat it like sackcloth?"

"I didn't buy it, exactly. I just paid for it. Aunt Dorrie wired a store in Dallas and asked them to send a dress on the train. She insisted, saying the wedding was doomed enough already without adhering to a few civilized proprieties. I had no idea the dress would be so noisy."

"Serves you right. It's a shame it's not bracketed with whalebone and barbed wire. It might make it too painful for you to go through with this. Just what do you plan to do about your wedding night, huh?"

"There won't be one," Abbie remarked coolly. "Rio agreed to the male preventatives, and they haven't arrived. They won't either. That's because I haven't sent for them."

"And if he happens to have one of those things with him? I've heard some men carry them as a practice."

Abbie hadn't thought of that, nor was she sure it was

true. She narrowed her eyes in suspicion. With the exception of her face and hands, Victoria had every inch of her body covered with her stiff-looking black-and-white habit. There wasn't even a strand of the woman's hair showing. She had hidden everything feminine about herself, not exactly a visual testament to any knowledge of the sexual practices of men. "Why would a nun know about such things?"

Victoria's cheeks flushed a bright red. "When I lived with the Sisters of Mercy near Houston, they provided medical treatment to the women of the, uh, well, the—"

"Whorehouses."

"You're vulgar, Abbie. And you're avoiding the subject. What will you do if Rio McCaine insists that you come to his bed?"

Abbie thought about it and decided there was only one thing she could do. "Then I suppose I'll have to do my wifely duty."

Victoria gasped and clutched her rosary again. "But you must know what he thinks of you. He no doubt believes you to be a defiled woman since you were with the Apaches."

"Is that a 'polite' way of saying he doesn't think I'm a virgin?"

"It most certainly is. And we both know you are. You are, aren't you?"

Abbie frowned. "Yes."

"And what happens when Rio wants to claim that part of your body? What will you do then?"

She shrugged and scratched her armpits. Lord, the fabric was itchy along with being noisy. "I suppose I'll just give it to him. It's not as if I had grand plans for it anyway."

Victoria's next gasp was significantly louder, and she mumbled a prayer. A very angry-sounding prayer. "I can't believe what I'm hearing. Do you mean to tell me that you'll sacrifice your body for this idiotic plan?"

"Sacrifice? Well, I suppose if I were a nun I'd look at it that way. I don't know how much of a sacrifice it'd actually be since it seems to be an activity people want to do all the time."

"Are you saying you intend to make this a real marriage?"

Abbie glanced at the woman's appalled expression. "No."

"Because that's what will happen if you have relations with Mr. McCaine."

"I guess." She shrugged. "Don't worry, Victoria. I'll find a way to discourage Rio."

"And if you can't?"

Abbie didn't have an answer for that. She would find a way, that's all. She couldn't let this become a real marriage, or all her plans would fail. "How hard could it be to discourage one man from the notion of bedding me? With the exception of Wendell Calverson, there haven't been too many trying to climb into my bed lately."

"That's because of the way you behave. This scheme is proof of it. But it doesn't matter what unsound reasoning has brought you to this point, I cannot in good faith let you do this." Victoria ended with a firm nod.

"Then do it in bad faith because I plan to marry Rio McCaine in less than a half hour."

A knock stopped Victoria from adding to her protest, and Abbie was so thankful, she threw open the door without asking who it was. Her intended was leaning against the jamb. Well, maybe not leaning exactly. Slouching perhaps, in his black frock coat and pinstriped trousers.

"My, you look . . ." She paused to catch her breath. "Dashing."

And he did. Abbie had thought he was a sight to see in his tight jeans, but this was enough to make her feel light-headed.

48

"I found the suit at the ranch. Must have belonged to my father." Rio eyed the askew sleeve of her dress. "Did I come at a bad time?"

Actually, he did more than eye her dress. He stared at it. When Abbie followed his gaze, she realized the bodice and the right sleeve were much, much lower than they should have been. Lord, another quarter of an inch, and he could easily see her nipple. She quickly tried to right it.

"You have most certainly come at a bad time." Victoria's voice and expression were filled with indignity. "As you can very well see, Abbie isn't dressed yet, and you shouldn't be here anyway."

Victoria tried to shut the door, but Abbie blocked it with her foot. "Something I can do for you, Rio?"

He handed her a large envelope. "These are the papers we discussed. The ones about the ranch. I just picked them up from your lawyer's office."

"Oh, come in, and I'll sign them. The money arrived at the bank this morning. I guess you heard?"

"Yeah, you should have seen the look on the bank manager's face. By the way, you didn't tell me that you were the one who sent the telegram to let me know the bank was about to take possession of the ranch."

"Oh, didn't I? Must have slipped my mind." And she hoped it would soon slip his. That was a connection Abbie didn't want him to make yet.

"He most certainly will not come in this room," Victoria howled when Rio took a step forward.

Abbie dismissed her with an annoyed glance and went in search of a pen. "Rio, this is Sister Mary Victoria Gonzales. Victoria, this is Rio McCaine, my intended."

Victoria's mouth thinned to a straight line. "He shouldn't be here. You're not properly dressed."

Abbie glanced at her dress again. Nothing vital was showing, so she didn't know why Victoria was in such a huff. Obviously, there was some sort of violation of convention here, but Abbie didn't want to take the time to figure out exactly what it was. That was one thing that had always puzzled Abbie—why make a rule if it didn't make any sense?

"Rio, will you finish buttoning me so I'll be *properly dressed?* And Victoria, I need a pen. Will you please get me one?"

With an outraged huff, Victoria hurried out of the room. Abbie shut the door and locked it. In the same motion, she retrieved a pen from the desk in the corner. "I love her to death, but not when she's worked herself up like this." She turned her back to Rio so he could begin the buttons.

"She doesn't want you to marry me?" Rio gave the sides of the dress a quick snap to pull them together.

"No. It's nothing personal, though. I think she had hopes that I'd join the Sisters of Mercy with her. Or something." The *something* was far closer to the truth than the part about the convent. Victoria hadn't ever mentioned Abbie as a suitable candidate for the religious community.

Abbie flattened the pages on the back of the door and started to read through them. The terms of the agreement were just as Rio and she had discussed and just as she had instructed the lawyer to draw up. The first document was the deed to the McCaine ranch, and the second was a document giving her half of it. The third was the newly deeded property returned to Rio—her wedding gift to him. Abbie quickly signed all three.

"I have the supplies ready for our trip," she told him. Rio finished the buttons, but he didn't move away. He kept one hand on the small of her back. A warm, firm hand. Not easy to notice something like that while she was wearing the dress, but Rio seemed to be able to make his touch felt even through the layers of fabric. "I was hoping we could leave after the wedding."

"Fine by me," he answered. "The sooner, the better. Perhaps you could tell me where we're going exactly?"

She slowly turned to him. Rio still didn't move his hand, and her shift in position made it seem as if he had embraced her. A warm, firm embrace. Like his hand, she could feel it through the dress. "South."

His eyebrow rose. "South?"

Lord, but he had beautiful eyes. Dark blue with tiny specks of silver. Oil black eyelashes framed them and seemed to make them sparkle. Abbie got so caught up in his eyes that she almost forgot he was waiting for more information. "Uh, well, we'll have to go southwest actually. To a place called Cedar Bluff. It's hardly more than a stretch of mesquites and a half-dried-up creek."

"I know the place."

Too bad about that. If he knew about Cedar Bluff, then he knew this ride wouldn't be comfortable. "You haven't changed your mind about collecting this woman, have you?"

He shook his head and inched her slightly closer to him. "No, I'll keep my end of the bargain. I'm just surprised, that's all, that you'd want to ride the trails. I didn't think a woman of your means would prefer a saddle to a leather train seat."

"My means don't actually dictate the way I live my life." He obviously still thought she was a well-bred lady. After the ceremony she'd have to tell him the truth. Or maybe she'd just let him find out. No matter which way she went, she still needed to be polite to him until they reached Kingston.

He looked at her and then the papers. "When exactly will I get those? We didn't work out the timing."

"Oh." Abbie glanced at the papers, forgetting that she even held them. "Right after the ceremony."

"After?" His mouth angled to a half smile. "You're not afraid I'll run out on you, are you?"

"Of course not. I just like the idea of holding onto them until we're properly wed." And she did actually want to make sure he didn't run out on her. Rio might look like a mouthwatering feast, but she couldn't let his looks make her stupid. "Uncle Henry and Reverend Waddill didn't try to talk you out of this again, did they?" she added.

"They did, but I persuaded them otherwise," he said. "I just told them you weren't likely to get a better offer since everyone's so convinced you're ruined."

"As ruined as the sky is blue." She imitated Reverend Waddill's high-pitched voice.

Rio smiled at her. "What about you—did Dorrie try to get you to change your mind?"

"Dorrie, Uncle Henry, and Victoria. As they soon found out, my mind isn't an easy thing to change. Don't worry, everything will be fine. You'll see. Once we're married, they'll leave us alone. If not, I'll figure out a way to force them to leave us alone."

"You're a woman of conviction. I'm learning that about you." Rio snagged one of her loose curls and let it coil around his finger. "Was your mother's hair this color?"

God, how could a touch to her hair seem so intimate? Perhaps it wasn't the touch, but the look in his eyes. Or maybe it had something to do with how close he stood to her. Abbie detected the faint smells of mint and soap. And man. All man.

"Yes, this was Mother's hair color. At least I've been told it was. I never saw her. My father didn't even have a picture." There was too much breath in her voice, and Abbie fought to keep it under control. This wasn't the time to act like a simpering schoolgirl.

"Tell me about your ordeal with the Apaches."

"Uh, I'd rather not talk about it." For about a million reasons, but probably not one he'd considered.

Rio brought the curl to his mouth and kissed it. "I'm sorry you had to go through something like that."

His words were so gentle, so sincere. And they had an effect on her. A warm, settling effect that seemed to spread through her whole body. Abbie firmly reminded herself and her body that this was a business deal. Under no circumstance could she be attracted to Rio. It would complicate her plan in the worst kind of way. Because if she started to care, then . . . no, that couldn't happen.

She needed a man about as much as a longhorn needed a corset.

"I survived my ordeal," she finally answered. Too breathily. She cleared her throat, hoping that would help.

"Had you been with a man before that?"

Another difficult question. Another throat clearing. At this rate he'd think she was coming down with something. "No."

She saw one sleek muscle in his jaw twitch, and his eyes turned dark. "Not all savages act like savages, Abbie."

Savages. The term was a reminder of how difficult Rio's life had probably been. She'd heard snippets about his hardships from Aunt Dorrie and some of the house help. The bastard son of a wealthy rancher, abandoned by his Indian mother, and unwanted by the Comanches and many of the whites.

"You're not a savage," Abbie said softly.

There was a moment, a long moment, when they just looked at each other. It was also a moment when Abbie felt incredibly guilty. She had manipulated this man into marrying her and had lied by omission. How could she—

"Abbie!" The doorknob rattled violently, and the pounding began.

"Lord, it's Aunt Dorrie," she said to Rio. When she

spoke to her aunt, she tried to take some of the irritation out of her tone. "Yes? What is it?"

"Victoria said Mr. McCaine was in there with you."

Abbie cut off anything Rio was about to say by placing her hand over his mouth. "No, he left a few minutes ago."

The knob rattled again. "Then why is the door locked?"

"I just wanted a moment to myself. To pray."

There was a noted silence on the other side of the door. A very long silence. Abbie glanced at Rio, lowered her hand, and whispered, "You might want to go out the window, just to avoid them."

He nodded. "I want you to know that I intend to pay you back."

"For what?"

"For the money you used to pay off the ranch, of course."

"Oh, that," she answered, hoping she didn't sound too relieved. "You don't have to do that."

"Yes, I do. We'll consider it a loan."

"But I don't want—"

The finger he touched to her mouth stopped the rest of what she was about to say. It also sent a shiver down the center of her body. A shiver that settled in an unmentionable place.

How the devil could his touch on her mouth go all the way down there?

"So, you really plan to go through with this?" he asked.

Even after he moved his finger, it took her a moment to catch her breath. "Of course. How about you?"

"I do."

Chapter Five

"I do," Abbie vowed.

She crossed her fingers beneath the bouquet of pink roses and hoped God didn't strike her dead for making such a pledge. She had just promised to love, honor, and cherish Rio McCaine until death. In truth, she was looking at about three weeks, give or take a day or two.

Hardly a lifetime.

But then, she could say the same thing about the promises he'd just made to her. Rio certainly wasn't looking for a lifelong commitment. He was looking for a ranch, and that made this the best of partnerships.

"You may kiss your bride," Reverend Waddill announced somewhat unenthusiastically.

Abbie had forgotten about that. The kiss. Something men and women were supposed to do after getting married. Something she hadn't counted on doing any time soon with Rio. Well, maybe it wouldn't be so bad. Rio was attractive, and she did seem to get an odd feeling when she was around him.

She turned to him and saw that he was watching her intently. Too intently. Maybe he'd forgotten about the kiss too. Or like her, maybe he was trying to figure out what to do about it.

"A peck on the cheek will be fine," she whispered.

He made a slight sound of disagreement and went for her mouth. It was still a peck, but a mouth peck. A generous mouth peck. His lips were warm and soft, something Abbie hadn't expected. And the kiss had a little bit of a jolt to it, like French champagne. That particular drink tasted sweet, but the one time Abbie had tried it, it'd left her a little dizzy. Just like Rio's mouth peck.

Abbie ran her tongue over her lips and tasted him there. "Well, then. That's that."

He gave a resolute nod. "Guess so."

Reverend Waddill cleared his throat and lifted his hand in presentation. "Mr. and Mrs. Rio McCaine."

Abbie didn't notice how silent the Fall Creek Presbyterian Church was until then. She glanced at the somber-faced attendees. All three of them. Her aunt and uncle looked horrified, and Sister Victoria was scowling. Well, so much for the merriment of the joyous occasion. They could easily have been attending a funeral.

"We're finished now," the reverend said. It seemed obvious he was in a hurry to get them out.

"Well," Dorrie said, fanning herself. She blotted a tear from her eye. "I guess what's done is done. No use crying over it now. I've prayed about it and honestly believe God will forgive me for allowing this to happen."

Abbie decided there was no good answer for that. She finally settled on a mumbled *yes*.

"I've prepared a small wedding party," Dorrie continued. "Something tasteful and simple. I mean, I didn't think Abbie would turn up her nose at all convention.

Perhaps we should go back to the house and get on with things?"

Abbie was afraid she would indeed have to continue to turn up her nose—for a little while anyway. She had to complete the next step in her deal with Rio.

"You and Uncle Henry go on ahead back to the house." Abbie caught onto Rio's arm with one hand, and with her other, she wadded up enough of the dress so she could walk without tripping. "Rio and I have a little matter to discuss first."

Rio didn't say anything until they were outside and away from the others. "Now, do I get the papers?"

"Absolutely. I tucked them in my undergarments. I didn't want to have to explain them to Aunt Dorrie if she went snooping in my things." Speaking of Dorrie, the woman had been watching them like a hawk since they'd left the church. "I'd really counted on this being a private discussion. Besides, I can hardly get the papers with her looking at us."

Rio pointed to the landau carriage they had ridden to the church. "How about we ride out to the McCaine ranch? It seems like the best place for me to take ownership."

"It does."

Thankfully, he helped her into the carriage, or she wouldn't have made it. Her dress seemed to be gaining pounds and volume with each passing moment. He also took the reins—another thoughtful gesture since she couldn't fully extend her arms in front of her body. The snug silk and lace had done an effective job of bundling her.

"Don't be long," Dorrie called out to them.

Abbie waved so her aunt would know that she'd heard her, then motioned for Rio to get the carriage moving. Fast. "If we don't leave now, she'll just keep talking."

Rio snapped the reins. "You and Dorrie don't get along?"

"We do, I suppose. It's just we don't always see eye-to-eye." Of course, Abbie could say that about almost everyone in her life. She always seemed to be at odds with people.

They rode through the center of town, past the shops and businesses that lined each side of the narrow road. All in all, Fall Creek reminded Abbie of Elliot's Grove, the town near her home. Small but thriving. Clean. Somehow, the citizens of Fall Creek had managed to keep the less reputable establishments away from the town center.

Once they'd reached the outskirts and passed the infamous Buffalo Clover, Abbie began to retrieve the documents. In this case a retrieval meant she had to run her hand under her dress and under the layers of petticoats to get to her corset.

"Problem?" Rio asked.

She glanced at him and saw that he was watching her every move—not a good time for that because she'd hiked up the dress and petticoats past her knees. She hadn't worn the ribbed cotton hose that Victoria had put out for her, so she was showing some bare leg below the hem of her pantalets. A lot of leg, actually, since the bottom of her pantalets had worked their way up to her thighs.

"Perhaps you could just look in another direction or something?" she suggested. There was no sense fanning fires that didn't need fanning. "I tucked the papers in my corset."

He turned his gaze back to the road, but not before she was sure he'd taken in an eyeful. "Need some help?"

If it hadn't been for the subtle lift of his mouth, she would have thought he was serious. "No, I can manage."

Well, she hoped she could. Even without the clothing items she'd hidden under the bed—the ribbed hose, the extra petticoat, and the corset cover—there was still a lot to work her way through.

She finally gave a frustrated groan when her finger tangled on a silk bow at the bottom of her corset. "There has to be a better way. If men had to wear this many clothes, they'd never win a fair fight. Heck, they wouldn't even be able to draw a decent breath."

"No argument there. You sure you don't need any help?"

Abbie glanced at him out of the corner of her eye. He seemed to have his attention on the road, and that's exactly where she wanted him to keep it. "No." She gave another groan, followed by a soft grunt. "I can get the papers once I get this bow unraveled from my finger."

"Bow? There's a bow underneath there?"

"It's some kind of trim on this accursed corset. God knows why the maker of the garment felt the need to put a blue silk bow on something that wouldn't normally see the light of day."

"Blue silk," he mumbled. Then he took a deep breath. His gaze drifted in her direction, then Rio took several more deep breaths and apparently saw fit to change the subject. "The ranch is straight ahead."

Abbie freed her fingers and caught onto the folded documents. "Got 'em." Giving them a tug, she pulled them out. "Finally. I was beginning to think I'd have to cut this corset right off me."

Rio took yet another deep breath.

"Are you all right?" she asked. He looked just a little pale, and there was some sweat above his top lip.

"Fine." But he'd said it through a tightened jaw, making her wonder if he was being honest.

Lord, she hoped all that show of her legs and undergarments hadn't worked him up into a state. Any state. She didn't need his manly desires getting in the way of what had to get done.

"I'm sorry," she finally said. "I shouldn't have raised my dress like that around you. It's just sometimes I forget."

"You forget that I'm a man?"

As if she could forget something like that. She would have an easier time forgetting she had on a corset. "No. Sometimes I forget I'm a woman."

He slipped his gaze in her direction and frowned. "Of course you do."

"You don't believe me?" She leaned against the seat. "Well, it's true. You'll probably learn this soon enough, but I don't always behave like a lady."

"Really?" he asked with a heavy dose of sarcasm. "I had a faint notion of that when you climbed through my window at the Buffalo Clover. That notion became a full-blown feeling when you asked me to marry you. Ladies don't usually do those sorts of thing."

"Well, I suppose I could have found a more ladylike way of doing things, but I didn't want to wait for us to be properly introduced. And I certainly couldn't waste time while you courted me. Uncle Henry and Aunt Dorrie would have kept interfering, and somebody else might have bought your ranch from the bank. Besides, while I was biding my time and trying to act more ladylike, Harmony would have had to wait around for us to rescue her."

"I see your point."

Maybe. But there was still a gallon of mockery in his voice. Abbie tried not to let it hurt her feelings. After all, she didn't really care what Rio thought of her. Well, maybe she did. A little, anyway. "If you had your heart set on marrying a lady, then I guess I'm sorry."

"I didn't have my heart set on marrying anyone, lady or otherwise." He smiled at her. A smile not like the cocky grins he'd been generously handing out. This had to be his lady-killer smile. Ironic. A lady-killer smile could still have a powerful effect on her even though she wasn't a lady.

She felt her heart slam like a fist against her chest.

"And you don't have to apologize for being what you are, Abbie. *If* I'd been looking for a wife, I would certainly have looked in your direction, and I wouldn't have been looking because of your money."

Since her heart was still slamming, Abbie didn't hear what he said at first. It took her several moments to figure out he'd just paid her a compliment. Well, sort of. A smile tugged at one side of her mouth. A frown tugged at the other. The frown was about to win out and with good reason. Because of her arrangement with Rio, she didn't need him to look in her direction for any reason.

"There it is. The McCaine ranch." Rio maneuvered the carriage up a crushed shell and gravel road and stopped in front of the house.

Abbie slid to the edge of her seat to get a better look and studied the property that stretched all around them. "This is a nice place you've got here."

The two-story white stone house needed a few repairs, but it looked sound, and the wide front porch gave it a homey feel. There were two barns, several other outbuildings, and miles of fence.

She knew from the deed that there were just over four hundred acres to the property. Not massive by Texas standards, but there was easily enough land for the ranch to become profitable again.

The gardens and flower beds were overgrown, but like the house it wasn't anything that couldn't be fixed. She was fairly certain that Rio would indeed fix it up. It made her feel good to know she was helping him achieve a dream. And he was helping her achieve one too. Well, in a manner of speaking.

He just didn't know it yet

"I can see why you wanted the place so much." She

passed the papers to him. "And it's all yours now. Lock, stock, and barrel. Congratulations, Rio, you are now the owner of your own ranch."

The papers felt like gold in his hand.

Rio looked at his name on the deed. His name. On the deed for the McCaine ranch. He only wished his mother was still alive to see it. Few things had given her pleasure, but this certainly would have done it.

He glanced at the woman who was responsible and smiled. "Thank you for this."

"Trust me, it's my pleasure. Well, this part was anyway." She clawed at the beaded neckline of the dress. "I could have done without the fuss of the ceremony and this torturous garment, but Aunt Dorrie insisted."

"I thought most women liked the fuss of a ceremony."

"Guess I'm not like most women."

No, she wasn't. His new bride was one of a kind. A good thing, too. The world wasn't ready for two of her.

Rio started to slip the documents into his coat pockets when he realized how warm they were. And that they still carried Abbie's scent. Since her attention seemed to be on righting her clothes, he brought the papers to his nose and inhaled deeply. Yes, it was Abbie's scent all right. Again, it was one of a kind, and it unfortunately ran through him like wildfire.

Hot, racing wildfire.

Rio hoped he didn't have to wait long to deal with these strong urges he felt toward his wife. The corset-blue-silk-bow incident in the carriage had made him very attentive to her.

Abbie stepped down from the carriage. "So what will you do with the place now that it's yours?"

It took him a moment to get his mind back on the ranch. That wildfire had settled somewhere in the region below his waist and seemed to be gaining heat and intensity. "I'll work it and try to build it back to what it was before my father died."

"You'll need money for that. I could give you—"

"No, you can't. I won't take any more money from you. As I said, this is a loan. I intend to pay you back."

She shrugged. "I don't see why. I've got more money than I'm likely to use in this lifetime."

"But that's just it, it's *your* money."

"True, but it's not as if I did anything to earn it. I was born to my father's only legal wife—that's it. A mere twist of fate."

Rio knew quite a bit about twists of fate. Some were good. Some weren't. Having Abbie come into his life might turn out to be the best thing that had happened to him.

Despite her dress, she stepped upon the bottom rung of the fence. "You've got some good pasture land here. How about water? Isn't there a creek just on the other side of those live oaks?"

He nodded, but his attention wasn't really on the creek or his newly acquired ranch. The sunlight was doing something amazing to Abbie's face. The rays picked up all the amber flecks in her green eyes and made her hair sparkle. For a moment, she made Rio forget everything except her.

"How long has it been since someone kissed you?" he asked.

Her eyes widened. "A half hour at the most. You just kissed me right after the ceremony, remember?"

"That wasn't a kiss. That was a, well, I don't know what that was. How long has it been since you've had a real kiss?"

"I can't remember exactly, but I'm sure it hasn't been that long."

"Months?" Rio questioned.

"Maybe."

"Years?"

Her chin came up a notch. "Men have kissed me, all right? Dozens of times."

"Dozens?"

"Dozens!"

"And these were men not related to you?" he clarified.

She frowned and stepped down from the fence. "Of course by men not related to me."

She was lying, but he didn't know to what extent. "Then you won't mind if I add one more."

It wasn't a question. Rio fully intended to kiss her. With that sunlight on her face and the deed in his pocket, it was just too good a moment to pass up. This was as good as life would get for him, and he wanted some icing on his cake. He wanted to kiss Abbie.

She opened her mouth, most likely to protest, when he lowered his head and brushed his lips across hers. Again, it was no more than a borderline peck. Well, maybe it had some punch to it, probably because her mouth had been open. Her breath was warm. Her lips, soft. And maybe it had a punch because she made a tiny noise that sounded like a sigh.

She looked up at him and swallowed hard. "All right, then. Now, I can say I've been kissed dozens of times, plus one."

He shook his head. "No, you can't say that at all. When I've really kissed you, *then* you can say it."

Rio caught onto a handful of that flame-red hair and hauled her to him. His eyes narrowed. Hers widened. She didn't even have time to blink before he put his mouth on hers. At first touch, when her soft lips met his, he could have sworn he felt a jolt of lightning pass between them.

The kiss was just plain potent. And it was slightly rough, with a surefire promise that it might quickly get out of hand if he didn't stop.

He didn't stop.

She didn't stop.

Her kiss was a little inexperienced, a little awkward, but she soon fell into the natural rhythm that man and woman had found since they first discovered how good it felt to put their mouths together. Rio nipped at Abbie's bottom lip with his teeth and deepened the kiss.

She pressed her hands against his chest, maybe to resist, but if so she didn't put up much resistance. She became warm and yielding. Rio certainly hadn't expected that, but then he'd expected her to push him away by now.

His tongue brushed over hers, sipping again at her sweet taste. She made a low, throaty moan of satisfaction and slipped her hand around his neck and into his hair. All right. Her inexperience had started to disappear real fast.

Rio skimmed his hand down her back, all the time edging her closer. Even through her layers of clothes, he could feel her breasts press against his chest. He deepened the kiss even more, angling her mouth to his. Her lips were damp, and he used that to move over hers without restraint. He felt her little shiver of desire, the slight trembling of her fingertips on his neck.

And he knew he was in a helluva lot of trouble if he didn't put an end to this right now.

He broke away and looked down at her. Her eyes were half closed as if she'd just awakened, and her mouth was curved into what he thought might be the beginning of a smile. She looked a little, well, drunk.

"I've never been kissed quite like that," she said softly.

"Then it's a day for firsts. I've never been the sole owner of a ranch."

"Yes." She took a deep breath and squared her shoulders. "Uh, we have to get back."

Since she hadn't said that with a lot of conviction, Rio

decided to test the waters. "We could do that, or I could show you the house."

She might have been naive in the ways of kissing, but Rio could tell from the startled look in her eyes that Abbie knew exactly what he had suggested. Sex. Hot, sweaty sex.

"We can't. I mean, we don't have time. We have to get back." Abbie turned and started for the carriage. "If we don't show up for the party, Aunt Dorrie will work herself into a lather."

Probably. Rio understood all about lathers and just how easy it was to work oneself into one. That kiss had done it for him. But that kiss had done a lot more than that—it made him realize just how much he was looking forward to his wedding night.

Yes, indeed.

Tonight, he planned to get more than icing on his cake.

"This is a *small* wedding party?" Rio asked when he stopped the carriage in front of the Marsh house.

Abbie groaned. Maybe it was Dorrie's idea of small, but it seemed half the town of Fall Creek had shown up. There were paper lanterns hanging from the trees and a fiddler on the porch sawing out *Little Brown Jug*. People were dancing. And laughing. Abbie had barely gotten down from the carriage before people began to call out congratulations and good wishes.

"Lord, why does she do these things?" Abbie shook her head. "Aunt Dorrie knows how much I hate parties."

"I'm not too fond of them myself."

"All right." Abbie eyed the revelers as if they were desperadoes there to pillage the place. "We'll just get something to eat, talk for a little while, and then we'll tell Aunt Dorrie we're anxious to get started on our wedding trip."

Rio didn't say anything, but Abbie quickly noticed the

change in his expression. There was a lot of desire gleaming in those intense blue eyes. Desire no doubt fired up by that kiss. Well now, thanks to a momentary lapse, she had her work cut out for her. One way or another, she would have to keep Rio out of her bedroll and anything else he wanted to get into.

It served her right. She shouldn't have been such a willing, eager, enthusiastic participant in that kiss. And she darn sure shouldn't have enjoyed it as much as she had. It'd been her first, even though at the time she hadn't realized it. Abbie thought she'd been kissed before. Was dead sure of it, but those others must have been something else. Rio's kiss had curled her eyelashes and consumed her flesh with a slow, hungry itch. And that certainly hadn't happened before.

It probably shouldn't happen again either.

Just hours earlier Abbie had made a point of telling Victoria that she could easily dissuade Rio from the notion of bedding her. That was before the kiss. Now, Abbie could see how future kissing would make it hard to dissuade Rio: It would make it hard to dissuade herself from encouraging him. Maybe that was why women allowed men to bed them—to get more of those eyelash-curling, itch-inducing kisses.

Yes, Abbie could see how that could happen.

For years, she'd been puzzled by the number of women that her father had been able to coax into his bed. But if he'd kissed them the way Rio had kissed her, then it was no wonder she had so many half-siblings. That was the best reason of all to prevent Rio from kissing her again. There were no preventatives, and she couldn't risk becoming pregnant. She had to go back to her original plan of dissuasion.

Dissuasion started with no more kisses.

Dorrie came out of the house and met them as they

crossed the yard. "It's about time you came back. I've been waiting for you."

"We weren't that long. Aunt Dorrie, why did you invite all these people?"

"You might shun convention, but I can't. This is my home, and I have to do what's expected of me. You'd do well to learn that yourself."

No, she wouldn't. Abbie was reasonably sure she didn't want to do what people expected of her. Still, this was Dorrie, and the woman was family. Strange family, but family the same. Abbie wouldn't humiliate her by walking out on her own wedding party. She'd just leave really early, that's all.

"Guess what Victoria and I have been discussing?" Dorrie asked, her tone becoming authoritarian.

Lord, this wouldn't be good. No more sermons about conventionality, just the ominous remark that she'd spoken with Victoria. She knew that Victoria could provide a multitude of things to displease Dorrie, so Abbie decided not to venture a guess for fear of giving something away.

"Victoria said you were riding home instead of taking the train," Dorrie continued. "My God, Abbie, didn't you learn anything from your ordeal with the Apaches?"

Abbie patted her arm. While she was at it, she allowed herself a short breath of relief. So, that's all Victoria had told her. It could have been worse. Much worse. "Everything will be fine. I'll be more careful this time, and Rio will be with me."

"That doesn't give me much comfort. Both of you could be taken captive."

Since Abbie knew this discussion could go on for hours and would be utterly futile, she kissed her aunt's cheek. In the same motion she looped her arm through Rio's. "I'm starving. Is that a cake I see over there?"

Beneath a large shade tree there was a long table

spread out with food. In the center was an enormous six-layer stack cake topped with frothy white icing and nuts.

"It is," Dorrie answered, though from her tone it was evident she didn't want to discuss something as mundane as a stack cake. "Go ahead and eat, but remember I want us to have that little talk I mentioned this morning."

"What talk?" But she quickly remembered. *The* talk. Dorrie had been somewhat vague about the details of her proposed discussion, but her aunt had mentioned that Abbie would have to know what would be expected of her tonight, on her wedding night. Abbie was sure she wanted to skip that talk altogether.

"Ah, there's Victoria with Gussie. You haven't met Gussie, have you, Rio?" She didn't wait for him to answer, mainly because she knew he didn't have a clue who Gussie was. The little girl was something else Abbie had forgotten to explain to him. "We'll just go and say hello to everyone."

"Gussie?" Rio questioned when they walked away from Dorrie.

"She came on the train with Victoria." Before they could reach the child, however, Gussie disappeared. On purpose, Abbie was sure. The child had a knack for avoiding people.

"A special song for the bride and groom," the fiddler called out. "Time to dance with your bride, McCaine."

Abbie shook her head. "I'm not a good dancer." She repeated the protest a little louder so the fiddler would hear, but he started to play "I'll Take You Home Again, Kathleen." Of course, he would have to play a ballad, a song that required couples to dance close together. And of course, everyone was staring at them, waiting for them to get on with it.

"I'm sorry," she whispered to Rio. "To save Dorrie from keeling over with embarrassment, perhaps we should dance. It's either that or we'll have to listen to her complain for the next hour."

As if he'd done it a thousand times, he took her hand in his and pulled her close. She was sure her eyes widened in surprise when Rio led her through the fluid steps of the dance.

"What?" He stared down at her. "You didn't think half-breeds could dance?"

That was a question without a good answer. No matter what she said, she would be wrong, so Abbie just shrugged. "I got sent home from finishing school before we got to dance lessons. I'll probably step on your toes before this is over."

The warning had hardly left her mouth when she did crunch his toes. Rio grunted softly but didn't miss a step.

"You're really good at this," she commented. And it wasn't nearly as bad as she'd thought it would be. It was hard to move around in the dress, but it was pleasant being in Rio's arms. Unfortunately, the closeness reminded her too much of the kiss, so she made sure she didn't get her mouth anywhere near his.

"Carlotta taught me how to dance," Rio commented.

Abbie stiffened. She didn't like the sound of that. "You mean the woman from the Buffalo Clover?"

"The very one. No lessons at finishing school for me either."

"But Carlotta? I didn't think she gave dancing lessons. I thought she, well, I thought she just, uh, did other things with men." Specifically things with her mouth.

She could tell Rio was fighting back a smile. He lost. "She does that too. The dancing was just something she taught me on a slow night when she didn't have anything else to do."

That sounded a little better. After all, if they were dancing, they probably hadn't been doing other things. At least Abbie didn't think so.

"How many times did you do things with Carlotta other than dance?" she asked hesitantly.

"A few."

That estimate was no doubt on the low end. Way, way, way on the low end. It probably wasn't a good idea for her to keep talking about Carlotta, but it was hard to put aside that Rio had actually been with a woman like that. It was even harder to put aside what Rio and Carlotta had done together.

"Why go to her?" Abbie asked. "Why not just find a woman who'd welcome you into her bed?"

After all, Rio was a fine-looking man. If she'd had an inclination to invite men into her bed, she would have certainly extended an invitation to him.

"Carlotta is a woman," he pointed out.

Abbie frowned. "You know what I mean."

"You mean why did I pay to bed down with her? It keeps things simple, that's why. No sentimental attachments. No expectations. I come and go as I please without worrying about hurting anyone's feelings."

She could see the advantages of that. And the disadvantages. "Exactly how many times do you think you kept things simple with Carlotta?"

"I didn't keep count." He edged her closer to him until they were actually touching, her breasts against his chest. Of course, the corset had pushed her breasts up and out so far that touching his chest didn't require much effort. She no doubt looked like a top-heavy, uncomfortable turtledove. "I haven't been with scores of women, but I know how to pleasure you if that's what you're worried about."

"Pleasure me?" she whispered.

Then she gasped. Lord, now she'd gotten him right back onto something she didn't want to discuss. Except, the word *pleasure* piqued her interest. What a strange term for an activity that seemed so odd. And how did a man learn to pleasure a woman? Did women like Carlotta teach them and, if so, who taught women like Carlotta? Better yet, who taught women like herself?

Maybe she should have that talk with Dorrie after all.

"Don't worry." Rio kissed her forehead. "I know what you're thinking."

"You do?"

"Yes, I do. I won't hurt you, and before we're done, I'll make sure we're both satisfied."

She swallowed hard. That was what she was afraid of. He would teach her. And satisfy her. And do things she probably shouldn't be doing with him.

The song ended, and Abbie glanced at the crowd that had assembled to watch them dance. Strange, but she'd gotten so involved with her conversation with Rio that she'd forgotten they weren't alone.

"Another dance?" the fiddler called out.

Rio waved him off. Instead, he and Abbie ate and talked with some of the guests. She was thankful that he didn't seem anymore interested in staying at the party than she did. They glanced at each other dozens of times during the festivities.

After an hour of pretending to be gracious and lady-like, Abbie caught onto Rio's arm and pulled him away from a one-sided conversation with Reverend Waddill. "I've had all I can stand of this dress. I'm going to change for the trip, and then we can leave right away."

He smiled at her. "It's about time."

"Good," she confirmed.

At least Abbie had thought it was good that he agreed to leave right away. His smile threw her off a little. It was the same smile he'd given her in the carriage ride out to his ranch. And the same smile he had smiled right before he kissed her.

Those kind of smiles might make the trip much harder

72

than she'd planned. Because those smiles could lead to . . .

Staying much longer wouldn't make things easier though. Just the opposite. The sooner they left, the better. If Victoria spent much time around Dorrie, Abbie feared her sister wouldn't be able to keep a secret. Her aunt would learn everything. And everything was exactly what Dorrie couldn't learn. Because if Dorrie knew, she'd tell Rio.

And if Rio knew, well, he wouldn't be doing any smiling, no matter how many kisses she gave him.

"I'll help you change," Dorrie said, following Abbie into the house. "That way we can have that little talk."

Abbie tried not to groan. Despite her earlier thought that the talk might be a good idea, she'd changed her mind. Somehow, she didn't think Dorrie would be an expert in such matters, and if by some miracle she was, Abbie didn't want that expertise passed onto her.

Dorrie closed the bedroom door behind them and locked it. "Abbie, since your mother isn't here to say these things to you, I feel it's my duty to say them in her place."

"It really isn't necessary—"

"Yes, it is. Now, I know you had a horrid calamity with the Apaches, so you are not unfamiliar with what takes place between a man and a woman."

She wasn't quite as familiar as Dorrie thought.

"So, I have just one thing to say to you about your wedding night," Dorrie continued. "Saddled."

Abbie had been about to try to tell her again that the talk wasn't necessary, but she hadn't expected Dorrie to say that. "Saddled?"

A blush crept over Dorrie's cheekbones, and she gave a brittle nod. "Think of the whole embarrassing ordeal as being saddled, and then, uh, ridden."

"You mean like a horse?"

"Very much like that. Rio will likely climb on you, just as he would a saddle. Well, almost like that anyway. Then you'll close your eyes, and he'll take care of his manly business."

"His manly business?" Abbie repeated before she could stop herself.

Dorrie's blush increased significantly. "Yes, and think of that part as churning butter."

Churning butter? Well, that wasn't a pleasant image— especially when Abbie considered what Rio would be churning with. And what he'd be churning.

Dorrie fanned herself with her handkerchief. "Of course, when you were with the Apaches, you could let them know right off that their manly business was disgusting. I mean, they forced themselves on you. But you can't let Rio know how much he disgusts you because he's your husband. You'll just have to lie there and bear it without making an ugly face or anything."

This was a very confusing conversation. "I will?"

"Yes, you will. And while he's taking care of his manly business, you can use that time wisely. You can think about what you'll wear the next day. Or plan meals. I came up with my recipe for tea cake while your uncle was saddling me one Christmas Eve."

Abbie twisted her mouth. She was reasonably sure she wouldn't be coming up with recipes since she was also reasonably sure she wouldn't allow Rio to do these things to her. And to think Rio had said he could pleasure her!

Being saddled and churning butter didn't sound like anything pleasurable.

They sounded more like chores.

Chapter Six

Rio came out of the Marshes' house after changing his clothes and stopped in his tracks. "I don't believe this," he mumbled under his breath. He'd thought the wedding party was surprise enough without adding anything else to it.

There was plenty wrong with the activity going on by the barn. For one thing there was his wife, looking very ladylike in her split riding skirt, except for the fact she was saddling her own horse. She hoisted the saddle onto the buckskin gelding as if she had the strength of a man double her size.

Well, that explained the calluses on her hands.

However, his wife was only a small part of the eyebrow-raising scene. Abbie wasn't alone. There were also Sister Victoria, a kid, and a mangy-looking dog. Rio couldn't quite tell if the kid was a boy or a girl.

"What's going on here?" he asked Abbie. He set down

the basket of food that Dorrie had given him minutes earlier and caught onto her arm.

She smiled. It wasn't her tentative smile either. This one was dazzling. She actually seemed relieved to see him. "I'm glad Uncle Henry didn't keep you too long. What did he want to talk about?"

Sex. And something about saddling a woman. Rio didn't want to repeat Henry's suggestions to Abbie. "What did Dorrie want to talk to you about?"

Abbie glanced away and started to nibble on her bottom lip. "Her recipe for tea cakes."

"Oh." Rio shrugged. So Abbie didn't get wedding night advice after all. He wished he could have skipped his discussion with Henry. Abbie's uncle didn't know a darn thing about pleasuring a woman. He actually felt sorry for Dorrie.

"I've already said my good-byes to my aunt and uncle," Abbie let him know. "I'm ready to go. How about you?"

"We can leave anytime." He tipped his head to Victoria. "What's she doing out here, and why is she holding that bay mare's reins?"

Abbie's smile became tentative. "She'll be riding with us."

"She what? You didn't tell me your friend was coming with us on our wedding trip!" Actually, he figured there was plenty she hadn't told him, but this particular omission didn't please him. He'd thought Abbie and he would travel alone.

"You won't even notice her," Abbie answered.

"Oh, I'll notice her all right. And so will everyone else. She's a nun, and she's wearing those clothes that nuns wear."

"She's also my half-sister. I can't possibly leave her behind. She doesn't get along with Aunt Dorrie."

"Your half-sister?" The woman was Mexican. He'd

noticed that earlier when they met in Abbie's bedroom.

"Yes, I told you my father had a roving eye."

"Eye?"

Abbie frowned.

"And what about the child?"

"Her name is Gussie. I think she might be a half-sister, too, but I can't say for certain. Her mother worked at Kingston and died not too long after Gussie was born. She refused to tell anyone who Gussie's father was."

"I wasn't asking if she was your sister," he ground out in frustration. "Is she coming with us too?"

"Well, we can't leave her behind. She came with Victoria."

Of course she had. Not that Abbie's explanation explained anything. He picked up his saddle and put it on Smoky, his midnight black stallion. "Where do they live?"

"At Kingston, with me. Victoria is a Sister of Mercy, and she teaches at the school in Elliot's Grove."

"And what about the dog?"

"He lives at Kingston too. His name is Beans, and Gussie never goes anywhere without him. Besides, Aunt Dorrie would never let me leave him here. She hates dogs."

"We're traveling with a nun, a child, and a dog."

Maybe he'd return only three-fourths of the money Abbie lent him.

This certainly added a new wrinkle. The trip would be considerably harder than he'd planned. And Rio had planned for a rough ride. He could deduct some money for the nuisances that he'd no doubt encounter along the way. The way things had started out, there would probably be plenty of nuisances.

"You led me to believe we'd have a wedding trip," he pointed out. "Alone. You said something about sleeping under the stars and how romantic that would be. Hard to be romantic with your sisters around."

"Well, I thought we would be alone, but then Victoria showed up with Gussie. They don't want to go back on the train without an escort, and they can't stay here. I can't very well tell them they can't come."

"Why not?"

She stared at him and made a flustered sound. "Because I just can't. They're my sisters. Don't worry, you'll hardly notice them."

"You've already said that, and I didn't believe it then anymore than I believe it now."

Her mouth tightened. "Well, I'm sorry, but it can't be helped. Oh, and by the way, until those male preventatives arrive, I'm afraid we won't be able to have marital relations."

Wanta bet? Rio kept that thought to himself. Despite Henry Marsh's notions, there were other ways to make love that wouldn't risk Abbie becoming pregnant. He was looking forward to teaching her a few of them. Still, it wouldn't be quite the same as taking her the old-fashioned way. Nope. He fully intended to explore that way too.

"Any idea of when the preventatives will arrive?" he asked.

"They should be there by the time we get to Kingston."

"And when will that be?"

"Oh, a week or so."

A week or so. If that *so* stretched out too long, he'd go nuts. He'd forgone Carlotta's company after accepting Abbie's offer, and he didn't want to go much longer without a woman. Since he now had a wife, it seemed only reasonable . . . well, it just seemed reasonable. Not much, including nuns, sisters, or dogs would stop him from bedding down with Abbie. He was a man in need, and when the need was this strong, there was always a way.

With or without preventatives.

He finished saddling his stallion and checked the pack horse that carried their supplies. The kid, Gussie, was already astride a young roan mare, and both the child and the animal looked more than ready to leave. For that matter, so did the dog that tried to hide behind the mare's front leg.

By now, Sister Victoria had mounted, sidesaddle. Straight-backed, she was trying to settle down the side-stepping bay mare. Rio tried not to look too disgusted. The rugged Texas hill country was no place for sidesaddles, but he could say the same thing about it being no place for a nun.

Or a child.

Or a bony, mangy dog.

Or even his surprise-a-minute wife, who seemed to have no trouble getting herself into the saddle. Astride. Thank God. At least she seemed to know what she was doing when it came to a horse.

Rio climbed onto his stallion, leaned his forearm on the pommel and gave each woman an impatient glance. "I'm guessing everybody can ride so I don't have to play nursemaid to any of you?"

The three women, even the youngest, gave him equally potent hell-freezing looks. From that angle, though none of them had the same coloring, he could see a definite resemblance. Something about the rigid set of their mouths. And something about the way they carried themselves.

Definitely sisters.

As if they had rehearsed it, they snapped the reins, and their horses took off. Apparently, everyone could ride fine, but Rio wasn't about to count his blessings just yet.

Nope.

This hellish little adventure had no doubt just begun.

They rode in pairs with Gussie and Victoria trailing behind Rio and her. The sun was low in the sky, and there was finally a breeze to give them some relief from the heat. Abbie could hear her sisters chat about the wildflowers that littered the countryside. Gussie laughed when Beans started to chase a butterfly.

Under different circumstances, Abbie would have enjoyed the ride. Being outdoors was certainly better than the past couple of weeks she'd spent at Aunt Dorrie's. However, the man riding next to her put a damper on what would have otherwise been a pleasant trip. Abbie couldn't quite get past the feelings that started to nag her. A guilty conscience, Victoria would have probably called it. Victoria would probably be right.

The trouble was Abbie didn't know how to relieve her guilty conscience, other than telling Rio everything— something she couldn't possibly do. Not yet anyway. Besides, there was a lot of truth to tell, and if he heard it all at once, she was afraid he'd turn around and head right back to Fall Creek.

It made her wish she'd hung onto that deed a little bit longer. Since she hadn't, she only hoped Rio was a person who kept his word.

Unlike her.

"How many more secrets are you keeping from me?" Rio asked.

The silence had gone on so long between them that his voice was startling. Her gelding whickered in protest when Abbie jumped at both the unexpected sound and the question. Especially the question. Secrets weren't something she wanted to discuss yet, so she took the easy way out and pretended she hadn't heard him. "Uh, what?"

"The secrets? In other words, the half-sisters. How many are there exactly that you haven't told me about?"

Oh. That kind of secret. She could talk about that. "To be honest with you, I don't know."

"Then how many live with you?"

"Just Victoria and Gussie. Harmony will stay with a distant relative after you collect her."

"She's a half-sister too?"

Abbie shrugged. "Most likely. Her mother worked at Kingston for a while. Like I said, my father had a roving, well, you know."

"Yeah, I know." He swatted away a bee that flew in front of his face. "You never did tell me how Harmony managed to get taken by the Apaches."

And she wouldn't tell him now either. Not the whole truth anyway. This was one of those secrets that was best kept for a while longer. However, she did have to come up with some explanation, or he would only get more suspicious. "Harmony was traveling with me when we were both captured."

He didn't say anything.

Abbie didn't like that. He gave her hesitation and partial explanation some thought. Too much thought maybe.

"Where exactly were you traveling?" he asked.

Now she would have to lie. Rio just wasn't ready to hear the truth because it would lead to more truths and more revelations. Blast it, why hadn't she held onto that deed? "I was on my way to visit Aunt Dorrie and Uncle Henry. Harmony and I decided we'd ride instead of taking the train."

"Like now?"

"Like now," she confirmed. That question was something else she didn't like. He hadn't said it inadvertently, but with purpose. Rio definitely sounded suspicious. "Anyway, we crossed paths with Gray Wolf's renegades, and they held us captive. That's really all there is to tell."

"Not quite."

Abbie stiffened. "What do you mean?"

"I mean you haven't explained why you were rescued and Harmony wasn't."

That was more of that truth he wasn't ready to hear yet. Lord, the man could ask a lot of hard questions. "We got separated from each other. I guess someone told you that I didn't want to leave when the Texas Rangers showed up?"

"Reverend Waddill mentioned it." He paused again. A long time. "Do you think Harmony's still alive?"

"Oh, I'm sure of it." Abbie wrinkled her nose, wishing she hadn't answered so confidently. She was confident, of course, but there was no reason to let Rio know. "What I mean is, I don't think Gray Wolf will hurt her. He'd better not, anyway."

Another pause. At this rate Abbie figured she wouldn't be able to eat supper because of the tightening knot in her stomach.

"How is it that you and Harmony were alone anyway?" Rio wanted to know. "A woman of your means should have had someone with you."

Ah, that. At least this wouldn't be a lie. "This goes back to that ladylike discussion we had this morning at your ranch. I don't always do things the conventional way, and traveling without an escort is one of them."

And it was past time she changed subjects. Her stomach couldn't take much more of this. "Tell me about yourself," she said quickly before he could speak. "Were you raised on the McCaine ranch?"

From the way he wrinkled his forehead, she didn't think he appreciated the question. She didn't care. His questions about Harmony had to stop before he somehow worked out the truth.

"I came to the ranch when I was five."

"And did your mother live there too?"

His eyebrow flexed with . . . not quite amusement, but something. Something that made Abbie uncomfortable. "No. She died."

"Died?" Abbie forgot all about her ploy to distract him. This sounded like something she really wanted to know. "How?"

Rio stayed quiet so long that Abbie wasn't sure he would answer. Finally, he did. "It was a fever of some kind. I don't remember much about it. My mother was working as a cook at the Billings ranch over in Eagle Pass. When she died, Mr. Billings didn't know what else to do with me so he took me to my father. My white father, Andrew McCaine."

Abbie started to reach across the distance and touch his arm, but the steely look in his eyes stopped her. No touch would heal the hurt she saw there, and she was sorry she'd brought it up. "Your father knew about you?"

Rio shook his head. "He said he didn't. His wife died when Julian was just a baby, and he'd brought in my mother to take care of his son. I guess he had one of those roving eyes like your father. When my mother found out she was carrying me, she left because she didn't want him to have to choose between his way of life and her. She'd thought it was for the best."

Maybe, but Abbie didn't think it was for the best for Rio. "Your father treated you well?"

"He treated me like a bastard. So did my half-brother, Julian, and half the town of Fall Creek for that matter. That's why I rode out of there as soon as I was old enough to leave."

She hated the hurt she heard in his voice. Hated that people had treated him so cruelly just because his mother was Comanche. Abbie reached across and placed her hand over his where it rested on the pommel. "I'm sorry."

"No need to be. All of that was a long time ago. I didn't look back when I rode out of town."

He might not have looked back, but he hadn't forgotten either. She sighed heavily and gave his hand a gentle squeeze. Their skin colors caught her attention. Her pale ivory fingers against his nearly bronze hand. That was the difference that had made her life charmed and his a living hell.

"Life's not fair," he said as if reading her thoughts. "Like I said, I didn't look back. I wouldn't have even returned to Fall Creek if I hadn't learned that Andrew McCaine was dead and left me half the ranch in his will. Too bad Julian ran it into the ground before I could get back and claim what was mine."

"Well, now you can show him. All of them," she hastily corrected. She gave his hand another squeeze and then moved it. "You are now the sole owner."

The bitter expression cleared from his face, and Abbie saw some hope creep into his eyes. It made her feel better that she was in some small way responsible for it. It also made her feel guilty again for tricking Rio. She suddenly couldn't wait until she could tell him everything. It wouldn't be pleasant, but the truth had to feel better than all the lies.

Abbie pointed to a small clearing west of the trail. "That's a good place to set up camp."

She'd been through here several times before and knew there was a creek nearby. Later, she thought she might be able to sneak off and get a bath.

They all pitched in and set up the camp. Thanks to Dorrie's basket, they didn't have to cook, but Victoria made coffee. They feasted on fried chicken and leftover stack cake from the wedding party.

The night settled in quietly around them, but even with the earlier breeze, it was muggy. There would be mosquitoes. It was a small problem compared to the one Abbie thought she might run into with Rio. She watched him as he helped himself to a cup of coffee. He looked up and winked at her.

Yes, there might be a problem.

After all, it was their wedding night, and they had shared that kiss earlier at the ranch. He might want to kiss her some more. And he just might expect more than kisses. That's why she was glad Victoria and Gussie were along. Her sisters would certainly put a damper on any of Rio's wedding night plans. No saddling. No churning butter. No special time to plan recipes.

Abbie rubbed her hand over the back of her neck and felt the grit. That she didn't mind so much, but the trail dust hadn't done much to take away the smell of the wedding dress. Before she'd worn that thing, she hadn't known lace had a scent—one that didn't appeal to her at all.

She caught onto Victoria's arm and pulled her aside. "Will you keep Rio occupied for a little while?"

"Occupied?" Victoria flattened her hand on her chest. "And just how am I supposed to do that?"

"Talk to him. I'm going upstream to wash off the smell of the wedding dress. It's making my horse skittish."

Victoria tried to stop her, but Abbie dismissed it with the wave of her hand. "But I don't know what to say to him!" the Mexican woman called out.

"Oh, between you and Gussie, you should be able to figure out something."

Chapter Seven

Rio eyed the little girl as she inched her way across the camp toward him. Gussie. Abbie's half-sister. At least now he knew she was a girl. Before Abbie had told him the child's name, Rio hadn't.

"Well," she said, stopping a couple of feet in front of him. She quickly stuffed her hands into her pockets. "I'm guessing it's time I introduced myself. I'm Gussie."

She was borderline scruffy, he thought as he took in her short-cropped reddish hair and scraped chin. There was a ragged tear on the right knee of her overalls. Her freckles didn't help either. They were so dark against her pale skin that they looked like specks of dirt.

He nodded in greeting. "Good to meet you, Gussie. I'm Rio."

She dropped down beside him, picked up a stick, and started to poke at the fire. "I guess I like you well enough. I mean, you haven't yelled or me or anything. So far. I 'spect you will a time or two before we get home."

Rio tried to smile to put the child more at ease. After all, he liked her well enough too. She hadn't been any trouble and had managed to keep up with them on the ride along the trails. Still, she was here on his wedding night, and he didn't care much for that. No sense blaming the child for it, though.

That was entirely the fault of his bride.

"So I guess it's time we had a real long talk," Gussie admitted.

"Oh? About what?"

"About Abbie. You really oughta know what you got yourself into by marrying up with her." Embers sparked and crackled when the child shoved her stick deeper into the fire. "Abbie always, always, always, likes to be in charge of doing things, and she gets all mad if she can't be."

Yes, he could see that. So far, she'd dictated everything. Rio frowned. Heck, Abbie had even dictated the terms of their wedding night. No preventatives, no sex. That didn't sit right with him. He'd never felt as if he had to be in charge of everything, but there were some things a man had to dictate. Making love to his wife was surely one of them.

"There's more," Gussie went on. "A lot more. Abbie says really bad words sometimes. Sister Victoria says it's not a habit fitting for a lady, and I better not try it or she'll wash my mouth out with the biggest cake of lye soap she can find. She smokes sometimes, too."

"Who, Sister Victoria?"

"No. *Abbie*. And she takes a bath every night when she's at Kingston. Every bloomin' night and makes me do it too. Miss Ina says we're gonna wash the skin right off our bones." Gussie looked up at him worriedly. "You think that might happen?"

He shook his head, amused. "No, I think you're safe."

"Hope you're right. Wouldn't want to walk around

with my bones showing." She sniffed and wiped her nose with the back of her hand. "Now, that's Abbie's bad side, which you never, never want to get on. But she's got a good side to her too, and you oughta know about that part just as much as the other. She takes care of all of us, and she doesn't even have to."

Rio was quickly learning that. The smoking and the cursing didn't bother him—he did some of that himself. He could even get used to her desire to be in charge all the time. Probably. But this devotion Abbie had for her sisters grated on him; she seemed to go way too far out of her way to help them.

Still, a part of him had to admire her for it. Julian had never given him one kind word, and there were times when Rio had needed one from him. Or from anybody. He certainly couldn't imagine Abbie mistreating her sisters.

"Gussie?" Almost running, Victoria came toward them. The hem of her long black skirt kicked up dust around high-top shoes. "Whatever are you doing over here with Mr. McCaine?"

"Rio," he corrected. "And we're just talking about Abbie."

Victoria started to rub her fingers over her rosary again, and she mumbled something in Spanish under her breath. "Gussie, it's not your place to be telling Mr. McCaine about Abbie."

"I just told him she sometimes swears," the child admitted with a shrug. "And that she smokes every now and then."

"Then I hope you also told him that Abbie's the one who puts food in your belly, clothes on your back, and gives you a roof over your head."

"I was getting to that. I was just telling him how she takes care of us when she doesn't even have to."

Rio looked to the horses, where he'd last seen his

bride. "Speaking of Abbie, where is she anyway?"

Victoria mumbled something else and put her fingers on the rosary again. "I'm not really sure—"

"Abbie said she wanted to get the smell of the dress off her, remember?" Gussie interrupted. "She's not used to wearing fancy dresses, something else you probably oughta know about her. She says she bet that woman, Eve, from the Bible, never had to wear no fancy dresses. Abbie can't stand the blasted things."

Victoria's hands went on her hips. "Augusta Marie Burge, if I ever hear you use language like that again, I'll wash your mouth out with the biggest cake of lye soap I can find."

Gussie rolled her eyes and looked pleadingly at Rio. "Told you that's what she says all the time."

Victoria's tone became even stricter. "And don't you sass me either. I think it's time you turned in for the night, and you say your prayers twice, understand?"

"Aw, I don't know why you're getting so mad." Gussie got to her feet and tossed her stick aside. "I didn't tell him nothing I wasn't supposed to."

That caught Rio's attention. He knew in his gut that Abbie was keeping something from him. He just didn't know what. It hadn't occurred to him to try to get information out of her half-sisters, but it would probably be easier than getting it from Abbie. "What exactly weren't you supposed to tell me?"

"Buckets full—"

But Victoria quickly smashed her hand over the child's mouth before Gussie could finish. "Three times on saying those prayers, Augusta Marie Burge, and if you utter one more word, I'll make it four. Now get to bed."

Gussie screwed up her face into a frown. "I'm going. I'm going." She kicked at a patch of dandelions, mumbled something under her breath, and walked to her bedroll.

"I don't guess you're willing to tell me buckets full of whatever Abbie's keeping from me?" Rio asked.

The nun started to caress her rosary again. "There's really nothing to tell. Not, uh, really."

"Isn't lying a sin, Sister Victoria?"

The woman's mouth tightened, and she gave an equally tight nod. "If there is anything to tell you, buckets full as you put it, then it should come from Abbie. Not me."

"I'd rather hear it from you. Might be less work that way. Does this have something to do with Harmony?"

Victoria didn't say anything for several moments. "There are a few things about Harmony that Abbie perhaps forgot to mention. I'm sure she'll tell you all about it the first chance she gets."

Not likely. "And those few things Abbie forgot to mention—what would they be exactly?"

"Well, it's just, well, it's just Harmony is in a little spot of trouble right now, and that's all I'd rather say on the subject if you don't mind."

"I do mind actually. Is this little spot of trouble more than just her capture by Gray Wolf?"

She moved her shoulder, an indifferent shrug, but there was nothing indifferent about her expression. "It's possible that, well, maybe the law might be looking for her."

Rio groaned. "The law?" The law! Ah, hell. He didn't want to get involved with tracking down somebody wanted by the law. Now, this was something Abbie definitely should have told him. "What did Harmony do?"

"Nothing. I mean . . . if I tell you this, Abbie will be furious with me."

"*I'll* be furious with you if you don't. And remember that part about sinning. I've asked you right up front, and if you don't tell me the truth, it'll be a lie."

Sister Victoria's fingers raced over her rosary. "You won't tell Abbie that I'm the one who told you?"

"I won't tell her. In fact, I'll just wait until she says something about it, then pretend I'm hearing it for the first time. How's that?"

She swallowed hard and nodded. "It's very kind of you, Mr. McCaine."

"Rio," he corrected. "Now what's this about the law looking for Harmony?"

"Well, they want to question her about some part she might have had in a crime, which she most certainly did not. And before you ask, I'll tell you that I'm not even sure what this crime entails, but it doesn't matter. Harmony just isn't capable of breaking the law. She's as meek as a lamb. Now, Abbie possibly . . ." She stopped and crossed herself. "I shouldn't have said that, and I'm sorry. She wouldn't break the law either."

Rio wasn't so sure.

"You won't mention this to Abbie?" Victoria asked.

"No."

She blew out a long breath. "Thank you. It's just that Abbie can be so, well, stubborn at times. I'm sure you've figured that out for yourself."

"She does have a way of getting her point across." He set his coffee cup aside and crushed out his cheroot. "Where exactly did you say Abbie was?"

She hadn't said, but Rio felt sure she would now. After all, he was doing his sister-in-law a huge favor by keeping his mouth shut about what he knew about Harmony. Except when he thought about it, he didn't know much more about Harmony than he had before their conversation. The law wanted to question Harmony. Maybe. She might have had some part in a crime. Or maybe she hadn't.

Nope. He didn't know much about Harmony at all. And he was sure that's the way Abbie wanted it. The only thing he couldn't figure out was why. Maybe she thought he wouldn't try to rescue Harmony if he knew the whole story.

"Abbie," he asked when Victoria still hadn't answered him. "Where is she?"

She started the rosary again. "At the creek. She's bathing."

Bathing? Now, that got Rio's attention in a way that nothing else could have. His wife was somewhere out there bathing? Well, now, that was something he wouldn't mind catching a glimpse of. Or maybe even more than a glimpse.

A real long look.

"I think I'll just go for a little walk myself. Good evening to you."

Victoria snapped to attention. "But—"

"Sleep tight. Don't forget to say your prayers."

Rio grabbed his flask from his saddlebag and walked in the direction of the creek. Maybe, just maybe, things would start to look up for him.

Abbie had interrupted him that night at the Buffalo Clover, and he'd lost interest in seeing Carlotta after Abbie's offer of marriage. That interest had suddenly returned—except it wasn't Carlotta he had a hankering for. It was Abbie. That hankering was blossoming into a full-fledged need, and it aimed itself at the former Miss Donegan. He wanted to see his wife at least partly naked.

All the way naked would be even better.

Beyond that, he tried not to think about what expectations he had, but just about anything was possible. After all, they were married. They were adults with adult needs. At least, he had needs. He wasn't sure about Abbie. That nearly caused him to turn around, but then he remembered their kiss at the ranch.

Yes, Abbie had needs, too.

Ducking under a low-hanging oak branch, Rio walked on and finally spotted her. Lord, did he spot her, and it was a sight he didn't think he'd forget anytime soon. With the moonlight glimmering all around her, Abbie sat by the side of the creek, her weight resting on one hand. Her copper hair was loose and hung in damp curls down her back. She was smoking a cheroot and brought it to her mouth in a slow, easy motion.

And she was practically naked.

That's what made the sight especially memorable.

She wore only her camisole and pantalets that she had rolled up to her knees. In doing so, she had exposed plenty of her long legs. Both garments were wet and clinging to her like skin. He could see the outline of her breasts.

Rio went from mildly interested to rock hard in a matter of a heartbeat.

Her shoes and clothes were in a heap beside her. The water lapped at her bare feet. She took another draw off the cheroot and flicked the ashes aside. Even with the scents of fragrant tobacco, wildflowers and the creek water, Rio could still smell her—a mingling of everything that was female, everything that made him remember he was a man.

A man with needs.

"Want some company?" he asked.

"Oh!" Abbie gasped and awkwardly snuffed out the cheroot in the dirt. She batted her hand in front of her, scattering the smoke. "I didn't know you were there."

Obviously. "Just thought I'd take a little walk." He dropped down beside her and offered her his flask. She took it, drank some and returned it to him. "Uh, I just had a bath. The water's a little cold, but it felt good."

"Maybe later I'll take one myself." And maybe he could even talk Abbie into joining him. Rio took off his boots, rolled up his jeans, and put his feet into the water. "Are you in the mood to talk?"

"About what?"

He took a drink from the flask. "Whatever you want to talk about. We haven't had a chance just to sit around and get to know each other."

"You want to get to know me?" she asked cautiously.

Oh, yes. He especially wanted to get acquainted with every inch of her body, but she probably meant something else. She probably meant did he want to get to know her mind. Well, sure, while he was at it, he could get to know that part of her too. "Why don't you tell me about your childhood?"

She blinked, smiled. "All of it?"

Rio liked her smile. It lit up her whole face. And it was unusual that he would notice her smile at a time like this. Now that his eyes had adjusted to the moonlight, he was having trouble keeping his attention off her breasts. With reason. The camisole covered but didn't hide them. He could even see the dusky shadows of her nipples beneath the flimsy fabric.

He was sure that lit up *his* whole face.

"Well, maybe you don't have to tell me all about your childhood, just the parts you want to tell me."

She hesitated. "I will if you will."

His mind was still on her breasts. And those dusky shadows that he knew were nipples. It was hard to concentrate with that kind of distraction. "You will if I will what?"

"Tell me about your childhood."

"Oh." He shook his head, hoping to clear the fog. He'd thought this might turn into a very interesting game, but she apparently just wanted to talk. "You go first."

"All right." Abbie eagerly nodded. "I had a wonderful childhood, except that I didn't have a mother. My father just sort of let me do what I wanted and didn't make me follow a bunch of useless rules."

"You grew up at Kingston?"

"Yes. My father traveled a lot because of his business, but there always seemed to be sisters around—though I wasn't really supposed to know they were my sisters. Still, I knew in my heart they were."

"What about school?" he asked, though he was more interested in other things.

She shifted her position, and her breasts jiggled under the camisole. The jiggling had an effect on him. He moved his arm over his lap so she wouldn't see.

Talk about wearing his heart on his sleeve. One glance at his lap, and Abbie would know just how interested he was in this conversation about her childhood. The thing that most interested him now was the possibility of her jiggling again. And him finding out exactly how well they could jiggle together.

". . . Tutor me," she said.

He'd missed the first part of what she said, but that last bit really grabbed his attention. *Tutor me.* Yes, indeed. Rio planned on doing plenty of tutoring tonight. Something along the lines of *Abbie, wrap your legs around me and let me sink deep into your—*

"Ear," she provided.

"Ear?" One side of his top lip rose in a puzzled gesture. "What exactly are you talking about?"

"I asked if there was something in your ear."

He brushed his hand over the part of him in question. "No, why?"

"Because you didn't seem to hear me, that's why. I'd finished telling you about the tutor my father hired to school me, and—"

"Tutor?" Oh that kind of tutor. The dull kind.

"Yes." She looked at him the way someone might look at a mentally deficient person. "Are you sure you want to keep talking? If you're tired, we could just head on back to the camp."

"No!" Since he'd practically shouted, he quickly tried

to level his voice. "I don't want to go back right now. I want to talk some more." And then get onto other things. Talking about mundane things just might give him time to act like himself rather than some horny half-wit.

"All right, then it's your turn."

Apparently, the horniness didn't plan to leave any time soon. That sounded like a full notice invitation to sample her wares. "My turn for what?"

"To tell me about your childhood."

Oh, that. Rio hadn't actually expected to talk about his childhood, or for that matter say anything about his past. Unlike Abbie's, it had been far from *wonderful* and it was something he wouldn't share with anyone. Not even his wife.

"How about we discuss our marriage instead?" He placed his hand over hers and curled his fingers beneath it until they touched her palm.

Abbie's head snapped quickly toward him. "What are you doing?"

With his attention focused on her fingers, he brought them to his mouth and kissed them one at a time. When he got to her thumb he nipped it gently with his teeth.

"I'm kissing your hand," he answered calmly.

"That's not a good idea." Abbie narrowed her eyes. "We still don't have those preventatives."

"We don't need them. I just want to kiss you. Can't a man kiss his wife without having preventatives?"

"I . . . guess."

Reluctant as she was, it was the only invitation he needed. If she hadn't accepted that one, then he would have kept trying until he found an invitation she did like.

Rio closed the few inches of distance between them. Lowering his head, he placed his mouth solidly on hers. She made a whimper of protest, just enough to part her lips. Just enough so he could kiss her the way he wanted. And that's exactly what he did: kissed her, the way he wanted. Still, he didn't linger too long. No sense over-whelming her right at the start. And there was a good chance too much of this would overwhelm him, too.

"See?" he said, smiling. "Just a kiss."

Abbie noisily gulped in a mouthful of air. "It's hard to catch my breath when you do that."

"Then I'm doing it right." It had felt right to him too. So right that he couldn't wait to get on with things. "Why don't we try another one? Except this time, let's do it this way."

"What way? You're not going to do anything odd to me, are you?"

"Odd?" he questioned.

"Anything involving saddles."

Oh, that. Apparently Dorrie had spoken to her after all. "No. Right now we'll just keep kissing."

Leaning closer, Rio kissed her again. Slow. Easy. No demands. Yet.

He took hold of her shoulders and kept his touch gentle so she wouldn't notice what he was doing, which was slowly easing her to the ground. She went down on the grassy bank like a feather.

He went with her.

Rio quickly covered her chest with his. Damn, it felt good. Maybe too good. She was soft and yielding. Jiggly. And he could feel her nipples through the thin camisole that clung damp and cool to her skin.

He deepened the kiss and gradually slid his leg over hers. Her pantalets were up just enough that he could feel her bare leg on his where he'd rolled up his jeans. Skin to skin. They were both damp and warm.

He prayed he could be patient with her. After all, just a few weeks earlier, Abbie had gone through a terrible ordeal. She didn't need him to act like a savage. But he wasn't sure she needed him to be so slow and patient either. Beneath him she was purring. The muscles in her body quivered. Her breathing was rapid and shallow. These were signs he understood well. She wanted him.

Rio covered her breast with his hand. The fabric of her camisole wasn't really a barrier because it was thin cotton and still wet. He gave a throaty growl of approval when her breast filled his hand. His fingers feathered over her nipples, bringing them to peaks.

She moaned.

Things were happening fast, and he knew it wouldn't be much longer before he could pleasure her. He decided he would take her here. Or least that's what his body decided. He would take her here on the warm grass while the water rushed over their feet.

"Rio," she whispered when he kissed her breasts through her camisole. "We probably shouldn't."

"It's all right." He kissed her ear, nipping her lobe with his teeth. A tiny yearning sound tore its way past her throat. "I want you, and you want me."

"Yes, but—"

He gripped the backs of her knees and bent them until they cradled his hips. He kissed her again, stroking her with his tongue in such a way that it imitated exactly what he wanted the rest of their bodies to do.

"Rio," she said again. It was more breath than sound.

"Yes?" Without waiting to hear what she had to say, he skimmed his hands over her upper body.

"We can't do this."

"Sure we can. We're married, remember?" He lowered his hand until he reached the tape on the waistband of her pantalets. "We can do whatever we want."

"No, we can't. We don't have the preventatives."

He loosened the string and slipped his hand into her pantalets. Her muscles twitched and rippled as his fingers moved over her stomach.

She stopped his hand from wandering any lower. "We can't."

"There are other ways, Abbie. Ways we can enjoy each other, and you wouldn't be able to get pregnant."

She stared at him, her gaze locked with his. "You mean what Carlotta was going to do to you?"

No! Absolutely not. That wasn't an image he wanted in his head right now—Abbie doing to him what Carlotta had planned. Her mouth on him . . . No, that wasn't something he could ask of his bride. Well, not tonight anyway.

Some other time perhaps.

"No. Other ways," he assured her. "I could just touch you."

"Touch me? Where?"

Lord. This wasn't something he'd ever had to explain. It was always something he'd just done. Deciding it was easier to show her, Rio eased his hand lower inside her pantalets.

Abbie quickly latched on to his hand. "Ohmygod, not *there. There?* That's what you meant when you said you'd touch me? I don't think so."

"But I promise it'll feel good, Abbie. Not like when the Apaches violated you."

She went stiff beneath him, and Rio wanted to kick himself for bringing that up. Now, when she'd just started to respond to him.

"I can't," she said on a strangled gasp. "I just can't."

Yeah, that's what he figured she'd say—and he couldn't very well pressure her to change her mind. Abbie had probably been through hell and back with Gray Wolf, and she definitely didn't need him trying to force her to do something she wasn't ready to do. It'd been less than a month, and it was possible she still had injuries—something his lust-driven body hadn't considered until now.

"I'm sorry." He rolled off her and sat up.

"It's all right. I'm all right."

No thanks to him. Rio sandwiched his head between his hands and stared at the glassy creek. What he wanted to do was pound his head against a rock. "I wasn't thinking. Did I scare you?"

"No," she said quickly. "It's just I'm not, I mean, I didn't, oh, hellfire, this isn't something I can talk about."

"Yeah, I know. That's why I should have never started it. Why don't you get dressed, and I'll walk you back to camp?"

"But—"

"Just get dressed." Rio tried not to sound gruff but realized he'd failed miserably. Now, she probably thought he was mad at her. Mad at himself was closer to the truth. Still, it wasn't a good idea to sit around here with his reticent wife, considering how little she had on. And especially considering the part of his body that wouldn't let him forget.

"Please," he said. "Let's just go."

Chapter Eight

Abbie swiped the sweat off her face with her faded red bandanna and looked out at the dusty trail in front of them. Texas had some pretty places, but this certainly wasn't one of them.

Gone were the succulent pastures and colorful wildflowers. In their place were rugged limestone hills, tall grass that looked like spindly weeds, and the scrawny-leafed mesquites that hadn't given them much shade all day. There wasn't even a butterfly in sight for Beans to chase.

Everything seemed hazy, slightly out of focus. And even though it was close to evening, it was miserably hot. The sweltering summer heat still escaped in steamy waves off the boulders.

She mopped the perspiration off the back of her neck and put away her bandanna. "We should get to Cedar Bluff in the morning," she told Rio when he rode up beside where she stood.

He just nodded.

All right. It might be just a nod, but at least he was communicating with her. Well, sort of. "Maybe it won't take us long to find Gray Wolf and Harmony once we get there."

Another nod. This time he added a grunt.

She thought maybe it was a grunt of approval. Hard to tell though. Most grunts sounded alike to her. Too bad it seemed to be Rio's favorite form of communication. "I think Gussie and Victoria are getting a little tired. We'll set up camp over there in that clump of mesquites."

He nodded and gave another of those uncertain grunts.

And so that seemed to end their conversation. That's the way all their conversations had gone over the past three days. Nods. Grunts. Shrugs. An occasional raised eyebrow. At night he'd even made a point of putting his bedroll as far away from hers as possible. A couple of times she'd started to ask him if he wanted to make himself a camp away from her, but Abbie was afraid he would say yes.

For the most part, Rio had just plain ignored her as if she were a speck of dirt. Abbie couldn't blame him. She wished she could ignore herself too. Or punish herself for what she'd done.

She felt lower than bunions.

Abbie didn't dare look Rio straight in the eye, even though they were riding practically side by side. It was just as well. It didn't seem as if he could look her in the eye either.

Of course, Rio probably felt guilty because he'd tried to have marital relations with her. No great misdeed, really. Most men would have expected that from their new bride. But when she'd stopped him, he no doubt thought she was still recovering from her terrible ordeal with the Apaches.

He probably felt lower than bunions, too.

Still, it was for the best. He no longer seemed the least bit interested in her, and that was a good thing. It would make it easier for them to part company after they arrived at Kingston. Unfortunately, his lack of interest in her didn't feel nearly as good as she thought it would.

To make matters worse, Abbie hadn't told Rio anywhere near the truth about Harmony's capture. Still, maybe—just maybe--she wouldn't have to tell him either. If luck was with her, then they could find Gray Wolf soon, and Rio could negotiate with him for Harmony's release. Maybe that would happen without the men exchanging too much information.

She could hope anyway.

If not, she'd have to do some fast talking.

As usual.

Rio got her attention by clearing his throat. "I want to walk ahead and see what's over that ridge."

Since it was the most he'd said to her in three days, Abbie nodded and got off her horse. "All right. I'll go ahead and set up camp."

Rio dismounted, and she took the reins of his stallion. Without even a farewell grunt, he headed off the path and across the rock-littered field.

Victoria walked over to Abbie, and the two watched Rio disappear into some dense brush. "What did you do to him?" Victoria asked.

Abbie slipped her a whose-side-are-you-on glance. "I didn't do anything."

"Don't give me that. Rio's been avoiding you, and you've been avoiding me. That spells trouble. It seems all of this started after that night he went looking for you. What happened, anyway?"

"He found me."

"And?"

Abbie shrugged and looked up at the sky. "And nothing."

"Not nothing. Something. Now, tell me what happened."

"We kissed, that's all."

Victoria frowned. "He found out, didn't he?"

"Found out what?"

"That those Apaches didn't do a thing to you."

"No, he didn't find out. I stopped things before they got too far."

Well, he had gotten his hand inside her drawers. Abbie supposed some might consider that too far, but the point was that she had stopped it.

"Ah," Victoria said knowingly, a little too smugly for Abbie's liking. "So, you stopped him with a reminder of the horrors you endured during your captivity. Now, you feel guilty for lying to him."

"What? How can you figure all of that out just by looking at me? Do you have some kind of straight connection with the Almighty?"

"As a matter of fact, I do." Victoria sighed and started the coffee. "Well, in this case, not telling the truth might have been the right thing to do."

"Glad you approve."

"I do. Nothing good could come from consummating this mockery you've made of something that should be sacred and holy. After all, when everything is said and done, Rio will return to the ranch in Fall Creek."

Abbie paused, shrugged. "Yes."

"And you'll have to stay in Kingston."

A longer pause. Another shrug. "Yes."

"Besides, after he learns everything, he probably won't speak to you anyway."

True. So, this really was for the best. Wasn't that exactly what she had told herself? Now her sister had confirmed it. That didn't give Abbie as much comfort as she thought it should. Victoria and she rarely agreed on anything, and she had just answered *yes* to everything the woman said.

"This way, you'll be able to get an annulment," Victoria added.

Again, that was true. Abbie bobbed her head in agreement. An annulment would certainly be easier, and it would mean Rio wouldn't have to live with the infamy of being a divorced man.

"Just how many times did Rio kiss you anyway?"

Abbie frowned. "Why would a nun want to know something like that?"

"A nun doesn't, but your sister does."

Of course. Victoria would use that to get her to confess. Unfortunately, it always worked. How could she possibly deny telling her sister the intimate details of her life? If Victoria had had any intimate details, she would have certainly shared them with her. "He kissed me a few times, that's all."

"If that's all there was to it, you shouldn't be blushing."

"I'm not blu—"

"You are too. Now, don't make me find a mirror so I can prove it. You're blushing, and you wouldn't do that if all Rio had done was kiss you. What else happened?"

"All right." Abbie gave a series of awkward nods while she tried to figure out how she could say this. "He touched me, uh, places."

Victoria's mouth flew open, and her hand caught a loud gasp. "Places? You don't mean *the place down there?*" Her nods were just as awkward as she tried to motion toward the spot in reference.

"No," Abbie said quickly.

But he'd gotten pretty darn close. Another inch or two, and she would have probably broken a few commandments. Except maybe she wouldn't have broken anything. Rio was her husband, after all. In fact, maybe it was breaking commandments to not let him touch her down there. . . .

That was certainly something to think about anyway.

Actually, she'd thought a lot about how his hands felt on her skin. How his skillful fingers had touched her. On her breasts. And on her stomach. But as good as all that was, and it was very good, Abbie thought maybe it would have felt even better if she'd let his skillful fingers go an inch or two lower. And maybe inside. Deep inside. Where there seemed to be a dull unexplainable ache. She shivered.

"You're blushing again," Victoria pointed out. "A lot."

Abbie had forgotten that Victoria was anywhere around. Actually, she'd forgotten her own name. "It's just hot out here." She was hot. Hot in a way she couldn't really explain. "I didn't think I'd like for a man to touch me in those places," she confided.

"But you did?"

"I did. It wasn't at all like Aunt Dorrie explained." She definitely didn't feel saddled. "It made me feel kind of itchy all over."

"Itchy?" her half-sister repeated in a small voice.

Victoria's hands went on her hips, and her voice rose to an ear-piercing level. "Augusta Marie Burge! Get out here this minute."

The girl peered out from behind a huge boulder only a couple of feet away. "What?" she asked innocently.

"What do you mean *what?* What are you doing back there listening to private conversations that you shouldn't be listening to?"

The child shrugged and moved closer to them. "Getting in trouble, I guess?"

"You're right enough about that. You'll have to say your prayers four times tonight."

"I'll say 'em five times if Abbie'll tell me what she meant by Rio making her feel itchy."

Abbie smiled softly and gave Gussie a playful swat on the bottom. "I'll tell you when you're older. And taller. And when you're smart enough not to get caught eavesdropping. Now, you'd better get started on those prayers. You might not get finished with them before daylight."

"Awww." Gussie kicked at a rock and headed for her bedroll.

"Honestly, she reminds me of you." Victoria clucked her tongue disapprovingly and shook her head. "I have no idea what I'm going to do with her."

Abbie held up her hand to silence her sister when she heard the noise. A bird, maybe. And maybe it was exactly the noise she'd been waiting to hear.

"What?" Victoria whispered.

"I'm not sure. I think I'll go for a little walk."

"A walk? Now?"

"Yes. I think we might have a visitor."

"Do you mean—"

"Maybe. Keep the rifle close, but for heaven's sake don't shoot unless you know who you're shooting at. I don't want you taking any shots at me or Rio."

"But what do I tell Rio if he comes back before you do?"

"Tell him I'm taking another bath."

Before Victoria could protest, Abbie retrieved her Colt from her pack and headed out.

Rio leaned against the tree and took in the night: the chirping of the cicadas, the night breeze rustling the leaves, limestone boulders still warm even though the sun had already set. There was a sky full of stars and a hunter's moon.

And he was alone.

Normally Rio would have considered this just about as close to heaven as he could get, but tonight it didn't feel much like heaven. He hadn't been able to shake his disgust with himself for pressing Abbie to make love with him. He'd pressed a woman who'd been violated only weeks before.

What in the hell had he been thinking?

That was just it—he hadn't thought. He'd reacted and let another part of his body move him. Rio knew for a fact that part of him rarely made good decisions. In this case, it had failed miserably. Abbie probably never wanted him to come near her again, and he understood. The problem was, his body still wanted her. And he would continue to want her as long as he was around her. Fortunately, that wouldn't be for long.

The first step was to find Gray Wolf, or maybe a better way of putting it was the first step was for Gray Wolf to find them. Rio had no doubt that would happen soon. In fact, he highly suspected that Gray Wolf or one of his men had trailed them all day. Someone had been, anyway. Rio figured once that person decided it was time to show himself, negotiations could begin.

Hopefully, he could get them to release Harmony right away. He didn't like the idea of spending a lot of time in Gray Wolf's territory, especially with Abbie and the others close by. In fact, he wanted to kick himself for allowing them within fifty miles of here. If he'd been in his right mind, he would have insisted the women ride by train. He could have come out here on his own to negotiate. Unfortunately, he hadn't been in his right mind for some time now.

Rio only hoped it wasn't a critical mistake allowing Abbie to distract him as she had. The distractions couldn't continue. He had to focus on what he needed to get done, and that started with negotiations for Harmony's release. That would only leave him to deal with getting Camellia out of Abbie's house. Then he could be on his way back to the ranch.

A soft sound snared his attention. Someone stepped

through the woods to his left. It was the same person who'd followed them all day, but he was closer now. It probably wasn't Gray Wolf, but the renegade leader was likely somewhere nearby. That's why Rio hadn't wandered too far from the camp.

There was a blur of movement in the brush. The same man again. Two steps and a pause; he slightly favored one leg.

Rio didn't move a muscle. The low-hanging mesquite branches didn't completely hide him, but moving now would certainly give away his position. Without lifting his rifle, Rio eased his finger into the loop and over the trigger.

The man stepped out into a small clearing. He was armed with a carbine and was definitely Apache. He wore light-colored trousers and a bulky overshirt. Bandannas were tied around his head and at his throat. His boots were loose, soft leather that he'd pulled up to his knees. There was a knife strapped to his leg.

He paused in the clearing. Not really paused, it was more of a hesitation. Rio could sense the subtle difference. The Apache had detected something. Maybe not him, but something.

Rio slowly raised his Winchester, aimed it, and waited to see what the man planned to do. Thankfully, the camp was behind Rio, and anyone headed in that direction would have to get past him. That wouldn't happen.

There was another sound to his right. Someone else was coming. Fast. There was no hesitation in these steps. A snap of a twig. The swish of a tree branch being moved. This one wasn't an Apache. Too much noise, and the gait wasn't right. It had to be a white—

Ah, hell.

He saw Abbie come from behind a rangy cedar, and she moved right into his line of fire. He didn't dare call out to her to stop because it would alert the Apache, and at that range the Indian could kill her with one shot. Rio only hoped Abbie would see the man and dive to the ground.

It was too late. The warrior's chin came up, and he shifted his posture toward Abbie. Thankfully, he didn't raise his weapon. Rio took aim, praying that Abbie would move, knowing if she didn't, he might have to fire anyway and hope that he got a lucky shot. She continued to walk in a straight line, a line that would take her directly to the man.

She put her hands on her hips when she got closer. "Well, it's about time you got here. Where in the Sam Hill have you been?"

It took Rio a moment to realize that she had spoken not to him, but to the Indian. And then Abbie did something that stunned him.

She wrapped her arms around the man and kissed him.

Rio thought maybe his feet had frozen to the ground. His wife had her arms around an Apache renegade, possibly the same man who'd held her hostage. Rio didn't like the thoughts that started to go through his head. Reverend Waddill said that Abbie hadn't wanted to leave her captors, that she'd resisted the Rangers' attempts to save her. Rio thought that was maybe because Harmony was still there.

But maybe not.

Maybe it was because Abbie was . . . what? In some kind of partnership with this man? In love with him maybe? That didn't sit well with Rio at all. No, not well at all.

His wife had some explaining to do.

Chapter Nine

The embrace lingered a moment longer before Abbie pulled away from Chey. "Where were you anyway?" she demanded. "Do you know how worried I've been about you?"

"I can guess." He pushed a lock of hair off her forehead. "Some bounty hunter was after me, and I had to lay low for a while until my leg healed."

Immediately Abbie's anger turned to concern. "Until your leg healed? He shot you?"

"The bullet went straight through. Nothing to worry about, but it kept me laid up for a while. That sweet little German widow near Harpersville nursed me back to health."

"Why did the man shoot you?"

"A case of mistaken identity. How about you? Are you all right?"

Abbie pressed her head against his arm. He smelled of saddle leather, and even though she hadn't seen or heard

111

his horse, she figured it was nearby. "I've been better. A lot better. Do you have any idea what's going on?"

"If you mean did I know Gray Wolf had taken you— yes. I ran into one of his men about two weeks ago, and he told me all about it. By then, you were already in Fall Creek. Did he hurt you?"

"I don't want to talk about me. It's Harmony I'm worried about. You have to do something to help her."

"And I will. But first, I have a question for you. Who's the man standing over there by that tree? The one with the Winchester aimed at my head?"

Abbie's breath rattled in her throat. God, a man. That could mean only one thing. This was not good. Not good at all.

She turned, slowly, bracing herself for the stern expression that she would see on Rio's face. And she saw it all right. Even in the darkness, she couldn't miss his formidable scowl.

"Rio," she said, but her voice had so much breath she had to repeat it to give it sound. "You're, uh, here."

He stepped closer, his rifle still aimed and ready to fire. "It appears that way."

"Rio?" Chey repeated.

Abbie tried to swallow the lump in her throat and failed. She decided she didn't want to see either man's expression now, so she looked up at the stars. "Rio McCaine. He's my, uh, husband."

"He's *what?*" Chey didn't sound happy. Abbie hadn't expected he would be. She only prayed he didn't give away everything before she had a chance to explain a few things to both men.

Rio stopped only a few feet in front of her and finally lowered his gun. "Care to tell me what's going on here?"

Abbie supposed he directed that question at her. She took a deep breath before she answered. "This is Chey."

His eyes narrowed. "Your lover?"

Stunned, her mouth dropped open. "My lov—absolutely not. He's my brother."

"Your brother?"

"Well, my half-brother."

"And what are you doing here with him?"

Lord, this wouldn't be a short explanation or an easy one. Abbie started to suggest they all get comfortable and sit down, but Rio didn't appear to be in a getting-comfortable kind of mood. Her brother probably wasn't either. "I'm here because I wanted to see Chey, and I think he wanted to see me too. I believe he's been following us for a couple of hours."

"He's followed us since this morning," Rio corrected. He tipped his head to Chey. "Care to tell me what's going on here? My wife seems to be sketchy about why she sneaked off to meet you."

Chey stepped out from behind her and stood by her side. "Your *wife* is usually sketchy about telling people her plans. I wouldn't mind hearing what she has to say myself. Abbie?"

She glanced at Rio, and then Chey. This was one conversation she would have preferred to avoid, but it didn't seem she could. "First of all, I didn't sneak off to meet Chey. I didn't even know for sure that he'd be out here. I heard something and came to see who or what it was."

"Go on," Rio said when she stopped.

"All right, I will. If it was Chey, then I wanted to tell him about my ordeal with Gray Wolf."

"He doesn't ride with Gray Wolf?"

"Lord, no. Chey wouldn't ride with a renegade like that, though he seems to get accused of it often enough."

Rio lifted his hand in a gesture to indicate *go ahead*. "Then by all means tell your brother about your ordeal. I'd like to hear what you have to say, too."

Chey probably already knew everything, but it wouldn't hurt to have him hear her version of events.

Gray Wolf had no doubt gone on and on with his own lopsided account.

She cleared her throat first. "Harmony and I were on our way to Fall Creek, and I thought I'd try to find Chey. I mean, I hadn't seen him in months, and I wanted to talk to him. Anyway, we were riding near Cedar Bluff, and before I knew what was happening, we were surrounded by over a dozen wretched, sweaty Apaches." She glanced at her brother. "Sorry about that, but they *were* sweaty and wretched. Then Gray Wolf grabbed Harmony and me and wouldn't release us."

That was close to the truth anyway. Abbie decided not to mention that Gray Wolf had been more than willing to let Abbie herself go, but he hadn't been so accommodating when it came to Harmony.

Chey stepped closer. "The man I spoke to a couple of weeks ago said Gray Wolf took you captive because you shot him."

"Oh, that." She dismissed it with the wave of her hand. "It was hardly more than a scratch on the arm."

"Gray Wolf didn't think so."

"Well, I don't care what he thinks. He's an Apache warrior, for heaven's sake. He should be able to handle a little bullet wound without whining about it to everyone."

"You shot that man?" Rio asked.

"Grazed his arm," she corrected. "It barely bled at all, and I'd have shot him again if I'd gotten the chance. He deserved worse after what he did."

Rio nodded. "I agree."

"Thank you." But it occurred to her that Rio had said that because of the things he thought Gray Wolf had done to her. Maybe this was a good time to go on with her explanation and not mention anymore about that.

Rio gave Chey a stern look. "Did you settle things with Gray Wolf for taking your sister?"

"Sisters," Chey corrected. "He took Harmony, too. I haven't had a chance to speak to him, but I will."

"Well, good." Abbie gave an approving nod. "He still has Harmony, and he wouldn't even talk to me about releasing her. Do you know what he said?" She didn't wait for Chey to answer. "He said I had to find you or some man to do my talking for me, that he wouldn't listen to another word coming from a trigger-happy woman. Can you believe that? He treated me like I was some bullheaded, rattlebrain female who can't think for herself."

A smile tugged at Chey's mouth. "He obviously doesn't know you. You're bullheaded but hardly ever rattlebrained. And you do more than enough thinking for yourself."

Abbie scolded him with one narrowed eye. "As I was saying, Gray Wolf insisted I had to find a man to talk for me, but I couldn't find you, Chey. Then the Rangers came and forced me to go to Fall Creek before I could settle all of this and get Harmony back. That's when I got the idea that maybe Rio could negotiate with Gray Wolf."

"And you thought the only way I would do that was if you married me?" Rio asked in disbelief.

"That's not why I married you." Blast it. That would have been a good time to keep her mouth shut. "I mean, yes—that's one of the reasons I married you."

"But now that your brother is here, you won't need me, will you?"

"Maybe not for that, but I still need you to make Camellia leave Kingston, and I want to introduce you to Wendell so he'll know he can't pester me any longer."

A long silence followed, and during that time Rio didn't take his attention off her. "Anything else you forgot to mention?"

"No. Nothing I can think of." There was nothing she

wanted to think of though. Absolutely nothing. In fact, she was completely sure she didn't want Rio to learn any more about this situation. "Let me say good-bye to my brother, and we can go back to camp. Victoria will be worried if we stay out too long."

Before Rio or Chey could object, she caught Chey's arm and pulled him aside. "How soon do you think you can get Gray Wolf to release Harmony?" she whispered.

Chey shrugged. "If she wants to leave, I could have her out of there as early as tomorrow."

"What do you mean *if* she wants to leave? Of course, she will."

"Maybe not. The man I spoke to said he thought she and Gray Wolf might have worked out their differences."

Abbie groaned and almost forgot to keep her voice soft so Rio wouldn't hear. "Has she lost her mind? Harmony said she was finished with him. The man will never, never make her happy. Now, she's the one with a rattle-brain."

"I think it runs in the family. I could say the same about you and this hasty marriage. It smells rank, like one of your cockeyed plans gone awry. What exactly are you up to anyway?"

She glanced at Rio. He had his gaze fixed on her. "It's a long story. One I don't intend to get into here."

"I have time to listen," Chey assured her, a hint of amusement in his tone. "I always enjoy a good laugh."

Her hands went back on her hips. "Just speak to Harmony, and if she wants to leave Gray Wolf, then I want her on a train to New Orleans. Send her to Aunt Maddie May's in French Town. It isn't safe for her to be on her own."

"You could say please, you know. Everything that comes out of your mouth sounds just like an order."

"It does not." Yes, it did. And her demands seemed to get worse whenever she was in a difficult situation.

Which seemed to be most of the time. "All right, *please.*" But it sounded a lot like the profanity she mumbled next. "Why do you have to make things so difficult?"

"Because I'm your brother. It's something I live for." He chuckled and kissed her cheek. "You don't have to worry about Harmony. She'll be safe with Gray Wolf. That man would die for her."

Abbie rolled her eyes and huffed. "I don't know why men always say stupid things like that. Dying's easy. Incredibly easy. People do it all the time without meaning to. But dying won't do a darn thing to protect Harmony. What I want is for her to be safe. She won't be safe at Kingston or even with Aunt Dorrie in Fall Creek. Not after what they think she did. Just make sure she understands that."

Chey nodded.

"And I need you to do something else," Abbie whispered. "Could you get someone to go into town for you?"

"Of course. What do you need?"

"If you manage to get Harmony to someplace safe, send a telegram to Ina at Kingston and let her know so she won't worry. Can you do that? Please," she added when he only gave her that blank stare.

He laughed. "Much better. Next time, we'll work on 'thank you.' Before long, you might actually get through a conversation without bossing somebody around."

"The telegram," she ground out. "Will you *please* send it to Ina?"

"Most certainly. I think you'd better go. Your, uh, husband seems to be getting restless."

Since Rio did look impatient, Abbie kissed her brother's cheek. "I don't know when I'll see you again, but if you need any money, I left some beneath the floor of the line shack near Whiskey Creek."

"Just go, Abbie. I don't need money."

"And tell Gray Wolf I'm, well, sorry about shooting

him in the arm. It really was an accident. And don't forget about that telegram."

"Please?" Chey teased.

She stuck out her tongue at him. Abbie stepped away from her brother and cautiously trudged toward Rio. A very stern-faced Rio. Her earlier explanations obviously wouldn't be enough to satisfy his curiosity. It was just as well. It was time he heard the truth anyway.

Well, most of the truth.

Rio and Chey stood for a moment and just looked at each other, the span of a dozen or so feet separating them. In profile she thought they seemed as unlike as two men could. Chey, with his light clothing and silk black hair sheeting down his back to his waist. Rio, dressed in his dark jeans and deep blue shirt. His hair lay against his neck. Both were half-breeds, but they had taken two entirely different paths.

It occurred to her, watching them, that they were the two most significant men in her life, and yet they didn't even know each other.

"Comanche?" Chey asked Rio.

Rio nodded.

"You'll watch out for her?"

Another nod.

Chey lifted his hand in farewell, turned, and disappeared into the darkness.

"Good-bye," Abbie called out to Chey.

She shook her head. "Just like him to leave without saying a word to me, and yet he wants me to say please and thank you to him." She glanced at Rio. "You didn't have to tell him you'd watch out for me, you know."

Yes, he did. If Abbie had been his sister, he would have demanded the same thing and would have expected the same confirmation that he'd just given her brother. Despite Chey's assurance that he'd talk to Gray Wolf about Abbie's abduction, however, Rio still hadn't ruled out finding the Apache leader on his way back to Fall Creek.

That was one score he'd like to settle personally.

Rio checked over his shoulder to make sure Chey wasn't following them. He wasn't. Not that he'd expected him to. The best he could tell the man had headed west. That was probably the direction of Gray Wolf's camp and Harmony.

"Go ahead," Abbie said as they walked through the woods toward the camp. "I know you have questions. Ask them."

Oh, he had questions. The problem was, he didn't know where to start. Abbie had just handed him another surprise. Actually, more than a surprise. He didn't think he could soon get the image out of his head of her kissing her half-brother on the cheek. It hadn't felt good to see her with another man.

"Well?" she prompted. "Are you just going to keep stewing and not say a word to me? Look, I know you're mad—"

"I'm not mad."

She stopped so abruptly, he nearly ran into her. "You're not?"

"No."

Even in the moonlight, he could see her puzzled expression. "Then why did you stop talking to me?"

Had he done that? Rio went back through the past three days. Yep, he supposed he had. Hardly a word. Nods, head shakes, and grunts, that was about it. Definitely not much talking. "I guess I didn't know what to say to you. I was mad at myself for what happened at the creek."

"Oh. But not mad at me?"

"No. You didn't do anything wrong, Abbie. You were just taking a bath, and I—"

"Please, there's no reason for us to go back through all of that again. Let's just forget that it happened, all right?"

He couldn't forget something that still had his body in knots, but he wouldn't press her to talk about it. Not when they had so many other things to discuss. "Is there any reason you didn't tell me your brother might be out here?"

That got her walking again. She scratched her eyebrow and started up the trail. "The truth?"

"That'd be nice for a change."

"He's always wanted by the law for questioning regarding some raids that I'm certain he didn't do. The Rangers assume because he's Apache that he rides with Gray Wolf and those other renegades. He doesn't."

All right. That was probably the truth. There had been at least a dozen raids on nearby towns, and any Apache within a hundred miles of Gray Wolf's men would have come under suspicion.

Abbie pulled in a deep breath. "But Chey should be able to work out Harmony's release. Thank God we ran into him when we did. I didn't like the idea of you having to face Gray Wolf."

"Believe me, I would have managed." And would have enjoyed every minute of it. "Tell me about your brother. When he's not hiding out from the law, does he live at Kingston?"

"Not anymore. His mother worked at Kingston, and they left when Chey was about fourteen."

"Because your father didn't want them there?"

"Oh, no. My father wasn't like that. Despite his roving eye, he only kept one woman at a time, and he *kept* Chey's mother for years. It was her decision to leave. Needless to say, it wasn't a good decision. If they'd stayed, I'd have been able to protect them better. Chey, especially."

"Maybe he doesn't want you to protect him."

"I can't imagine why." She shrugged. "He's my brother. It's what I'm supposed to do."

"What you're supposed to do?" he repeated. "What if Chey wanted you to move out here so he could protect you?"

Abbie laughed, a single harsh burst of air. "That'll be the day. I don't need anyone to protect me." The moment the words left her mouth, she stopped. Paused. Then she started walking again. Well, she actually started to stomp a little. "Oh, I get it. You're trying to make me see that it isn't necessary to impose myself into my brother's life. Well, you're wrong. I'm the oldest. It's my duty to make sure they're safe and happy."

Rio didn't want to remind her that those two things weren't always in agreement. Besides, maybe Abbie was beginning to see on her own that she didn't have to boss everyone around under the guise of it being her duty.

He stopped when they neared the camp and caught her arm. "Before we go any farther, I'd like to ask you something else, something I'd like you to answer honestly."

"What?" she asked cautiously.

"Are there anymore of these surprises waiting for me?"

She paused and bunched up her forehead as if giving that some thought. "Not really."

The indefinite answer nearly caused him to groan. There was something else. Something Abbie obviously didn't want to tell him. Definitely more surprises. "Why do you find it so hard to trust me?"

"I do trust you," she answered slowly. "About most things. I'm just, well, I'm just not used to relying on anyone but myself."

He cupped her chin, forcing her to look at him. "I know why you married me, and it wasn't so you could have a real husband or so you could experience a night of passionate lovemaking. I've already said I'm sorry for what happened at the creek. I scared you, and I—"

"You didn't scare me."

"I did. I know I did."

"You didn't. In fact, I maybe liked it when you kissed me."

Oh. Rio hadn't expected that. "You did?"

She nodded. "It didn't scare me at all, but it did confuse me a little. Remember when I told you I'd been kissed dozens of times?"

"Yes."

"Well, that wasn't exactly true. I think maybe I hadn't been kissed at all, or else the others didn't know what they were doing. I'm pretty sure you knew what you were doing. It made me feel, well, I don't even know how to explain it. It made me feel sort of itchy all over, like I was missing out on something and didn't even know I was missing it. Does that sound stupid?"

Rio had to swallow. "No." It sounded like an open door to do some more kissing, that's what. In fact, he'd wanted to kiss Abbie again for days now. But this time, things would be different. He would take it slower. Keep it nice and sweet. Let Abbie set the pace. Then, maybe he could show her what she'd been missing.

Since his hand was already on her chin, he brushed his thumb over her bottom lip. It trembled under his touch. Abbie trembled. He saw the small shiver work its way down her body. Rio took a step closer, closing the distance between them. He put his rifle aside and slipped his hand around the back of her neck.

"Is this all right with you?" he asked. "Because I'd like to kiss you."

"Yes," she whispered breathily.

Rio paused a moment longer, wondering if this would be a mistake. Suddenly he didn't care if it was. She'd said yes. Yes meant yes. He had never wanted to kiss a woman as much as he wanted to kiss Abbie. Never.

He lowered his head, brought their mouths together, and kissed her.

Their bodies naturally angled to adjust to each other. His bottom lip moved between Abbie's slightly opened mouth. He felt the warmth and moisture from her breath. When his tongue slid across her lips, she opened her mouth to him, and the kiss swallowed their coupled moans.

"Yes, there it is," she whispered, her mouth still against his. "That itch I was talking about."

Her words turned his body to fire. His attempted tenderness suddenly seemed a lost cause. Something primal kicked in, his body responding to a need that would not be denied. A need to claim, to possess. To mate. He didn't want to think about anything else. He needed. She needed. What needed to happen, would.

Pushing her off the trail and beneath a scrub oak, Rio landed his shoulder hard against the rough bark. Abbie crashed against him since he still had a tight hold on her.

The kiss continued.

He reached for her. She reached back. Abbie clutched his shoulders and dragged him closer. Not that he needed to be dragged. Not that he could get much closer. They were already pressed to each other, the tree supporting them both. To get closer, he'd have to be inside her.

The way they were going, that would happen very soon.

He forced himself to consider the consequences of that. Unfortunately, those thoughts got muddled by the tiny yearning sounds she made and the way she grabbed onto him. He couldn't risk getting her pregnant though—and not just because it was something that frightened her. No, he couldn't risk it because it was something that frightened him. It scared the hell out of him, actually. He couldn't just walk away from his own child, couldn't do what his father had done to him. A baby would mean he'd be bound to Abbie and the child for the rest of his life. Rio didn't want that kind of commitment.

Something like that would mess up all of his plans.

"Just kissing," he mumbled, more for himself than Abbie. "Nothing more."

"Sure. All right."

From the way she said that, he got the feeling that he would have to be the one to slow things down.

"When I say stop, we'll have to stop," he added.

"Sure."

She latched her hands onto his hair and pulled his mouth back to hers. Rio feasted on her. Her lips. Then the base of her throat. Lowering his hand, he cupped her breast. First one and then the other. It wasn't enough.

He wanted more.

Through her shirt he stroked her nipple until it tightened, fitting itself into the snug space he'd allowed between his thumb and forefinger. There he played with it. First with his fingers, then he closed his mouth over the thin cotton and the sensitive bud beneath it.

"Yes," she hissed, practically shoving her body into his.

Yes, was right. But soon that wasn't enough either. He could go a little further and still stop. Or he was fairly certain he could.

Abbie grabbed his hair again. "Do something, please."

Ah, hell. Now, he had her begging him. That didn't sound like stopping.

It didn't *feel* a lot like stopping either because Rio began to pull at the buttons of her shirt. His hand was too unsteady to be gentle. It didn't seem to matter. Abbie wasn't gentle either. Her fingers dug into his back.

When he had enough of the buttons undone, he ran his hand inside and stretched down her camisole to expose her breasts, her soft skin. She was all woman. He wet his fingertips and slipped them over her nipples.

She gasped. "Yes."

Abbie closed the distance between his mouth and her breasts, offering herself up on her tiptoes. He lowered his head and took. Kissed. Slowly. Thoroughly. He roughly flicked his tongue over the nipple and brought it into his mouth.

Another gasp. "Rio?"

"What?"

"I can't breathe again."

Yes, she could. He could feel her breath was coming hot and fast. So was his. "You'll be all right."

"I don't think so. I feel so itchy. God, Rio, can't you do something? I don't think I can stand this much longer."

He groaned. Oh, he could do something all right. He could strip off her clothes, pull her to the ground and sink right into that warm wet place between her thighs. Neither one of them would feel itchy after that. But then, there was the problem of making a baby. He could give them a whole world of pleasure now, but he might have to pay for it the rest of his life.

"Please," she whispered again.

That did it. Something would to have to give here. He would die of need if he didn't stop the pounding ache in his groin. And obviously Abbie would do some dying of her own. What he had in mind wouldn't be pretty, but it would get the job done.

He ran his hand down her thigh and caught the back of her knee, lifted it so that it hugged the outside of his leg. The centers of their bodies met in precise, direct alignment. Even through the split-skirt he could feel how soft she was. Unlike himself. The fit was perfect. So much so that he ground his hard heat into the soft vulnerable notch of her body.

Again, though he was rough, she was rougher, latching on to handfuls of his shirt and his flesh to bring him against her, to create more contact. More pressure.

"Yes, that," she mumbled. "Lots more of that."

Not that she had to tell him. Rio knew she was finding her own version of paradise by the way she rubbed herself against him. The rhythm of her hips was as old as time itself.

"More," she demanded.

Then she mumbled something about churning butter, but he didn't know what she meant. He didn't want to take the time to figure it out either. Rio wanted just one thing. To drop down to his knees so he could give her a kiss she'd never forget. That would certainly qualify as *more*. More for him and a heck of a lot more for her. But something stopped him.

A sound.

Abbie must have heard it too because she quickly untangled herself from him. Somehow, without bumping into each other, both of them caught up their weapons and whirled toward the sound, ready to fire. Later, although he'd been surprised to see she had a weapon, Rio wanted to tell her how impressed he was with her maneuvering. Some considered him to be a fast draw, and Abbie had matched him.

Forcing his attention back to the sound, Rio heard the barking, but it took moments longer before he realized what it was. It took him even longer than that to figure out the dog was crashing toward them. Beans, however, wasn't alone.

"Gussie," Rio said, moving away from Abbie.

She made a sound of protest and tossed her gun aside. "Gussie? Not now. Where?"

"Coming up the path." He quickly tried to right her clothes but knew there was nothing he could do about his own condition. Even in the darkness the bulge in his jeans was painfully obvious. He adjusted his rifle so it covered that particular part of him.

"Gussie?" Abbie called out. "What are you doing out here?"

With her hands stuck in her pockets, the little girl walked closer. "I'm just out walking. I didn't see much. Well, except for Rio kissing you."

Abbie shook her finger at her. "You shouldn't have seen anything at all because you shouldn't be out here. It's dangerous for a little girl to be wandering around these woods at night. Now get on back to camp."

It seemed the child would. Gussie turned, stepped forward . . . then turned right back around to face them. "Is that what you meant when you said Rio makes you feel all itchy?"

"What!" Abbie howled. "Augusta Marie Burge, you—"

"I know, I know. I gotta say my prayers four more times."

"Ten," Abbie corrected as the child walked away. With the annoyed look still on her face, she glanced at Rio. "I'm sorry about that. We probably shouldn't have been doing this out here anyway."

He nodded. "Are you all right?"

She gave her camisole an adjustment and finished buttoning her shirt. "Just a little light-headed."

There was nothing light about any part of his body. Rio leaned the back of his head against the tree and tried to catch his breath. Gussie's interruption was a reminder that he had done this all wrong. Again. This wasn't any place to make love to Abbie. Especially not against a tree.

In a day or two they'd arrive at Kingston, and they would have the preventatives. They might also have some privacy there. Or at least a bed. It seemed reasonable that he should make love to her the first time in a bed. Rio didn't want to consider that making love to her at all was an unreasonable notion.

No, he didn't want to consider it.

Not when his body still begged for the woman next to him. And he didn't want to consider it after the way she'd just responded to him. After all, what harm could it do for a man and woman to enjoy each other's company at least once?

Or twice.

Chapter Ten

"She's gone, Abbie."

Abbie was stooped over, washing her face in the creek, but she looked over her shoulder at Victoria. "Who's gone?"

"Gussie. She's not here."

"Sure she is. I saw her when we were eating lunch."

"That was nearly a half hour ago. She said she was going to relieve herself, and she hasn't come back."

Abbie dried her face on her shirtsleeve and glanced around the woods. "She's probably playing and just lost track of time." She cupped her hands around her mouth and yelled, "Gussie."

Nothing.

Abbie stepped away from the creek and called for the girl again.

Still nothing.

Victoria caught her rosary between thumb and index

finger. "Something's wrong, Abbie. I can feel it in my bones."

Abbie only nodded. Maybe something *was* wrong. Gussie's hearing had never been a problem, just the opposite, and the child knew better than to wander too far from camp. Also Abbie knew that Victoria had a special talent for sensing when things weren't right.

"What's going on?" Rio asked.

He was at the pack horse, checking the cinch, and Abbie motioned for him to join them. "Gussie might be missing."

"This isn't like her," Victoria added. "I think something's happened."

Abbie suddenly recalled the previous night when she'd scolded Gussie for going out into the woods, and for trying to watch Rio and her kiss. Now that she gave it some thought, Gussie had been quiet all morning. Not just quiet—sulky. Maybe Gussie decided to hide out so she could give them all a good scare.

Unfortunately, it was working.

"Let's split up," Rio instructed. "Victoria, you take the east side of the camp. Abbie, you go straight ahead up the trail. I'll follow the creek."

Abbie gave him a quick glare. Why did he think he was in charge of putting together a search party? He hadn't even given her a chance to assemble a possible rescue before he'd taken it on his shoulders. Well, she didn't want this on anyone's shoulders but her own.

"You have a problem with something I said?" he asked after glancing at her.

"Gussie's my sister. Probably. And I think I should be the one to come up with the plan to find her."

"Oh?" he asked with enough skepticism to put her teeth on edge. "And what exactly is your plan?"

Abbie realized she didn't have one. She also realized there was nothing wrong with his. It was just the principle of the thing. Much like saying please instead of issuing an order. "We'll do as you say. This time. Next time we need a plan though, I get to come up with it. I'm the one in charge of this trip."

Lord, that sounded petty, and Abbie frowned at herself. Her sister might be missing, so why should it bother her that someone else wanted to be in *charge?*

With an annoyed snarl, Rio began to walk toward the bank of the creek. "Take a gun with you," he called back. "Or maybe you'd like to come up with a different plan for that, too?"

Abbie glared at him and went up the trails. How could that man set her on fire one minute and burn her up the next?

She had no answer for that.

There also seemed to be no answer as to Gussie's whereabouts. After searching for over a half hour, Abbie's concern turned to full-fledged fear. She started to imagine all kinds of horrible things—a wild animal, a rattlesnake. Maybe Gussie was just plain lost and frightened. Maybe it was worse. Maybe she was lying hurt somewhere and hadn't been able to make it back to camp.

"Gussie?" Abbie called out again. "Answer me!"

In the distance she heard Victoria call out the child's name also.

"Over here," Rio yelled.

Breaking into a run, Abbie followed the sound of his voice. The brush was dense, and she fought her way through the thick cedars and knee-high grass. She didn't like what she saw when she came out into a clearing. Only inches from Rio's feet was a steep limestone embankment that went straight down about ten feet. At the bottom was a sliver of a creek that was nearly dry and littered with rocks. A partially uprooted oak angled over the gaping void.

And Gussie was on the tree.

Abbie gasped. "Ohmygod."

The girl was on her belly with her arms and legs wrapped around the tree. Her grip looked firm, but it was the tree that worried Abbie. If the roots gave way, the tree would fall, and so would Gussie. Abbie didn't think a fall from that distance would be fatal, but she would no doubt be hurt.

"Don't move," Rio said to Gussie. His voice was calm, but Abbie could see the concern on his face. She figured it mirrored her own.

"How am I going to get her down?" Abbie asked.

"*I'm* going to get her."

"What?" But she knew. He was already testing the base of the tree with his foot. "The tree might fall if you climb on it."

"I'm not going to climb on it. I'll stand here on the roots and see if I can reach her."

"Well, I can do that."

"My arms are longer."

She didn't have an argument for that. Besides, his arms *were* longer, and of the two of them, Rio stood a better chance of reaching Gussie. Still, it was dangerous. If the tree gave way, Gussie might fall. Rio might also. She might lose them both to the whim of some gnarled tree roots.

"You might not want to stand around there talking," Gussie said. "I'm out here for a reason, you know."

Not understanding, Abbie stared at her. "What do you mean?"

"If you look behind you, you'll figure it out."

Abbie didn't know what to expect when she looked behind her, and she was almost afraid to find out. It was a skunk. But not just a skunk. Skunks. With their tails lifted high in the air. Abbie counted at least five of them, and they were milling around less than a stone's throw away.

"Don't be making any suddenlike moves," Gussie added. "Cause there's more just off to the side there."

Rio mumbled some profanity under his breath. Abbie added some of her own when she glanced around and saw three more. "What in the Sam Hill is going on here? Is this a skunk family reunion or something?"

"More like mating season," Rio provided.

"You'd think for something like that they'd want more privacy and wouldn't invite all their relatives."

He gave her an odd look that Abbie thought might have something to do with her inviting Victoria and Gussie along on their wedding trip. Well, she gave him an odd look right back. If she'd intended to mate with him, she *wouldn't* have brought her sisters along.

"I thought I'd just wait 'em out." Gussie made it sound as if she were on the veranda sipping lemonade. "You might wanta do the same. Victoria always says to pretend you're a tree when you see a skunk."

"Pretend you're a tree," Abbie repeated. "Not climb one." But she couldn't actually blame the child. It was more than a little disconcerting to see this many of the critters in one place. If there had been another tree close by, Abbie would have climbed up it too. As it was, she couldn't do anything but stand, cringe, and watch.

Abbie got Rio's attention by catching his arm. "So what now?" She didn't know if skunks had good hearing or not, but she wasn't about to take any unnecessary chances. The idea of being sprayed didn't appeal to her at all. It'd happened to her father once, and it had taken days for the stinky scent to wear off.

"I was waiting for you to come up with a plan," he said almost indifferently. "You said the next time we needed one, you'd be the one to come up with it. Well, here's your chance."

Yes, she had said that. In hindsight it had really been

a stupid thing to say. She'd never been good at plans, and this time would be no exception.

"I can lie out here for a long, long time," Gussie said. "So don't be in a hurry to make me get down. It might be a good idea if ya'll just stand there and don't move around too much. That big one looks real mean, and he's walking toward Abbie."

Abbie made a soft gasp but forced herself not to make any sudden moves. Since Rio was at an angle that allowed him to see over her shoulder, she looked at him for verification.

"He does look mean," was his answer.

Oh, that helped at lot. She inched closer to Rio until they were toe to toe and her head was tucked under his chin. "Are you just saying that to try to scare me?"

"No. He's nearly twice the size of the others, and he looks riled that he hasn't found a mate."

Great. A riled lovesick skunk. That didn't create a good image in her head. Well, it didn't matter. Even if it were the size of a bear, she couldn't let it stand in the way of Gussie's rescue. Despite the child's assurance that she could stay on the tree for a long time, Abbie didn't want to take any chances.

"It might be hours before those skunks do whatever they're planning to do," she whispered to Rio. And she didn't want to consider how long it took skunks to finish having relations. "We can't wait around here all day."

"No, but it might be a good idea to wait another minute or two."

"Why?"

"Because that big one is just a couple of inches away from your foot."

"Oh God." She squeezed her eyes shut and tightened her grip on Rio's arm. "Maybe it's a good time to tell you that I'm not scared of snakes or spiders. Or anything else that creeps around." Abbie shuddered. "But the idea of a skunk next to my foot makes my skin crawl."

"Told you it was a good idea to stay still," Gussie hollered.

Abbie angled her eyes in the child's direction, hoping to give her a warning not to raise her voice. Gussie obviously didn't understand the look.

"When ya'll stand that close together, it makes me think ya'll will start kissing again like ya'll were doing by the tree."

"Shhhh," Abbie said to no avail. Gussie continued.

"Rio, do you get itchy when you kiss Abbie?"

She heard him groan. Softly, but it was still a groan. Husky and pained. He gave Gussie that same scolding glance and then slipped his gaze down to Abbie. His eyes were stormy blue. Narrowed. A muscle twitched in his jaw.

Abbie took a deep breath, wondering if his stern expression had something to do with their argument. He didn't seem so much angry as bothered.

He smelled good. Not that it was a good time to notice that. But the scent of the woods was on him, mingling with saddle leather and the coffee he'd had with his lunch. Beneath all of that was another scent she was coming to recognize. Man. Warm man.

"Don't breathe on my neck," he whispered.

Abbie looked up at him and blinked. "Huh?"

"Don't breathe on my neck. It's a ticklish place for me."

"Ticklish. What the heck does that mean? Oh—" Since they were pressed against each other, she was close enough to feel what he meant. There was a distinct bulge forming in the front of his jeans. A bulge she'd felt on two other occasions. Once when they were by the creek, kissing. The other when they were against the tree, kissing.

Good Lord. Just what she didn't need. Horny skunks,

a horny man, and her sister hanging on to an uprooted tree over a crevasse.

Abbie tried to lean her head back, but she didn't want to lean too far because she didn't know how close that skunk was. "Why did this have to happen now?" she mumbled to herself. "Can't you control that thing?"

"It's nothing really to do with you," he answered sourly. "Just a male reaction. It would have happened if any woman was standing this close to me and breathing on my neck."

"Oh." That put her in her place. Any woman, huh? For some reason the thought of that bothered her. Rio with a woman. Rio aroused because some woman was breathing on him. Rio doing something about that arousal with another woman. No, she didn't like the thought of that at all. "How long will it take this male condition of yours to go away?"

The look he gave her could have cracked stone. "It might help if you stop talking about it. It would also help if you didn't swish your hips back and forth. You're rubbing me the wrong way."

"I am not swishing my hips—" But she was. Actually her whole body was swishing. Shaking. She trembled like a leaf on a tree. "Well, I'm sorry, but I'm scared. Just think of it as a female reaction. Nothing to do with you, really. It would have happened no matter who was standing this close to me with a bunch of skunks around."

A harsh gasp stopped her from adding anything else. It took Abbie a moment to realize it hadn't come from Rio or Gussie but from someone behind her.

"Holy Mother," Victoria said after another of those gasps. "Gussie? What are you doing out there?"

"Shhh." Abbie eased her head around so she could see Victoria.

"Why are you shhhing me when Gussie's hanging on

to that tree? Why aren't you doing anything to get her down?"

"The skunks," Abbie quickly answered.

"What skunks?"

"They left a couple of minutes ago," Gussie happily provided.

Abbie stepped back from Rio and had a look for herself. The only thing black and white in sight was Victoria's habit. There wasn't even the whiff of a skunk. "Why didn't you tell me they'd left, Gussie?"

"I wanted to see if you and Rio would starting kissing again."

Abbie groaned.

Rio groaned.

Victoria gasped, then hissed, "You mean you were about to kiss while Gussie was hanging from that tree?"

"We weren't going to kiss," Abbie snapped.

Rio mumbled an agreement. Tossing his hat aside, he put one foot on the tree roots. "Gussie, I want you to try to reach my hand."

"I can do it all by myself."

Rio shook his head. "No, I want you to take my hand."

The child shrugged and unwrapped her arms from the tree. Rio caught her hand, then her wrist, then with slow tugs, he eased Gussie toward them.

Abbie held her breath. Despite the annoying conversation Rio and she had just had, she hadn't forgotten the danger. With each move, she worried that Gussie could fall or the tree roots would give way.

When Gussie was a foot or so from Rio, he leaned out and scooped her up. In the same motion he stepped off the roots and down to solid ground.

"Gussie, don't ever scare me like that again." Abbie grabbed the girl and hauled her into her arms. "What were you doing out here anyway?"

"Running away."

Abbie pulled back and looked at her. "Why would you want to run away?"

"I thought you were mad because I saw you and Rio kissing."

"No I wasn't mad about that. All right, maybe I was a little mad, but I certainly didn't want you to run away. We're sisters, Gussie, and we belong together. I don't want you to leave, ever."

The little girl nodded and moved away from Abbie. With her hands in her pockets, she slowly walked toward Rio. "I oughta thank you for saving my life. I don't think I woulda, but I mighta fell off that tree and smashed my head wide open if'n you hadn't come along."

He stared at her a moment and then playfully ruffled her hair. "Then I guess I'm good for something, huh? Just don't ever do it again."

"Don't worry, I won't. I said my prayers a lot of times when I was out there. Hope nobody wants me to say more." She looked around hopefully.

"You should thank God for being alive," Victoria snapped. But then, as Abbie had done, she caught Gussie and gave the child a fierce hug. "I'll thank Him too, just so He understands how glad I am that you're safe."

Gussie turned her gaze to Rio. "Are you mad at me?"

He put his thumb to the brim of his Stetson and gave it a slight adjustment. "Well, I'm none too pleased."

"You're not gonna turn me over your lap and spank me, are you?"

"I'll have to give that some thought. While I'm making up my mind, you might want to be on your best behavior. It just might turn my decision in the direction you want it to go."

Gussie nodded, even though she didn't seem especially concerned with any punishment he might give her.

Rio glanced around the woods. "We might as well go

ahead and make camp. I don't think we'll get much more riding in today anyway."

Abbie nodded in agreement. Her hands were trembling too much to try to ride rough trail. "I'll go back and get our things."

"I'll go with you," Victoria volunteered.

Rio slapped a hand on his jeans to get rid of some of the dust. "We'll all go." He paused a heartbeat. "Unless Abbie wants to come up with a different plan."

She tried to scowl but failed. "Not this time." She paused the same fraction of time that he had. "But maybe later."

Chapter Eleven

Abbie sat down, her back against a tree, and watched Gussie play fetch with Beans. "It's amazing," she said to Rio. "Just a little while ago she nearly killed herself, and now she seems to have forgotten all about it."

"That's the way kids are." Rio lit a cheroot, the match hissing to a flame when he struck it over the heel of his boot. "Are you all right? You still look pale."

"Gussie scared me half to death." And the proof of that was she still felt a little shaky. She thought it might take years to get over the image of Gussie hanging onto that tree. The skunks had been an annoyance, but having Gussie in danger wasn't something she wanted to relive.

"Yeah. She scared me some, too." He sank down beside her, using part of the tree to rest against. "I guess she's like your own kid."

Abbie shrugged. "In a way. I was almost twenty when she was born, then her mother died not long afterward. Victoria, Ina, and I have pretty much raised her."

"Ina? Not another sister?"

"No. She's the housekeeper at Kingston. Actually, more than a housekeeper. She's a friend too. She's married to Juan, and between the two of them, they pretty much run the place."

"Hard to believe you'd let anyone other than you run the place."

She started to give a sharp reply, but since it was true Abbie let it pass. Apparently Rio decided to do the same because he took a drag off his cheroot and quickly changed the subject.

"You never did tell me about Kingston. Is it a working ranch?"

"Hardly. My father never was good at ranching, so most of the Donegan land is just pasture. We keep horses, of course, but that's about it. I've heard some people say the only thing the Donegan place is good for is wildflowers and my father's outside children." She glanced at him and blushed. "Sorry. I didn't mean to offend you."

The corner of his mouth twisted into a smile. "You didn't. I prefer that to half-breed bastard." He paused, flicked the ashes off his cheroot. "How about your father's business? Who runs it now?"

"I do. Well, with the help of some bookkeepers. Before my father died, he'd pretty much turned it over to me."

"A businesswoman." He grinned around his cheroot. "I guess that shouldn't surprise me."

His grin stopped her for a moment. Or at least it stopped her heart. The man was too good-looking for his own good. She wondered how long it would be before she could make herself immune to that grin. "What, you didn't think I sat around all day and fanned myself, did you?"

"No. You might be an heiress, but I figured you'd be in the thick of something. It just didn't occur to me what exactly."

She only nodded. There was a silence. A slightly awkward one. Finally, Abbie said something she'd meant to say for hours. "I want to thank you for what you did today. You risked your life to save Gussie."

"Not really. I wouldn't have fallen."

Despite his bravado, Abbie knew very well he could have fallen. He knew it too, and in spite of that he'd still gone after Gussie. She supposed that said a lot about a man's character. He hardly knew her little sister, yet he'd risked everything to save her.

That suddenly made her feel incredibly guilty. She was lying to Rio about so many things she had lost count. Abbie hadn't remembered feeling queasy about lying before. She did now.

Rio stretched out his legs and stacked his feet one on top of the other. The sunlight filtered through the oak leaves and fell on him in golden streaks. There were times when she could look at him and not remember how handsome he was.

This wasn't one of them.

Definitely not.

She had even started to like those tight-fitting jeans. In fact, she'd started to like them so much that she paid attention whenever Rio climbed down from his saddle. Abbie particularly enjoyed the way the muscles in his thighs and backside flexed and responded when he did such a simple task.

Actually, she liked the way the rest of him responded too. The grin that could be cocky. Or easy. Or even sweet. The expression in his blue eyes could be all those things put together.

And here she was lying to him.

Lord, what a tangled web her lies had made.

She cleared her throat to get his attention. "Rio, just in case things get a little crazy when we get to Kingston, I want to thank you for what you did for Gussie. And thank you for agreeing to help get Camellia out of the house."

One dark eyebrow slipped upward and he frowned. "That sounds like a good-bye to me."

Maybe it was. It should have been, but in her heart Abbie didn't want it to be. Victoria had been right. She'd gone into this plan without considering all the consequences. Driven by revenge, Abbie hadn't really considered Rio. Him or his feelings. The McCaine ranch seemed a paltry price to pay for dragging him right into the middle of this hornets' nest.

She could tell him the truth now, of course. And, of course, he'd turn around and head in the other direction. There wouldn't be a thing she could do to stop him, and even though she would have some measure of revenge, it might not accomplish everything. Besides, her hands were tied until she knew Harmony was safe.

"Do you ever wish you could start over?" she asked.

He rubbed the back of his neck. "Sometimes. The problem is that I wouldn't want to go back into the past. Thanks to you, I'd rather think about my future."

Well, at least he felt that way now. She thought he might change his mind later. "I want you to promise me something, Rio."

"What?"

"If something goes wrong when we get to Kingston, please just give me a chance to make it right before you get mad and storm out."

He turned and stared at her. "What's going to happen? Why would you think I'd get mad and storm out?"

There were too many reasons for her to count. It could get really ugly once he learned everything she'd been keeping from him. "Uh, Camellia will say things, and I don't want her to turn you against me without giving me a chance to explain."

"You could explain now."

She shook her head. "Not here. Not now." Abbie continued before he could say anything. "There's something else I want you to know. If I had to be married to anyone, I'm glad it was you."

Rio smiled and touched the end of her nose with his finger. "And that coming from a woman who likes to be in charge. Does that mean you'll think fondly of me in your old age?"

Abbie smiled too, and she hoped it masked her guilty conscience. She also hoped it masked the sinking feeling she got in the pit of her stomach. Would she think fondly of him in her old age, or would she want to curse herself for what she'd done to him? Maybe she was making the worst mistake of her life.

"Of course I'll think fondly of you," she assured him.

He crushed out his cheroot and leaned closer to her. "I don't think it's my imagination that we have some physical feelings for each other."

"We do."

"Then why don't we act on them?"

She looked at him as if his ears were on backward. "What?"

"Not here," he quickly corrected. "I mean when we get to Kingston. You said the preventatives would be there when we arrived, so there's no reason we couldn't spend a night together."

Abbie hadn't actually considered that, but yes, they probably could do that. Except she hadn't ordered the darn preventatives. Maybe there were some in her father's things. Certainly he hadn't risked impregnating half the county with his escapades. Or the more she thought about it, maybe he *had* impregnated half the county.

But getting the preventative was only a part of the problem. There was something else to consider. "Having marital relations could complicate our arrangement."

"It could do that, yes. If we let it. We don't have to let it. If we go into it with the understanding that it's just one night, then it won't have to complicate anything. One night. That's all."

Maybe that's all it would be, and maybe it wouldn't. But it occurred to her that if she didn't make love with Rio, she might never experience what it was like to be with a man. She might die a virgin, a true spinster, something that hadn't bothered her until now. At the age of twenty-seven, she probably wouldn't get the chance to marry again, and she couldn't see herself slipping into some man's bed just so she could have a physical relationship. So, there was that side of the argument.

The other side was she wanted to slip into Rio's bed.

She wanted to feel his hands on her. She wanted to feel herself turn to warm mush when he touched her. He was very good with his hands. Very good at finding just the right spot to touch her.

When they were in the woods against the tree he'd wet his fingertips and slipped them over her nipples. She flushed just thinking about it. Then he'd suckled her. Not like a baby would have. Like a man. More of that would be memorable.

Her palms started to sweat.

The episode in the woods hadn't stopped there either. Rio had adjusted the way they leaned into each other. She'd felt him—hard, rubbing against the center of her body, against that unmentionable place between her legs. She'd rubbed him right back because it felt better than anything she'd ever known.

If they hadn't had on their clothes, if they'd been naked and in a bed, it probably would have felt even better. And something would have happened. Not churning butter, that's for sure. Something beyond him just going inside her, even though Abbie knew that's what happened when men and women mated.

No, she was sure something much grander than just a coupling would have taken place. She'd been on the brink of something. Her body had been itching, screaming for something. She thought maybe Rio knew how to get her past that brink and onto whatever could happen next.

She glanced at him.

He grinned.

Yes, he knew how. Definitely.

"Well?" he asked. "What'd you say?"

Abbie only nodded, knowing exactly what her agreement meant. But she didn't trust her voice to say it aloud. Maybe if luck was with her, it would happen before he learned the truth about her. It couldn't happen afterward, of course.

Because afterward, Rio wouldn't want to saddle her or churn her like butter. He'd want her tarred and feathered.

Rio glanced around the camp and couldn't believe what he saw. It was daylight, everyone had finished breakfast, and yet the Donegan females were sitting around. Victoria read a dog-eared Bible. Gussie stroked Beans' head. And Abbie sat with her back against a tree and her chin on her palms. She looked bored and annoyed.

"Any of you plan to ride today?" he asked.

All three turned to him, none looking too pleased with his question. Victoria's mouth tightened, and she went back to her reading.

"It's Sunday," Gussie finally answered, her voice lowered as if she were trying to whisper. "Pretty much nothing will get done today."

He didn't like the sound of that. Rio had planned to make it to Kingston by nightfall. "Why not?"

Victoria slammed the Bible shut and glared at him. "Because it's the Sabbath, and we can't work on the Sabbath."

"I didn't intend to work. I intended to ride."

"Won't do any good to argue with her." Gussie sighed heavily. "She won't budge on this one. Believe me, me and Abbie have tried."

Rio looked at Abbie for confirmation. She only nodded and sank her chin back into her palms. He glanced at Victoria. She certainly didn't seem pleased that he had questioned her Sunday habits.

"We can't hunt. We can't fish," Gussie went onto say. "We can't do much of anything except things we can't stop our bodies from doing. Pretty soon she's gonna make us all pray. Wait and see."

Again, he looked at Abbie. Another nod. Her mouth tightened.

"But we could make it to Kingston by tonight," Rio pointed out. "You could do your praying once you got there."

Victoria got to her feet and held the Bible in front of her like a shield. "But today's the Sabbath, and we're not going to ride on the Sabbath. If you wish to go on ahead, feel free to do so. We'll catch up with you sometime tomorrow."

"Ah, hell," Rio muttered. The nun was serious. And from Abbie's expression, it seemed she was serious too. They really weren't going to ride today. "Any reason no one told me about this sooner?"

"Because I was hoping Victoria would forget," Abbie supplied.

Gussie shook her head in disgust. "She never forgets."

"I'm trying to save your eternal soul, young lady." Victoria crossed herself. "Now, it's time for prayers. Everyone close your eyes and fold your hands."

Rio walked to Abbie and sank down next to her. "Is she serious?"

"Completely. My advice? Just hush and go along with her. Pretty soon we can sneak off."

He started to ask if sneaking off meant riding out of camp, but he didn't think Abbie would leave her sister behind. Victoria started the prayers, asking for spiritual guidance. She prayed for Abbie, Gussie, and even him.

Rio couldn't remember anyone ever praying for him before, and it would have pleased him except Victoria didn't stop there. She prayed for Abbie's and his marriage, for Gussie's wild and rebellious nature, and even for the erring habits of smoking and swearing. She asked for spiritual guidance for seemingly everyone she'd ever met in her entire life.

An hour passed, and it appeared Victoria had just warmed up. She moved onto political leaders and prominent people. Rio didn't know how much longer this would go on, but his legs were starting to fall asleep.

He opened one eye and glanced at Abbie. She had one eye open and was looking at him. She shook her head slightly and softly mouthed, "If you interrupt her, she'll just make it longer."

Rio didn't know how that was possible. It seemed she'd gone on all day.

It said a lot about Abbie's love for her sister to tolerate something like this. Or maybe Abbie really was a religious person. He glanced at her again. She was studying her fingernails. His bride might indeed be religious, but she wasn't enjoying Victoria's prayer anymore than he was.

Since he didn't have anything else to do and since it didn't seem he'd be going anywhere for a while, Rio did some praying of his own. Unlike Victoria, he kept his simple; he asked God to help him get to Kingston before the Donegan females drove him to the brink of madness. With all of Abbie's lies, Gussie's antics, and Victoria's praying, he didn't know how much more he could handle.

Maybe he'd only return half of the money he owed her.

Yes, half.

He'd earned at least that much on this trip.

Rio felt Abbie's elbow gently touch his. When he looked up, she'd drawn a small ticktacktoe grid in the dirt between them. She raised one eyebrow—a challenge for him to play. He raised his own. Abbie placed an *X* in one the boxes. And the game was on. Rio won the first, but Abbie took the next two.

They continued to play, but after a dozen games Rio could see Abbie was bored with it. So was he, but Victoria still droned on with the prayers. When he placed his next *O* on the grid, he put a little face on it. Abbie pressed her hand to her mouth to suppress a giggle. She put little feet and hands on her *X*.

Not to be outdone, Rio reached across to draw something else on his *O*. His finger brushed Abbie's thumb. She glanced up at him. For a moment. Then quickly looked away. He touched her thumb again, intentionally, then slowly moved his fingertip to her knuckle.

She smiled.

Since it seemed to be an innocent game, he moved his finger farther down to the channel between her thumb and hand. Her hand was warm, and that particular spot was soft. He slid his finger over it several times.

Her gaze went to his again, but this time there was something different in her eyes. A little heat, maybe. Definitely something he shouldn't encourage. Not here, anyway.

He wanted to.

Slowly he turned her hand over and trailed his fingertips to her palm, keeping his touch light. Abbie took in a soft breath, and her eyelids floated downward. All right. So this was obviously a sensitive place on her. Strange, but after seeing Abbie's reaction, it became a sensitive place for him too.

She opened her eyes and slanted them in Victoria's direction. She probably meant it as a warning for him to stop, but he didn't. She didn't pull away. With his hand cradling hers, he eased his finger into a circular motion over her palm.

"Sweet Jesus," Abbie mumbled.

"Amen," Victoria said.

Rio quickly lifted his head. Abbie and Gussie did the same. Gussie grinned, and Abbie seemed to be fighting off the effects of their game.

She stood, caught Rio's hand and practically pulled him to his feet. He rubbed his foot over the ticktacktoe grid so Victoria wouldn't see what had kept them occupied. Well, what had kept them partially occupied. It seemed anytime Abbie and he got near each other, their attention always settled on one thing.

And it sure wasn't praying.

"Thank you, Victoria, for all those prayers," Abbie said, sounding a little out of breath. "While you're doing your meditations, Rio, Gussie, and I will take a walk and, uh, contemplate nature."

Gussie eagerly nodded and ran to Abbie. The two looked at Victoria, and she finally nodded. With the approval given, Abbie hurried out of the camp and started through the woods. Since she still had a firm grip on Rio's hand, he had no choice but to go with her.

"What does contem-pate nature mean?" Gussie asked.

Even though Abbie was practically running and dragging Rio with her, the little girl had no trouble keeping up. "It means there's a shallow creek not too far from here, and we get to swim."

Gussie cheered. Rio felt like doing the same. Even though he would have preferred to be riding toward

Kingston, a swim didn't sound bad at all. He needed to cool off after all that hand touching.

Abbie led them through the woods, apparently well aware of the creek's location since she didn't hesitate. She navigated them through the dense brush of small cedars and wild berry briars.

"How long we got before afternoon prayers?" Gussie wanted to know.

Rio groaned. "There are afternoon prayers, too?"

"Yes, but not for hours," Abbie assured him. "We can enjoy ourselves for a while."

"Why do you put up with it?" he asked. "Since you're in charge, as you always like to say, why don't you just tell Victoria that prayers have to wait until we get to Kingston?"

"Believe me, we've tried that," Gussie answered. "It doesn't work. Victoria says she's in charge on Sundays 'cause she's a nun and all. We could argue with her until we've got no breath left in our bodies, but she'll only argue back, and we'll end up just wasting time. In the end she's just gonna keep on praying, and she'll make us do it with her."

"What day do I get to be in charge?" Rio asked.

Gussie giggled. "Same as me. Never."

Somehow that didn't seem so hard to accept at the moment. After all, taking a day off was a rare treat, and he would get to swim. With Abbie. There were worse ways to spend a Sunday.

"Are you gonna stay at Kingston a long, long time?" Gussie asked him.

Rio hadn't expected that question. Nor had he expected the hopeful look he saw in Gussie's eyes. He stopped and stared down at her. "No," he said honestly. "I'll have to get back to my ranch."

"You mean you aren't gonna live at Kingston with us?"

He shook his head. "I'll stay a couple of days. Maybe a week or so."

Disappointment consumed Gussie's face. Her voice was small, and her eyebrows slanted downward. "Then why did you and Abbie get married if you weren't gonna live at Kingston?"

Thankfully, Abbie answered. Or at least she tried to answer. "Rio and I got married for a lot of reasons, but we never planned to live together in the same house. I thought you understood that."

Gussie twisted her mouth. "I mighta understood if somebody had told me. I thought Rio was gonna stay with us and be like family. Maybe like, uh, a brother. Or something. Maybe even like a daddy. He's old enough to be a daddy. My daddy, anyway, not yours or Victoria's. So I just thought you married him so we could all be a family."

Rio looked at Abbie. She looked at him. It was clear neither of them knew what to say to the child.

This was something Rio hadn't considered. Abbie obviously hadn't considered it either. How did you explain to a child the deceptions that adults could come up with? Gussie had obviously taken the marriage at face value. And now she had grown attached to him.

He touched the tip of Gussie's nose with his finger. "Maybe you can come and visit me sometime at the ranch."

Gussie only shook her head, folded her arms over her chest, and walked ahead of them. "Wouldn't be the same."

No, it wouldn't be, but it was the best he could offer. His marriage to Abbie hadn't made him part of the Donegan family, and it never would. Rio was glad he wouldn't be around to tell Gussie about the annulment. He didn't want to see any more disappointment in the girl's face.

"I should have told her," Abbie said under her breath.

"She wouldn't have understood." Heck, there were times when he didn't understand the boundaries of this arrangement himself, so how could she expect Gussie to grasp it?

Abbie sighed heavily. "Still, I should have said something. I didn't think it would bother her this much."

"She'll get over it." He hoped. But something tugged at his heart too. Something he didn't really want to think about. He would get over it, but it wouldn't be as easy as he'd thought it would. "Maybe even like a daddy." Gussie had said. No, that wouldn't be easy to get over at all.

They walked over the ridge, and he saw the creek. The water was diamond-clear, with wildflowers dotting the banks. There were dozens of large, full oaks clustered around a wide bend.

Abbie immediately started to take off her clothes, but she stopped when her gaze connected with his. "Oh, I forgot again."

"Forgot what?"

"Well, you see, we usually strip naked to swim. That way, we don't get our clothes wet."

Rio wouldn't have considered stripping a problem if they had been alone. In fact, he would have enjoyed playing around naked in the water with Abbie. It seemed she could use some cheering up, and something like that could vastly improve both their moods. . . .

"Oh, well." Abbie shrugged. "I guess it wouldn't hurt if we just stripped down to our unmentionables."

"I don't have on any unmentionables."

Abbie stared at him. "Then what's under your jeans?"

"Just me."

She swallowed hard, then looked down at the area where unmentionables would have been.

"I could just keep on my jeans," he let her know.

Abbie blew out a breath of relief. "Good."

Gussie had already removed all her clothes except for her one-piece cotton underwear. She ran into the water and started splashing. Apparently, her dark mood was already gone.

Slipping off her split skirt and shirtwaist, Abbie hung them over a low branch. She ran into the water before he even had a chance to ogle her.

"Come on in," she called out. "The water feels heavenly." She closed her eyes, leaned back in the water and let herself float.

Heavenly. Yep, that described the view Rio had in front of him. Abbie, wearing only her unmentionables and floating in the creek.

He took off his boots and shirt and joined them. The water was barely up to his chest, but it felt good. "What did you call this? Contemplating nature? Well, I like the way you contemplate."

He swam toward her, caught her foot, and dunked her under. When she came back up, she splashed some water at him and laughed. He splashed her right back and before she could blink the water from her eyes, he slipped his arm around her waist and pulled her to him.

He looked down at her lips. It was a stupid idea to kiss her now. He should have had the sense to leave her and her mouth alone. That conversation with Gussie should have taught him to keep his distance from the whole lot of them.

He glanced at Gussie to make sure she wasn't watching. She wasn't. She was busy building a boat out of sticks and leaves.

"What do you see when you look at me?" he asked.

Abbie smiled and pushed wet hair off his forehead. When she'd finished, she let her hand rest where it was. She kept her fingertips on his cheekbone. "Is that a trick question?"

It should have been. He didn't know why he'd gotten into this with her. "What do you see?" he repeated.

"A handsome man."

He shook his head. Rio hadn't been fishing for a compliment. Besides, he'd been called a lot of things but never handsome. "I'm talking about my Comanche blood. Is that what you see when you look at me?"

She stared at him a moment longer. "No."

"Why not?"

Abbie gave an amused smile. "I don't know. Do you see my Scottish blood when you look at me? Or my mother's Irish blood?"

"I see your white skin."

"Only because you're thinking hard about it right now. If I think really hard about it, I can see Victoria's brown skin, and her Mexican blood. Or I can see Gussie's freckles. Most of the time I just see my sisters." She paused. "Do you think people only see the color of your skin when they look at you?"

"Not always."

Most of the time. But it seemed that wasn't true for Abbie. He didn't know why it was different when she looked at him, but it was. There were times, like now, when she gazed at him as if he were the only man in the world. Here she was rich, white, and pretty—and she made him feel so special. . . .

He moved even closer, his mouth hovering a fraction over hers.

"Are you going to kiss me?" she asked.

His gaze moved slowly to her mouth and stayed there. With the ease of a man who had all the time in the world, he visually traced her lips. "I was giving that some thought, yes."

"And?"

"And I decided . . ."

He trailed off, paused, but obviously for too long; Abbie kissed him. She grabbed onto fists full of his hair and wrenched him closer until their mouths were forced to meet. And they met all right. There were no more preliminaries, no long yearning looks, no soft caressing breaths, no gentleness. Just them. Two people kissing each other as if this would be the last kiss either would ever have.

"I got tired of waiting for you to decide," she said when they paused to breathe.

Apparently he'd grown tired of using common sense, too. That was the only reason he could figure out why he'd let that kiss continue. Oh, and the fact that he'd thoroughly enjoyed it.

It was hard to argue with passion, but Rio kept trying. There was that part about him leaving soon and the part about Gussie getting attached to him. Of course, Abbie understood he had to leave. And she wasn't getting attached. Well, she probably wasn't. She was just doing the same thing he was—enjoying some kisses.

He drew in a gulp of air through his mouth and took in her taste and scent at once. It raced through him, stirred his blood and body. Rio kissed her again, twisting and knotting his fingers through her hair so he completely controlled the movement of her head. He wanted to control the rest of her, wanted to take her. Not here, of course. But just as soon as they got to Kingston.

Rio put his mouth to her ear. "Tomorrow, you'll let me have you." It wasn't a question, and he didn't need her answer; Rio knew from the way she moved against him.

She turned, slowly, until her gaze met his. Her mouth was swollen from their kisses, and her eyes were hungry with the same need Rio felt. "I wish it could happen now," Abbie whispered.

He groaned. So far, he'd managed to keep an erection at bay. *At bay* went south in a hurry.

She brushed her mouth over his, her lips as slippery and wet as the rest of her. "It's hard to wait. I didn't think it would be. I mean, I've never wanted . . . well, I've never wanted a man. But I definitely want you."

Another groan. Rio did like the way Abbie could torture him. It was hell, of course, but it would make their lovemaking only that much sweeter.

Well, it would if he survived this swim.

"My, my," a woman's voice called out. "What's going on here?"

Rio reacted as if someone had taken shots at them. Even though she resisted, he shoved Abbie behind him and braced himself for a fight.

But there didn't seem to be anyone to fight.

There was a young dark-haired woman standing by the water's edge. She had a small build and carried a frilly parasol. Unless he counted the parasol, she had no weapon, and it didn't look as if she could whip even Gussie. She also looked a little like Abbie, except for sooty black hair.

With a wide grin on her face, she put her parasol aside and waved. "Interrupting anything, am I?"

And she leaned back and laughed.

Chapter Twelve

Abbie pushed herself away from Rio. "Harmony! My God, Harmony!"

Gussie squealed with delight, and the two sisters began frantically swimming toward their third sibling. Sopping wet, they each grabbed Harmony and hugged her.

"You're here," Abbie said, sounding out of breath. The sudden dash from the water was partially responsible for that, but Rio's recent kisses had practically sucked the air right out of her. Still, that sort of thing had to wait; Harmony came first.

Abbie looked the young woman over from head to toe. No bruises. No signs of mistreatment. And especially no signs of Gray Wolf. "And you're safe."

"For right now anyway." Harmony scooped up Gussie in her arms and kissed her cheek. "What kind of mischief have you been getting into, young lady?"

"All kinds. I've been having to say my prayers lots. Are you coming back to Kingston with us?"

"Not this time." Harmony glanced at Abbie and carefully stood Gussie back on the ground. "I understand the Rangers are still looking for me."

Abbie nodded and glanced around the woods. "Are you alone? Where's Chey? He was supposed to find you."

"He found me. He's with Victoria right now. She *talked* him into staying for prayers and meditation. I escaped just in time. I told her I'd do my prayers on the way to the creek."

"Chey's here too?" Gussie asked. She started to hop up and down with her hands clasped in front of her. "Can I go see him? Please, Abbie? Pleeeease?"

"Of course. But go straight back to camp and don't dawdle."

Gussie had already started running. "I don't ever dawdle when I can see Chey," she called back.

Abbie waited until the child was out of earshot before she said anything else. "Chey said he'd heard you mended fences with Gray Wolf? Is that true?" She didn't bother to conceal the displeasure in her voice.

"I tried, and failed." She kissed Abbie's cheek. "Don't worry. I've learned my lesson this time. That man will never mend his ways. He'd rather spend the rest of his life on the run from the law than negotiating peace and getting on with his life."

"Humph, I could have told you that."

"It's not polite to gloat when you're right, Abbie." The younger woman tipped her head to Rio. "I guess that's your husband?"

Abbie turned to look at him just as Rio stepped from the creek. His soaked jeans clung to him like a second skin. His hair was wet, too, and tangled onto his forehead and neck.

Lord, he was beautiful.

God, it was not a good time to notice that.

"He doesn't know everything that's happened," Abbie whispered. "So don't say anymore than you have to say."

"Naturally. I don't want my secrets out anymore than you do. He's a sight to look at, that's for sure," Harmony said, her easy drawl brushing each word. She kept her voice low and her gaze on Rio. "Chey said he's part Comanche. Definitely a good mix of bloodlines. Tall, lean, and delicious. I can see why you want him."

There was no polite answer to that. "I didn't marry him because he's good looking."

Harmony smiled as if she'd tasted something sweet. "Oh, but I'm sure that helps."

No, it didn't. If he'd been bone ugly, she might have an easier time resisting him. As it was, she couldn't even get her mind off him. The latest around of kissing had proven that.

Rio started up the bank toward them, the muscles in his thighs and legs responding to each step. Abbie couldn't look away. She tried, but failed. She was suddenly damp with sweat. The pulse on her neck pounded. She firmly reminded her body that it was preparing itself for something it couldn't have.

And her body obviously didn't care one bit.

He stopped only inches away and smiled. "Harmony?"

"Yes. You must be Rio. Chey told me all about you." She smiled and extended her hand. Actually, Harmony did more than smile. She glowed. Abbie was well aware that her sister was a truly beautiful woman. One glance at Rio, and Abbie saw he was aware of it too.

Abbie wasn't jealous, of course. But she caught Rio's arm after he shook Harmony's hand. "Chey's back at the camp with Victoria," she let him know.

"Praying," Harmony added with a knowing wink.

Abbie loved her sister, but she intended to step on the girl's toes if she kept smiling at Rio. He was looking at Harmony, too. Really, really looking at her.

Thrill to the most sensual, adventure-filled Romances on the market today...

FROM  LOVE SPELL BOOKS

As a home subscriber to the Love Spell Romance Book Club, you'll enjoy the best in today's BRAND-NEW Time Travel, Futuristic, Legendary Lovers, Perfect Heroes and other genre romance fiction. For five years, Love Spell has brought you the award-winning, high-quality authors you know and love to read. Each Love Spell romance will sweep you away to a world of high adventure...and intimate romance. Discover for yourself all the passion and excitement millions of readers thrill to each and every month.

Save $5.00 Each Time You Buy!

Every other month, the Love Spell Romance Book Club brings you four brand-new titles from Love Spell Books. EACH PACKAGE WILL SAVE YOU AT LEAST $5.00 FROM THE BOOKSTORE PRICE! And you'll never miss a new title with our convenient home delivery service.

Here's how we do it: Each package will carry a FREE 10-DAY EXAMINATION privilege. At the end of that time, if you decide to keep your books, simply pay the low invoice price of $17.96, no shipping or handling charges added. HOME DELIVERY IS ALWAYS FREE. With today's top romance novels selling for $5.99 and higher, our price SAVES YOU AT LEAST $5.00 with each shipment.

AND YOUR FIRST TWO-BOOK SHIP-MENT IS TOTALLY FREE!

IT'S A BARGAIN YOU CAN'T BEAT! A SUPER $11.48 Value!

Love Spell ✦ A Division of Dorchester Publishing Co., Inc.

GET YOUR 2 FREE BOOKS NOW—AN $11.48 VALUE!

Mail the Free Book Certificate Today!

TWO FREE BOOKS

Free Books Certificate

YES! I want to subscribe to the Love Spell Romance Book Club. Please send me my 2 FREE BOOKS. Then every other month I'll receive the four newest Love Spell selections to Preview FREE for 10 days. If I decide to keep them, I will pay the Special Member's Only discounted price of just $4.49 each, a total of $17.96. This is a SAVINGS of at least $5.00 off the bookstore price. There are no shipping, handling, or other charges. There is no minimum number of books I must buy and I may cancel the program at any time. In any case, the 2 FREE BOOKS are mine to keep—A BIG $11.48 Value!

Offer valid only in the U.S.A.

Name_____

Address_____

City_____

State _____ Zip _____

Telephone_____

Signature _____

If under 18, Parent or Guardian must sign. Terms, prices and conditions subject to change. Subscription subject to acceptance. Leisure Books reserves the right to reject any order or cancel any subscription.

A $11.48 VALUE

Get Two Books Totally
FREE —
An $11.48 Value!

▼ Tear Here and Mail Your FREE Book Card Today! ▼

PLEASE RUSH
MY TWO FREE
BOOKS TO ME
RIGHT AWAY!

Love Spell Romance Book Club
P.O. Box 6613
Edison, NJ 08818-6613

He squinted one eye, and his gaze wandered over her. "You look very well, considering your ordeal with the Apaches."

Confidently, she glanced at Abbie, who glanced nervously at Rio. Of course, he would wonder about that.

"Well, I guess I'm tougher than I look," Harmony said calmly. "Gray Wolf let me go as soon as he and Chey, uh, talked."

Abbie stiffened. Gray Wolf and her brother disliked each other immensely. They wouldn't have just *talked.* "Is Chey hurt?"

"A few cuts and bruises—that's all."

"Well, I hope Gray Wolf had more than that?"

Harmony patted her arm reassuringly. "Don't worry, he did. Listen, I can't stay long. Chey's taking me to the train station."

Naturally, Harmony would have to go by train, but Abbie knew that wasn't without risks. Dozens of things could go wrong, including a lawman who might recognize her. "You have to be careful," Abbie cautioned. She hugged and kissed her sister good-bye.

Harmony didn't appear worried; she merely nodded and patted her sister on the shoulder. "Certainly, and don't worry, everything will be fine."

Abbie could only hope.

Harmony extended her hand to Rio again, and he shook it. "It was good to meet you."

"Same here." He paused and shook off some water dripping down his face. "Why are you leaving, anyway? Aren't you going to Kingston with us to report your abduction to the authorities?"

Abbie gave her sister a look to remind her not to say too much. It obviously worked. "Chey and Abbie are worried that Gray Wolf might come after me again. It's probably best if I disappear for a while."

He made a sound of disagreement, but Abbie was

thankful he voiced no more than that. She didn't want to go into the whole mess with Gray Wolf or Harmony's dispute with the law. If she did, she'd be forced to lie. . . . And she'd done enough of that already.

"I want Chey to send me a telegram once you're safely on your way," she called out as Harmony started to leave.

"I'll remind him."

For several long, awkward moments Abbie and Rio just stood there even after the woman disappeared from sight. She quickly tried to go over the entire conversation that had just taken place. She hoped that neither Harmony nor she had said anything to make Rio suspicious. One look at his face, however, and she knew he was.

Highly suspicious.

"Anything you want to tell me?" he asked. Both of his eyebrows arched high on his forehead.

Well, that had an easy answer. "No." There was absolutely nothing she wanted to tell him.

His mouth tightened. "That's what I figured."

He picked up his things and walked away.

His stallion gave a protesting snort when Rio maneuvered him through the ankle deep mud. "I know how you feel, Smoky," Rio whispered. "Don't much care for it myself."

Rain spat down from the dark evening sky, the water snaking off his yellow oilskin slicker and yet somehow making it beneath to his clothes. There were still no signs of clearing, even though the rain had kept up its drenching pace most of the day.

Appropriate, he supposed.

A stormy end for a stormy trip.

All day he'd thought about Harmony's visit. And about Abbie's vague comments about her sister's destination. His wife was hiding something again. Something no doubt about Harmony's abduction. What, exactly he didn't know, but he did know that Harmony didn't look as if she'd been through a terrible ordeal with the Apaches. She looked as if she'd been out for an afternoon stroll in the woods.

Rio mumbled profanity under his breath. What did he care about the secrets Abbie still kept from him? Harmony was free, and that meant a large part of his deal with Abbie had been fulfilled even if he hadn't had anything to do with it.

Tossing out Camellia should be easy. Discouraging Wendell Calverson would be easier still. And maybe even a little enjoyable. He'd be on his way then. He'd have his ranch and this would all be over.

That was a good thing.

Really.

"The house is just ahead," Abbie called out over the drone of the rain. "At least it should be if it's still standing."

"You doubt it will be?"

"With Camellia, you never know."

Beans started to bark and charged on ahead. Through the gray drizzle, Rio could see lights. Kingston. At last. And it was still standing, despite Abbie's concerns. There were times Rio felt as if he'd been traveling here half his life. He'd make it a point not to travel again with three females. Ever.

Even without the benefit of moonlight, Rio could still make out some of the house. There were lots of windows, and seemingly a lantern in every one of them.

"Someone's expecting you tonight," he commented. "They lit the way for you."

"That's Ina's doing. She's probably worried about us."

He tipped his head to the house. Now that they'd gotten closer, he could better make out its distinctive shape. If he hadn't been sober, Rio would have sworn he was seeing things. "It looks like a riverboat."

"That's exactly what it is."

"You live on a riverboat?" he asked in disbelief.

She nodded. "Amazing, isn't it? My father loved ships. He bought this one not long after I was born, dismantled it and had it brought here piece by piece. Personally, I think it looks ridiculous out here right in the middle of prime pasture."

Rio had to agree with her there. It was certainly ridiculous, and it wasn't even especially attractive. It sprawled and jutted out in every direction with decks, doors, and railings. The huge paddle wheel was still attached and had ivy wound through it.

They cut across a pasture surrounded by white fence. Just as Abbie had said, there was no cattle or livestock. Through the gray drizzle, Rio could make out a barn and several other outbuildings near the house.

Abbie reined in her gelding in the front yard. Rio and the others did the same. There was a tabby cat with its whiskers pressed against the window, its striped fur practically standing on end. The critter looked ready to tear him apart and probably would have tried if it could have figured out how to get past the glass.

"One of Gussie's pets?" Rio questioned, nodding at the cat.

"Victoria's," Abbie provided. "His name is Pig. My advice? Steer clear of him. He's ornery even on his good days."

Victoria quickly disagreed. "He's just a little scared around people. He's harmless, really."

"I don't mind Pig, but if Camellia's in there, I'm not going in," Gussie protested. "She's mean to me. She's always telling me I smell like boogers and that I need to wash my hair."

Victoria bobbed her head. "I'd rather not go in either. I'm too tired to deal with Camellia tonight. She always tells me I look like a fat skunk."

Rio looked at all three women. Abbie had a scowl on

her face, but the other two eyed the house as if it were the gates of hell. This Camellia was certainly a force to be reckoned with if she could put fear into Gussie and Victoria. Not much had frightened those two on the trip from Fall Creek.

"Is this Camellia really that awful?" he asked Victoria.

"She's worse than awful. I refuse to spend another night under the same roof with that woman."

Abbie climbed off her gelding and shook rain off her slicker. "Well, I'm not sleeping anywhere but in my bed. Remember, Kingston's your home more than it is Camellia's. If she keeps you away, it's like letting her win."

Victoria frowned and looked at Rio. "Are you really going to tell Camellia that she has to leave?"

"I'm really going to do that," he assured her. "All of you can wait on the porch if you'd rather not face her."

But Victoria shook her head. "No, if you're kicking her out tonight, then I want to watch."

"Me, too," Gussie heartily agreed. "Maybe I can tell her she smells like boogers and needs to wash her hair."

Abbie peeled off the oilskin slicker and draped it on the rocker on the porch. "Gussie, you don't need to hear anything Rio has to say to Camellia. I want you to go up the side stairs to your room. Take a bath and go to bed. In that order. And don't skip the bath part. Ina has enough work without washing dirty bed covers."

"Awww." She kicked at a lump of mud. "Why do I gotta go to my room? I miss all the fun stuff."

"And you're going to miss even more if you don't do as I tell you, young lady. I'm tired, hungry, and in an otherwise surly mood. Tomorrow we'll let you know what happened."

Giving the mud another kick, Gussie shoved her hand in her pockets and started up a set of stairs on the right side of the porch.

"And don't you let me catch you eavesdropping," Victoria warned the child.

The front door flew open and a round-faced woman with oil-black eyes rushed onto the porch. "Senorita Donegan, Sister Victoria, you're home. I so prayed you would get here tonight."

Rio thought the woman looked a little frightened. Her eyes were wide, and there were worry lines on her otherwise smooth forehead. Her silky graying hair was pulled into a tight bun.

Abbie greeted her. "Rio, this is Ina."

"The housekeeper," the woman clarified for him. She immediately ushered them inside and started to fuss with Abbie's clothes, trying to untie her bandanna. "You're soaked to the bone. Did you find Harmony?"

"Yes, and don't worry. Chey is taking care of her. I'm expecting a telegram from him. Did it come?"

"A couple of hours ago." She pulled the telegram from her pocket and handed it to Abbie. "Clayton Simpson's boy brought it all the way here in the rain."

"All is well," Abbie read.

Victoria looked over her sister's shoulder. "That's it?"

"That's all it needs to say. Thank God."

Ina mumbled something in Spanish, smiled and crossed herself. "So, Harmony is safe?"

Abbie took over the task of untying the bandanna and motioned for Rio to follow her inside. "She's safe. She should be on a train to New Orleans."

Pig, the cat, came barreling up the hall toward them. His fur stood on end, and he was on the tip of his toes. At least he was for a second or two. The display of aggression didn't last long. When he caught sight of Victoria, he sauntered toward her, and she scooped the feline into her arms.

There were two huge corridors on each side of the

entry, and a large circular staircase directly in front of them. Rio glanced down one of the halls and noticed the long line of doors. It seemed more like a hotel than a house, and it was certainly ornate. Or something. Bright red wallpaper and shiny gold lamps were everywhere. Even the picture frames were gold. The paintings seemed more suited for a saloon.

Ina leaned close to Abbie. "There's something you should know, Senorita Donegan. Something you're not—"

"What's all the fuss about out here?" a woman's voice bellowed from the other room. "You're making enough noise to wake the dead."

Pig hissed.

"Senorita Donegan and Sister Victoria are home," Ina answered. She quickly turned back to Abbie. "There's something I have—"

"Well, good God, do they have to be so loud?" the woman again.

Rio heard a woman's shoes tap on the polished wood floor. The swish of satin petticoats and expensive fabric came closer. Carrying a cut crystal glass of whiskey, she stepped into the entryway, the gold-gilded arch framing her and the pose that she struck. She eyed them the way a mountain lion would inspect its next meal.

Camellia, no doubt.

There was no look of worry on her flawless face. No real concern in her cool violet eyes. She stood easily six feet tall, and her body was lushly curved with full hips and breasts that her low-cut bodice generously revealed. A sleek column of blond hair was piled high on her head, some shiny coils dripping onto one shoulder of her blueberry-colored dress. Her full, richly painted mouth eased into a sardonic smile.

167

"Well, well," she purred. "Look what the cat dragged in."

Rio wasn't sure if he was the cat or what it'd dragged in, but was pretty sure he'd find out soon enough.

As if offended by the remark, Pig hissed.

Chapter Thirteen

Abbie was aware of the exact moment that Camellia's hungry gaze landed on Rio. The changes in the woman were about as subtle as a killer tornado in a wide-open field. Camellia's smile went from catty to brilliant. Her eyes glimmered. She shifted her posture, so her breasts were more conspicuous.

As if anyone could have missed those nippled watermelons.

If Camellia leaned another inch forward, Abbie figured those melons would come spilling right out of that dress—which was probably what she wanted to happen.

"Well, I hadn't counted on seeing you any time soon, Abilene." Camellia brought her glass to her mouth and took a drink of its amber contents. Even though she continued to speak to Abbie, she didn't take her lash-lowered gaze off Rio. "Last I heard you were in Fall Creek, recovering from your ordeal with some Apaches. You're ruined, I heard."

Abbie shot the woman a glance that she hoped would indicate that she was only mildly interested in what Camellia had to say. The muscles were so tight in Abbie's face, she nearly bared her teeth.

"As you can see, I'm fine," Abbie said, trying to sound impassive. Again, it was more like a Pig imitation. She was pretty sure she hissed.

"Really? You don't look fine at all. You look like a scarecrow. Your hair's stuck to your head in clumps. Dirty clumps from the looks of it. There's a questionable smear of something on your cheek, and your clothes look as if you've been riding herd for a month."

On that point Camellia was probably right. Abbie felt like a soggy piece of week-old moldy bread. Probably looked like one too.

She tried to brush some of the mud off the sleeve of her cotton shirtwaist but ended up smearing it instead. She had never wanted to dress like Camellia, but there was something uncomfortable about standing in the same room with a woman who looked ready to attend a cotillion.

Especially when that woman looked at Rio and licked her lips.

Abbie challenged Camellia's smugness with a smile of her own. It was probably stupid to be smug now with everything still so unsettled, but Abbie couldn't help it. Even if everything else blew up in her face, she would finally get this awful woman out of her home.

Camellia's long slender fingers gripped her crystal glass like talons, and she gave Abbie a venomous smile. "I had actually begun to wonder if you'd come back at all. I figured if you weren't back by the end of the week, I could have a memorial service or something."

"I'm glad my return saved you from all that trouble."

"Oh, it wouldn't have been that much trouble. I see you brought a guest home with you."

"He's not exactly a guest."

But before Abbie could elaborate, Rio stepped in front of her. He slipped off his Stetson and gave the woman a nod of greeting. "It seems you're actually the guest. That is, if you're Camellia."

She gave him her usual cat-lapping-cream smile. "That's exactly who I am. And you are?"

"Someone who wants you out of this house."

There was only a flicker of surprise in her eyes. That faded quickly enough, and the haughtiness returned full force. "You're obviously a stranger who doesn't have a clue about how things are around here."

"Oh, he knows," Abbie quickly assured.

"Then he knows all about the promise you made to your father?"

"At least half the state of Texas knows about that, and about your hellfired fairy wings. It was the latest gossip in Fall Creek."

Camellia didn't seem the least bit embarrassed. If anything, it amused her. "Gossip or not, it doesn't change anything."

"But it does change things. I made that promise to my father before I was married."

The surprise was no longer a flicker. Camellia's eyes had flames in them. "Married!"

Abbie grinned from ear to ear. "Yes, and this is my husband."

Camellia stumbled over the words when she first tried to speak. "Your what? Your husband? Husband!"

Abbie nodded happily.

"And this is supposed to change things, just because you're married?" Camellia yelled. "You have it all mixed up. You promised your father that you'd allowed me to stay here at Kingston until *I* got married, not you. This doesn't have anything to do with you."

"It does if my husband doesn't want you here." Abbie

paused a heartbeat to savor the only moment she might get to savor. "He doesn't."

Clutching her rosary, Victoria stepped forward. "They were married in a church. Their union is sacred, and scripture warns that no one should come between man and woman in these holy bonds. Abbie's promise to obey her husband is binding, and furthermore it makes him head of this house. If he tells you to leave, then it's your Christian duty to do so."

"Yes, that. What she said," Abbie quickly agreed, knowing she couldn't have possibly come up with something like that. She gave Victoria a nod of approval.

"My Christian duty?" Camellia repeated. "What the hell is that supposed to mean? Just because he tells me I have to go, you expect me to go?"

It was Rio who answered. "Yes." The one-word response had undertones of a cold warning.

"Well, what if I say no, huh? What if I refuse to leave? Just what will you do then?"

"I'll pick you up and toss you on your butt right out that door. If you try to come back in, I'll shoot you for trespassing. It's against the law to trespass, and it doesn't matter how many deathbed promises Abbie made. I made no such promise to her father."

Camellia's jaw tightened. "Who the hell do you think you are, anyway, ordering me around like this?"

"I'm Rio McCaine, Abbie's husband."

"Rio Mc—" Camellia drew in a sharp breath and squinted her eyes while she stared at him. "My God, it is you. It *really* is you."

"Do I know you?" Rio asked, frowning.

Abbie answered before Camellia could. "You probably saw her around. She used to visit Fall Creek years ago. She's my Uncle Henry's cousin, and he's the one who introduced her to my father."

"You're that *Camellia?*" But it came from Rio's mouth

like profanity. His frown turned to a scowl. "Yeah, I remember you. Not fondly either. You and my half-brother were friends."

Camellia slipped her poisonous gaze back to Abbie. "I can see what's going on here. Why you little conniver. You stinking little conniver. You actually married Rio McCaine? Just wait until I tell. I'm not alone here, you know. He's here. Right up those stairs."

All right. So, Abbie hadn't expected that. Not tonight. *He* was here. Hellfire. He wasn't supposed to be here. She'd sent him on that wild-goose chase to San Antonio. How could he have made it back already?

One glance at Rio, and Abbie knew that Camellia and she weren't the only ones in the room who were surprised. Even though Camellia had said little in comparison to what she could have said, it was enough. More than enough for Rio to realize he'd just stepped into a hornets' nest.

Abbie cleared her throat. "Remember when I told you things might get a little confusing when we got to Kingston?" She continued despite the dark look he gave her. "Well, it's about to get more than a little confusing. I really had planned to tell you this tonight—"

"Tell me what?"

"Everything. I thought we'd have some time after you tossed out Camellia. I thought we'd have a couple of hours at least, and I'd be able to explain everything to you. I didn't want to learn about it this way."

"Explain what?" he asked in a hoarse growl.

Before Abbie could answer, Camellia cupped her hands around her mouth. At a volume that could have shattered glass, she yelled up the stairs. "Julian! Get down here right now. Abbie's back, and you're not going to believe what this little conniver did."

There was a silence. A long one. Since Abbie didn't know what else to say, she let the silence linger.

"Julian?" Rio questioned. "My half-brother?"

Abbie managed a nod just as she heard the footsteps thundering down the stairs.

Rio just stared at her. "What's he doing here?"

"I'm sorry," was all she said. "For everything."

Rio couldn't believe his eyes. There was Julian coming down the stairs as if he owned the place. He sure as hell didn't look like a pauper or a man on the run from his creditors. He wore an expensive-looking suit with a silk vest.

But that wasn't what bothered Rio the most—it was Julian's mere presence. His half-brother was the last person he'd expected to be in Abbie's home.

"What the hell are you doing here?" Rio demanded.

Julian gave Rio an amused smile. "I suppose I could ask you the same thing." The smile quickly faded, though, and he looked in Abbie's direction. "What's this all about, Miss Donegan? First, you send me on a ridiculous trip to San Antonio to collect money from a man who doesn't even exist. Now, you show up here with my half-brother?"

"I'll tell you what it's all about," Camellia interrupted. "Abbie said she married him."

"Married?" Julian laughed. "That's ingenious. I wish I'd thought of that myself. I would have sent Camellia to Fall Creek instead of you."

"It wouldn't have worked," Rio let him know. "Camellia couldn't have given me what Abbie did."

"And what would that be?"

"The ranch. She paid off all the debts, and now it belongs to me."

He enjoyed the hint of surprise that went through his brother's eyes. The surprise didn't stay long though. "She tricked you, Rio. Can't you see that?"

"I don't know what you mean."

"That's what she does. She's a liar. Do you think for one minute a woman like Abilene Donegan would give you the McCaine ranch?"

"I have the deed," Rio insisted.

"What you have is a fake, a worthless piece of paper. The ranch was supposed to be mine. That's the deal I made with her."

Rio glanced at Abbie, at the unreadable expression on her face, and then turned back to his brother. He didn't like the sudden direction this conversation had taken. "What deal?"

"That she would somehow get you out of the way," Julian answered. "It's the *McCaine* ranch, and I have no intentions of sharing it with you. I told my father that when he wrote his ridiculous will. My guess is Miss Donegan had you sign something, a document with some very creative wording. Well, read through it again, Rio, because you might have just handed her my ranch."

Every muscle in Rio's body went stiff. His stomach began to churn. He didn't know what to believe. Julian was a liar. But then, apparently, so was his wife.

Rio turned to her. "Abbie?"

The color drained from her face. "He was blackmailing me, but—"

"Hell! It's true? What he said is true?"

"Parts of it, but—"

Rio aimed a finger at her to silence her. "Yes or no, did Julian tell you to get the ranch for him?" She frantically shook her head and started to say something, but once more Rio interrupted her. "Yes or no?"

"Yes, but—"

"I don't want to hear anything else!" He groaned. For days, he'd thought the ranch was his. His and his alone. He'd planned and dreamed. But this didn't feel much like a dream come true. This was a nightmare. "How the hell could you conspire with my brother?"

She shook her head again, but Rio turned his back to her. He couldn't take anymore of this tonight. His head pounded, his stomach was in a knot, and his temper was on a very short fuse. He looked around the room and spotted the Mexican housekeeper who was practically cowering near the door. "I need a place to sleep. I'm not going back out in that rain tonight."

She nodded timidly. "I had Juan take your things to your room. It's down that hallway, third door on the right."

Abbie caught his arm. "Rio—"

With more force than was required, he threw off her grip. "There's nothing you can say that I want to hear. First thing in the morning, I'm taking those papers to a lawyer to see if I can reclaim my rightful share of the ranch. My advice to you? Stay the hell away from me."

"No, I won't do that. Not until you let me explain everything."

"Why? So you can lie to me some more? That's all you've done since the minute I first laid eyes on you." He shoved his hands against the sides of his head. "I can't believe I actually agree with Julian on this, but you are nothing but a conniver!"

"All I ask is that you hear me out. You see—"

"I wouldn't believe anything you said if you wore an angel's halo and gave away Bibles."

Rio was so mad he could hardly see straight, but he did manage to notice her eyes narrow to slits. "Fine, if that's what you want to believe, then believe it. I'm tired, and I'm going to bed. Maybe tomorrow you'll be in a better mood to listen." She pointed at Julian. "And you get out of my house. Now!"

She didn't even wait to see if that's what Julian would do. Rio watched as she turned and stormed down the hall.

"You heard her," Rio said to Julian. "She wants you out of her house. Since that's about the only thing Abbie and I agree on, I'll be more than happy to show you and Camellia the door. In fact, I'll be more than happy to toss you out it."

"No need for such measures. We'll leave on our own. We can get a room at the hotel in town, but we'll be back first thing in the morning. Don't worry about getting a lawyer, Rio. I'll send for mine, and you can show him those worthless papers. Then you'll see exactly how big of a mistake it was to believe your wife."

Rio was dead certain he didn't need a lawyer to tell him that. He had been a fool to trust Abbie.

A damn fool.

Chapter Fourteen

Abbie threw open the door to her bedroom as if she'd declared war on it. The glass doorknob smacked against the wall with a loud thud.

"Hellfire!" Abbie snarled. "Hell blooming hellfire. Blooming blasted hellfire. Awwwww, hell!"

With his tabby tail raised high in the air, Pig came sauntering in. Not in the mood for the cat's ornery temperament, Abbie smacked her foot hard on the floor. Pig gave an indignant meow and scampered under her bed.

"Is there anything I can get for you, Senorita Donegan? Uh, I mean Senora McCaine."

She looked behind her where Victoria and Ina were huddled in the doorway. She tried to keep her anger out of her voice when she spoke. After all, it wasn't their fault she'd ruined everything. "No, I can manage. Go to bed, both of you, and get some sleep. And please check on Gussie. She probably heard everything."

"But what about—"

Abbie held up her hand, hoping it would quiet Victoria. For once it worked. "I'll work it all out tomorrow, I promise. Please, just go. I need some time to myself."

And to make sure they did leave, Abbie gave the door a push with her foot. It slammed in their faces. While it was rude, she really couldn't handle anymore questions tonight. She couldn't handle *anything* else tonight.

She looked at her father's picture on her dresser and groaned. Well, she'd made a mess of things. A real mess. Never in her wildest dreams had she thought success would make her feel this way. Even if she had managed to checkmate Julian and Camellia, it had come at a high cost.

Without bothering to unbutton it, Abbie ripped open her shirt and shoved it off her shoulders. She let it fall in a heap to the floor. Her boots came off next, which she threw against the wall. By the time she'd worked her way out of the soggy split riding skirt, the first tear made it's way down her cheek. It was hot and burned against her chilled, damp skin. She quickly wiped it away.

"That's right," she chided herself. "Go ahead and cry. Just what you need now. A red, runny nose and blurred vision. That'll make everything better."

"Meow." Pig strolled out from beneath the bed and began batting at a loose thread on the hem of her drawers. Abbie didn't do anything about it until one of the claws swiped over her ankle. She quickly pushed the cat away.

With his head tilted at a questioning angle, Pig studied her and let out a disapproving sound.

"Yeah, well life's not fair, is it?" Abbie mumbled.

Pig answered with another judgmental meow.

The door flew open, and in a quick rolling motion, she reached for the Remington revolver that she kept on the night table next to her bed. One look at her visitor, though, and she didn't think she'd need the gun. Well,

179

maybe she would. He certainly looked ready to kill her. She just might have to defend herself.

"Rio, I can't talk—"

"I don't remember giving you a choice. You'll talk to me all right, and you'll explain everything."

She pushed her hand through her hair to get it off her forehead. "If I thought it'd do any good, then I'd—"

"Just what kind of game were you playing, huh? Did you think you could do this to me, and I would just walk away? That I wouldn't mind that you made a fool out of me? Well, I'm not walking anywhere. We had a deal, and you're going through with your end of it."

"I have gone through with my—"

"I walked right—"

"Will you stop interrupting me? If you want me to tell you the truth, then you'll have to listen." Her hands went to her hips. Only then did she remember she had stripped down to her underwear—pantalets and a camisole. Thin cotton pantalets and a wet camisole. Along with being called a liar and a swindler, she supposed Rio would now call her brazen.

Abbie suddenly didn't care. She felt drained. Completely drained. And she really didn't care what names he called her.

"Nothing that comes out of your mouth will be the truth," Rio fired back at her. "Did it ever occur to you once that you should have told me about Julian and this cockeyed plan you had to steal the ranch from me?"

She paused a moment to make sure he'd finished. Abbie thought she might scream if he interrupted her again. Pig must have felt the same way because the cat made a throaty squawk. "Well, of course, it occurred to me, and I almost told you a couple of times. But I changed my mind. I figured if you knew Julian was here, then you'd turn around and go back to Fall Creek."

"You're damn right I would have. I sure wouldn't have

been traipsing through the state to rescue Harmony. And I wouldn't have come here to help you evict my half-brother's lover." He swore profusely and used his boot to push Pig away. The cat swiped a paw at him. "God-almighty, when will I learn not to trust white people?"

Abbie frowned. "Well, how very narrow-minded of you. What if I judged all Indians by the way Gray Wolf behaved? Then, I'd be saying ignorant things like 'when will I learn not to trust Indians?' "

"It's not ignorant if it's based on fact. I don't have any reason to trust white people."

Pig chose that moment to dig his claws into Rio's boots. Fed up with the cat's antics, Abbie scooped him up, opened the window, and put the cat outside on the porch. She quickly closed the window before he could get back in.

Abbie turned her gaze back on Rio. "It's your turn to leave. If you don't get out, I'll dump you on the porch, too."

"No, you won't."

"Yes, I will."

"Won't!"

Frustrated, she pulled back the covers on her bed and fluffed up her pillow. "God, we sound like Gussie. You've got me arguing like a child. Now, will you get out of here so I can go to bed? It's clear you're not going to listen—"

"And it's clear you're nothing but—"

"—to me or let me finish a sentence."

"—a lying little—"

Abbie picked up the pillow and threw it at him. It smacked him right in the head. She wished she'd given the action a little more thought because Rio's eyes turned the color of a huge, ominous storm cloud. A hoarse growl rumbled in his chest, and Abbie's breath backed up in her throat.

"Rio—"

He reached for her. Abbie darted to the side, but at the same time he did. His body collided with hers and sent them flying backward on to the bed. Even though the mattress was soft, the impact of his solid body rattled her. She thought maybe it'd done the same to Rio since she heard him sputter and cough.

"What do you think you're doing?" she managed. She struggled, trying to get out from beneath him, but he pinned her hands to the bed. His clothes were cool and wet against her, but his breath was so warm, it felt like fiery gusts on her face.

He didn't answer. He only stared at her.

"So, what are you going to do?" She swallowed hard. "Hit me?"

"No."

Abbie wasn't so sure of that. He looked ready to do serious harm to her body. She figured she could get him off her, that is if she resorted to violence. She wasn't helpless, and a knee shoved into his groin would certainly discourage him. It was the way she'd discouraged several of Gray Wolf's renegades when they tried to touch her. But she really didn't want to hurt Rio.

She'd already done enough of that.

"Rio—" she said, trying to soften her voice.

"Don't! Don't say anything else. No more lies."

"I—"

His mouth swooped down on hers, and she gasped at the unexpected contact. The kiss was brutal, and he thrust his tongue into her mouth. But somewhere in her mind, it registered that it was still a kiss. One from Rio.

"I'm not lying," she got out when he broke away from her. "The ranch really is yours."

She didn't think he even heard her. His mouth was on hers again, and she swore she felt flames rush from his lips. The kiss raged with anger and frustration, but it wasn't actually rough. She had no doubt he could be a lot rougher if he wanted to be.

"I swear I'm not lying," she repeated as Rio's mouth went to her neck.

God, that felt good. His wet, clever mouth on her neck. She hadn't realized how sensitive that area was before. She moaned and pressed closer to those kisses. To that clever mouth.

"I said I don't want to hear it," he snarled. "I just want you to do your wifely duty."

Abbie stiffened. "My what?"

"Your duty." He ran his hand between their bodies and cupped her through her pantalets. "This!"

He'd probably meant to disgust her with that crude gesture, and part of Abbie really wanted it to disgust her. But this was Rio. His mouth had kissed her. His hands had touched her. He was mad. Hurt. Wounded. And she was the cause of those hurts and wounds.

In her mind she might have justified giving herself to him just to soothe him. Or she might have justified it by saying this was indeed her duty, something she'd bartered away when she'd said "I do." She was after all his wife.

However, wifely duty didn't have a whole lot to do with this. His hand was on her *there,* and his middle finger was pressing on a delicious little spot that Abbie hadn't been aware she had. It was hard to think about duty when she saw stars and had trouble catching her breath.

"All right," she gasped. "Take me."

He paused for a moment, staring deeply into her eyes. Abbie thought he might stop then, that he might have come to his senses. She didn't want him to come to his senses just yet. This would probably be the last time she would ever be with Rio, and she wanted to make the most of it.

"Did you hear me, Rio?"

Oh, he'd heard. A moment later Abbie was absolutely certain he had not only heard but that he intended to *take*. He latched on to the front of her camisole, and with a furious jerk, he ripped the sides apart. Her breasts spilled against his clenched hands.

His hands didn't stay clenched for long. Abbie watched his gaze as it went from her face to her throat. And lower. His long fingers molded around her breasts.

A soft rush of breath left his mouth.

She thought that might be a good sign. Harmony had told her once that men liked to touch a woman's breasts. Well, if he touched her, then maybe—

Ohmygod.

Rio slowly lowered his mouth to one of her nipples and nipped it with his teeth. He didn't stop there. He roughly flicked his tongue over it and brought it into his mouth. The sound Abbie made was a full-fledged gasp.

"Ohmygod."

She felt her pulse scramble when he gave the same treatment to her other nipple. Yes, Rio liked breasts. And she liked that he liked them—very much. Abbie didn't, however, like the roaring heat she felt build inside her. She had somehow gone from feeling just plain itchy to wanting him more than her next breath.

Abbie gripped his wet shirt, pulling him closer. It was she who deepened the kiss when he eased his tongue over her bottom lip. Rio took things from there. His fingers sank into her hair, angling her head. He put his other hand on her hips and angled her body. And he adjusted their position, until even through his jeans and her pantalets, she could feel every inch of him.

Every increasing inch.

At first the sensation astonished her. Of course, Abbie had seen the stallions before they covered the mares, but she hadn't thought that male part of Rio could become as hard as stone. And big. My God, the man was huge.

Then, she remembered how the stallions had entered the mares, and her astonishment quickly turned to panic. This would probably hurt. Not probably. It *would* hurt. Badly. And then she remembered something else—she hadn't told Rio that she was still a vir—

"Ohmygod," she moaned.

He adjusted their positions again. Just a fraction. Now they fit the way a man and woman were supposed to fit. That hard-as-stone part of him actually fit itself right to the—*ohmygod*—place that his finger had touched. It didn't hurt at all. It was wonderful. Delicious. Like something she'd always wanted but hadn't known.

Abbie quickly amended her earlier idea. Yes, this would be pleasurable, and she didn't care a speck of dust if it hurt.

She dug her heels into the mattress and arched herself against him, but the contact went away as quickly as it had come. She groaned at the loss and reached for Rio, but he only moved his hands between them.

Roughly he tore the center seam of her pantalets, the sound stark in the otherwise silent room. She felt the movement of his fingers brush her flesh as he struggled with the buttons on his rain-soaked jeans. He freed himself but kept one hand between their bodies.

"Don't say you don't want this." His voice was a low rumbling growl.

Abbie had no intentions of saying that. Why would she? Even she wasn't *that* good of a liar—and there were some who considered her the best liar around.

Sliding his hand lower down her stomach, he slipped inside the gaping tear in her pantalets then recaptured her gaze. Pausing a moment, he lifted one eyebrow in a challenging gesture and eased one finger inside her.

Her breath hitched, frozen solid in her throat. "Ohmygod. Ohmygod. Oh. My. God."

"Don't say you don't want this," he repeated. "I feel the proof."

Other than the obvious, unexplained wetness between her legs, Abbie had no idea what proof he was talking about. Nor did she care. If he really wanted to see proof, all he had to do was look at her. Her eyes were probably glazed, and she was within seconds of demanding that he do his husbandly duty to her.

She was suddenly sure there was such a thing as husbandly duty.

If not, she'd invent it.

"I do want you, Rio."

He whispered something she didn't understand, then she slowly watched his expression soften. It was the only thing soft about him. Seeing the gentle look that crept into his eyes, Abbie didn't know why he'd had this sudden change of heart, but she hoped it didn't interfere with what he'd started.

"Abbie," he whispered.

She wanted to tell him not to stop, but he kissed her again, and Abbie immediately felt the difference. There was tenderness mingled with his need. It stirred her own, feeding it in a way that raw passion hadn't. She didn't want to think what it meant for him to be tender now. She didn't want to think about what it would cost them both later. But there would be a cost, something she never thought she'd want to pay.

All at once, she cared so much for him she was afraid it just might break her heart.

"Rio," she whispered. "Make me your wife."

He gripped her wrists and pinned them against the mattress. She felt that hard male part of him touch her. She stiffened. Relaxed. Arched toward him.

Briefly, she had time to realize that this was what she wanted. Exactly what she wanted.

Positioning himself, he pushed into her with a solid thrust.

His thrust didn't get Rio very far. It should have planted him firmly, deeply inside Abbie.

It didn't.

"Sonofabitch," Rio managed.

Abbie gasped and threw her forehead into his shoulder. Rio gasped, too, but for air. Abbie's fingers dug into his flesh as she struggled beneath him. She made little whimpers, her face contorted with pain.

Rio arched his neck and groaned, unable to do more than that. The tightfisted lock inside her trapped him. If he could have said anything, he would have cursed the vilest words he knew. As it was, he could do no more than appreciate Abbie's whimpers.

"Why?" he demanded.

She frantically shook her head.

He shook his also, and his shaking was just as frantic. "That . . . is not an answer."

"What's the question?"

"God, how can you even ask that? There was only one question. Just one! Why are you still a virgin?"

"I don't think I am one anymore." She looked between their bodies where they were partially joined. "In fact, I'm sure I'm not."

Groaning, Rio rolled off her and landed on his back on the mattress. "Ah, hell! Hell! Hell! Hell!" He sandwiched his hands on each side of his head and looked up at the ceiling. "Try a real answer this time, one that doesn't make me feel like I'm pulling teeth. Why were you a virgin until just a few seconds ago?"

"Uh, because I've never been with a man."

Of course. What answer had he expected her to give? It was a typical Abbie answer. And a really stupid one.

It was also probably a ploy to throw him off because she wasn't a stupid woman.

He wanted to curse, to let go of some vile words that would blister her ears. If that was even possible. Hell. He had married a virgin. A virgin! Never in his wildest dreams had he ever wanted to bed a virgin, and here he'd married one.

One that shouldn't even have been one. She'd lied to him again!

Abbie sat up and pulled the sides of her ripped camisole over her breasts. "I really didn't think you'd notice that I hadn't been with a man."

Slowly, he turned his head toward her and gave her a long cold glare. "You didn't think I'd notice something like that? Good God, Abbie, I'm not half-witted. I noticed, all right?"

Since she seemed to be trying to cover herself up, Rio got off the bed and did some covering of his own. He rebuttoned his jeans and stared at the floor so he wouldn't have to look at her.

"Why did you lie about this? *How* could you lie about something like this?" But Rio didn't even give her a chance to answer. "Forget that. I don't want to know. Anything you say would probably be just another lie. Well, I'm tired of hearing them. I'm tired of you."

She looked as if he'd slapped her. But she didn't even utter a word.

Turning, he went to the door and walked out. He decided the muffled sound he heard couldn't possibly be Abbie crying.

If she was, then her tears were probably lies too.

Chapter Fifteen

Abbie sank into the tub of water that Ina had prepared for her. The warmth eased the soreness between her legs, but it did nothing to ease the soreness in her heart. She didn't think she could do much about that.

The night before she'd finally experienced what it was like to be with a man, something she thought might never happen. Now, unfortunately, that man hated her with a vengeance.

Almost hesitantly she studied her body for any signs of change. There were none, since she had washed off the small amount of blood on the inside of her thigh. Such a small reminder of the monumental thing that had happened. Rio had kissed her and touched her. He had made her respond and feel. No man had ever given her that much, and she had never given that much of herself to anyone either.

She never would again.

Abbie slapped at the water to distract herself. It didn't

work. The agitated waves swirled over her breasts, reminding her of Rio's exploring hands. And his mouth. Her body started to itch, responding to a much too vivid memory. It was impossible to forget the way his body blanketed hers with his solid weight.

She shuddered and leaned her head against the tub, afraid to give a name to what afflicted her. It had a name, she knew all too well. She was suffering from a bad case of Rio McCaine. Abbie feared there was no known cure.

There was a soft knock at the door, followed by Victoria's hushed voice. "Can I come in, Abbie?"

"No."

Abbie knew Victoria'd come in anyway, and she was right. The door popped open, and Victoria entered. "I know you want to be alone, but I just had to see you."

"Since you're here, will you pour me a shot of whiskey?" Abbie motioned toward the decanter on her dresser.

Victoria's head whipped up. "I most certainly will not. It's still morning. You haven't even had your breakfast yet."

As if that had ever stopped her. "Get me a cheroot then. They're in the drawer of my night table."

"Not one of those either. Honestly, Abbie, you shouldn't even be smoking those things." Victoria crossed the room and stood directly over her. "What went on in here last night? Did Rio hurt you?"

"No." Well, he hadn't hurt her the way Victoria meant. Abbie didn't think she could very well blame Rio for the ache in her heart. She had to put that squarely on her own shoulders.

"Well? Then what did happen?" Victoria asked.

"A lot." Too much. And in some ways not nearly enough. "I did my wifely duty, except I forgot to tell Rio that I'd never been with a man—"

"Holy Mother." Victoria crossed herself and dropped

down into the chair next to the tub. Without asking, she poured some water over Abbie's hair and started to wash it with a cake of soap. "And now he knows you lied to him about that too?"

Abbie took a deep, frustrated breath. "Now he knows."

"He must have been furious. Why didn't you just tell him before you decided to, well, uh, do your duty?"

"I got caught up in the moment." A huge understatement. The moment had swept her completely away. But she had paid dearly for that lapse. If only she'd forced herself to tell Rio, then he might not have gotten so mad.

She eased forward so Victoria could rinse her hair.

"I've heard a man can beguile the moment, so to speak," Victoria said almost shyly. "I've also heard that a man practiced about such matters can touch a woman in such a way to make her forget what she's doing."

Oh yes, that was absolutely true. Abbie had firsthand knowledge of that.

"Don't worry," she told Victoria. "Rio didn't do anything to me that I didn't want him to do. Anyway, just as soon as he found out, he got right up. I guess you could say I didn't do my wifely duty after all. I just sort of started it." She glanced at Victoria. "Isn't a man supposed to get a lot of pleasure from marital relations?"

"You're asking me?"

Abbie shrugged. "You're right. Sorry. I figured since you knew that other part, you'd know about this too."

"I don't," Victoria quickly assured her.

"I'm pretty sure Rio was at least supposed to enjoy it a little. When I looked in the windows at the Buffalo Clover, those men looked like they were enjoying themselves." Abbie remembered the couple tangled up like eels. "Well, I guess they were. Anyway, I think if Rio had enjoyed it, he wouldn't have got up right away. I think he would have stayed around a little longer."

"Well, I'm sorry everything turned out this way. I like

Rio, and I had hoped he wouldn't get hurt by this scheme of yours."

"Please don't say I told you so."

Victoria didn't say anything for several moments. "I won't. You know what you've done, and it won't do me any good to remind you of it."

Now, that was a first.

"I do have some good news," Victoria added, her expression brightening. She took the towel and vigorously wrung out the water from Abbie's hair. "Camellia and Julian left last night."

"That's something at least." It didn't give Abbie nearly as much pleasure as she'd thought it would.

"I don't know about that. Camellia threatened that she'd be back."

"Good. Maybe I'll just beat the crap out of her, something I should have done months ago."

Victoria crossed herself. "You couldn't do that. Your father—"

"Our father," Abbie corrected, "was in the throes of carnality when his heart gave out on him. I wonder sometimes if he knew what he was asking me to do."

"He knew," Victoria said firmly. She took a barrette from the dresser and pinned up Abbie's thick mass of hair. "I was there, too, remember?"

Abbie didn't think it was a scene she'd likely forget. Her father, naked except for the bed sheet that Camellia had thankfully covered him with. His face, pale as ash. His words, weak and clipped.

During those last moments, Abbie had actually thought she hated him for allowing his libidinous appetite to kill him. Now, after she'd experienced a few of those libidinous moments with Rio, she better understood her father. She would never be able to understand why he'd chosen Camellia, of course, but the rest she could finally comprehend.

She'd put on those stupid fairy wings in a minute if it would make Rio forgive her.

"Have you seen Rio this morning?" Abbie asked.

"I saw him a little while ago out by the barn."

Her heart sank. "Was he leaving?"

"I don't think so. He mumbled something about not going anywhere until he'd spoken to you."

Abbie didn't know whether to be thankful for that or to run and hide. "You sure you won't pour me a glass of whiskey?"

Frowning, Victoria stood up. "No, I won't. I won't help you drink yourself into a stupor. The best thing you can do for yourself right now is to get dressed, have some breakfast, and try to mend fences with Rio."

She'd have an easier time learning to like Camellia. Abbie didn't say that. It would only give Victoria cause to keep scolding her. Besides, she could always get her own drink when her sister left.

"And don't wear trousers today, for heaven's sake," Victoria continued. The scolding tone became even thicker. "Put on a dress and fix yourself up a little. It won't hurt to remind Rio that you're a flesh-and-blood woman, even if you are prone to odd behavior and bouts of lying."

Abbie gave her sister a mock salute, and Victoria quickly left.

The silent room gave her plenty of time to think—about the night before, about everything that had happened.

About Rio.

He'd taken her. *Taken.* She lacked a better word. After that initial jolt of pain and after Abbie forced her muscles to relax, what remained was a somewhat satisfying sensation. Beneath the discomfort was the promise of something that could start to feel a whole heck of a lot better

193

any minute. Unfortunately, that's about the time Rio rolled off her and cursed.

There could be no annulment now, and that meant they would have to go through a divorce. Well, unless she lied again and said they hadn't consummated their marriage.

No.

There had been enough lies. It was time for the truth.

Abbie wasn't sure her heart could accept the truth. Somewhere between the time she'd crawled through the window at the Buffalo Clover and now, she'd really started to care for Rio. Maybe it was even more than caring. Maybe it was something she didn't want to believe. Could it be possible that she was falling in—

Abbie groaned at the sound of the door opening. "Not now, Victoria. Just give me another couple of minutes."

Silence.

An eerie silence.

Abbie turned her head slowly so she could see her visitor. Not Victoria. Not Gussie. Not even Ina.

It was Rio.

He just stood there and looked at her.

Rio froze at the sight of her.

Abbie naked. Thoroughly naked. In the bathtub.

He hadn't seen her completely unclothed the night before when he'd taken her so roughly on the bed. Both the apology and the argument he'd intended died on his lips. With reason. She took his breath away.

She'd piled her copper hair on top of her head, but only a fragile barrette held the damp mass of curls in place. Some of the wavy strands had already started to slump against her neck. Rio focused on that shiny gold barrette, knowing if it were to give way, Abbie's hair would tumble down onto her shoulders and breasts.

"Uh, I'm what you might call indisposed," she said softly.

All in all, it was a good word for it. Indisposed. Naked, was a better word though. Naked and beautiful.

Abbie's face was dewy, practically glistening, from the heat of the bathwater. Tiny beads of perspiration were on her forehead and above her upper lip. Her leaf-colored eyes were wide with surprise, and her mouth opened slightly. He heard her breath. Saw the pulse flutter in her throat.

"I'll be done in a minute or two if you want to come back," she added.

"I don't want to come back." He cleared his throat and put some gravel in his voice. "I want to talk. Now."

That probably wasn't the brightest idea he'd ever had—talking to a naked woman when he was furious with her. Especially because he wanted to stay furious with her until they'd straightened out some things. Nakedness had a way of tipping scales that shouldn't be tipped. Especially when it was Abbie's nakedness.

The bathwater was deep enough to cover her breasts. Well, almost. It gently sloshed from her earlier movement. With each ripping wave, the water revealed her puckered nipples, only to cover them quickly again as the water and soap suds shifted. It was rhythmic, a seemingly relentless taunting of his senses. Like watching a hypnotist's timepiece swing back and forth. Compelled, Rio watched, helpless not to respond. Hell, he responded. He got as hard as the tub where Abbie sat.

Definitely dampening his fury.

"I suppose there's a reason you didn't knock?" she asked.

Probably. But he couldn't think of it at the moment. He tried to blame that on the overly warm room and the scent of her soap. Nothing perfumy. Just soap on this naked woman's body.

Ah, hell.

He was in trouble here.

Rio wanted to speak or move—he wanted to do anything to break his gaze, but he seemed to be boneless. Though not bloodless; the blood raced through his veins. He was practically deaf from the roaring in his ears. And he was absolutely positive he'd never wanted another woman as much as he wanted this one.

Abbie anxiously slid her tongue over her lips to moisten them. She might as well have skimmed her tongue on his mouth. She might as well have kissed him. Really kissed him. One of those kisses that was as wet and hot as her bathwater.

"Well?" she prompted. "I guess you'll tell me all about it when you quit staring at me. At least hand me the towel so I can cover myself. I'm not used to sitting around bare-butted while an angry man watches me bathe."

Did he really look angry? Well, good. That was something at least. He'd rather look angry than aroused, especially right now.

He took her towel from the chair and thrust it toward her. "Get dressed. We have to talk."

Rio turned his back, then, but it didn't matter. He could see her reflection in the mirror over her dresser, every glorious inch of her.

With water sheeting off her body, she stepped from the bathtub. She didn't cover herself right away with the towel, but then she probably didn't know he was gawking.

Lord, the woman had a beautiful body. Creamy, flawless skin. From the swell of her ample breasts to the flare of her hips. Naturally, his attention went straight to the triangle of dark copper curls between her legs. Yes, that part of her was beautiful too.

Of course, he couldn't remember ever thinking one of those was ugly.

196

She dried herself. Starting with her arms, Abbie smoothed the towel over them, then did the same to her back and shoulders. She had to arch her body to do that, thrusting her breasts forward.

Rio nearly choked on his own breath.

With one foot anchored on the floor, Abbie slowly raised the other foot to the rim of tub and rubbed the towel over her ankle. Her calf. Her thigh. And higher. God, he'd never wanted to be a towel before, but this would have been a good time for it. She repeated the same procedure on her other leg, drying the inside of her thigh, and she then tossed the towel onto the chair.

While Rio watched dumbfounded in the mirror, she unclipped the barrette in her wet hair so that it slowly spilled over her shoulders. She gave her head a feminine little shake and sifted her fingers through the strands to smooth it away from her face.

Hell. Much more of that, and he'd drag her to the bed. Or the floor. Or—

No! That couldn't happen for a lot of reasons.

"You have some explaining to do," he snapped. "You should have told me everything before we got as far as we did last night. What were you trying to do, surprise me? Because you did, you know that? You shocked the hell out of me."

She reached in the wardrobe and took out her pantalets. "Believe me, it shocked me too."

"What does that mean?"

"It means I didn't expect what happened to happen. I haven't exactly had a lot of women in my life who could tell me about these things. Well, except for Aunt Dorrie, and she said it was sort of like being saddled."

"Saddled?" he mumbled.

"Yes, you know, as in riding. Well, I can promise you, it was nothing like that."

Rio remembered the way she'd grimaced in pain. Like

her naked body, it was an image he couldn't get out of his head. "I hurt you, and for that I'm sorry. If I had known—"

"I'm pretty sure it still would have hurt."

"Not as much. I could have, hell, I don't know what I could have done. I've never been with an inexperienced woman before."

"Then I guess that made us kind of even last night."

"No, it didn't," he assured her. "It doesn't make us anywhere even. You lied to me again."

Because he was still looking in the mirror, he saw her nod and then dip down her head. She said nothing. On a ragged sigh, she stepped into pantalets, pulled them up over her hips, and tightened the drawstring around her waist.

It was sight to see. Abbie standing there bare-breasted with a close-fitting pair of pantalets and a sad expression. Her rose-colored nipples had puckered, and her skin was still slightly damp from her bath.

Rio had to shut his eyes for a moment just so he could concentrate on their conversation.

"Why did you tell me the Apaches had violated you?" he asked. "Why would you lie about something like that?"

She sighed again, softly. "I didn't exactly lie."

His eyes flew open. "How can you deny that? That's *exactly* what you did."

"You asked if I'd been with a man before I was taken captive, and I said no. That was the truth." She pushed the fabric of her pantalets up to her upper thigh, gathered up her dark cotton stockings and slid them over her foot and up her long, slender leg. She repeated the unhurried maneuver with the other stocking and secured them with garters.

"All right," Rio continued after he unclamped his teeth

from his bottom lip. "But when we were by the creek, and you stopped me—"

"I only said I couldn't. I didn't say why, exactly."

"Exactly? Exactly! You knew what I was thinking," he accused. "You knew that I believed you'd been violated in the worst way a woman could be violated—and don't you dare say not exactly."

"Yes, I did know what you thought, but I had to let you believe it for a while. If I'd told you the Apaches hadn't violated me, then I would have had to explain why they hadn't."

She snatched a camisole from the wardrobe hook and slipped it on. Unfortunately, the fabric caught on her erect nipple. Caught, and Abbie had to pluck at it to unsnag it.

Ah, hell.

She pulled the garment down. Rio was thankful she had finally covered most of herself. He hadn't remembered a woman dressing being such a damn distraction. Usually it was more arousing for a woman to remove her clothes.

"Well?" Rio questioned.

"Well what?"

Rio groaned. "Explain why the Apaches didn't violate you."

"Oh, that." She put on a pale green dress and let it slide down over her body.

"Yes, that." Since the only thing she had left to do was button her dress, Rio faced her again. "That's the little detail you forgot to mention."

"They didn't violate me because Harmony and Gray Wolf are lovers. As awful as Gray Wolf is, he wouldn't have harmed me since I'm Harmony's sister." She motioned toward the back of her dress. "I don't guess you'd be kind enough to button me, would you? They make these stupid garments so a woman can't dress herself."

He wasn't in the mood to discuss women's dresses, but it would probably only prolong this ridiculous conversation. Rio got three buttons done before he realized exactly what Abbie had said. "Harmony and Gray Wolf are lovers?"

"Yes, and lower your voice. I don't want Victoria and the others running in here. Besides, Gussie's probably listening outside the window."

"Am not," the girl's voice called out. She peeked through a slit in the curtains of the partially opened window. "Not for very long anyway."

Abbie put her hands on her hips. "Augusta Marie Burge—"

"I know, I'm in trouble. I'll go say my prayers. Maybe sixty hundred times or something. But Rio should haveta say his too because he watched you in the mirror when you was dressing. Men aren't supposed to watch women dressing."

Abbie's eyes quickly turned in his direction. "Did you do that? Did you actually watch me?"

Frustrated, Rio lifted his hand to the mirror and then to her. "I saw a little, yes. I couldn't help it. There was no place to look except at that mirror or at you." Not exactly the truth, but it wasn't something he wanted to discuss right now. "Gussie, why don't you run along and let me talk to Abbie?"

Gussie nodded but didn't leave right away. "Are you gonna yell at her?"

Yes, he probably was. "Your sister will be fine."

"All right," Gussie answered, her tone unconcerned. She moved away from the window and stepped off the porch into the front yard.

"You watched me dress?" Abbie asked.

"I've already said I did. A little. But this isn't about me watching you. It's about the lies and the half-truths you keep telling. Why didn't you just let me know right from the start that Harmony wasn't really in any danger? Why did you make me think I had to rescue her?"

"Because I thought she needed to be rescued. She was on the outs with Gray Wolf when he took her, and I thought he was still holding her against her will. Chey's the one who said they worked out their differences. I asked him to find her anyway, and he did. He also apparently got her to safety since he sent that telegram."

Safety. Because Harmony was in some kind of trouble with the law. Still, that was no reason for Abbie to keep it secret. He balled his hands into fists to keep from grabbing her. "It's just one lie right after another with you, Abbie. I could never trust you. Never."

"Fine! Don't trust me. Just quit yelling and growling at me."

Rio turned to leave, but she cleared her throat. "What?" he barked.

"The buttons?"

Hellfire. He was furious with her, and she wanted him to button her dress? He started to tell her that it wasn't a good idea for him to get that close, that, he didn't know how much more of her he could take.

"Please," she added. But as usual it wasn't a nice *please*. It was an Abbie please, laced with a hint of an order.

Rio thought about it. About yelling at her. About shaking her until he shook some sense into her. But he didn't do any of those things. Instead, he latched onto her shoulders and stared at her.

Abbie suddenly looked frightened. "Uh, what are you going to do?"

Yes, what would he do? He considered all those other things. The shaking and the yelling. He also considered walking out and leaving her with her pretty back exposed for the world to see.

He even considered tossing her on the bed so he could

teach her a real lesson—not to mess with him again. And this time he damn sure wouldn't stop because she was a near-virgin. No, he would push himself into her as deep as he could go, and he would . . .

Rio had to put a stop to those thoughts. He was getting aroused. Hardly a bargaining tool for winning this argument.

"Rio?" Abbie said hesitantly. "What are you going to do to me?"

He roughly spun her around. "The buttons," he ground out. "Your damn buttons."

Chapter Sixteen

When Abbie walked into the dining room, Gussie's glass of milk stopped halfway to her mouth. "I didn't think you'd ever actually wear that dress. Did somebody die or something?"

Abbie tried not to snap at the little girl, but she wasn't in any mood to answer questions about her choice of clothing. "I wore this because I felt like it." She sat at the breakfast table and greeted Victoria.

"I see you decided to take my advice," Victoria remarked with a smile. "About the dress and about having breakfast."

Abbie made a sound of disapproval. "I just felt like wearing a dress, all right? Now, can't anyone think of something else to discuss?"

Gussie gulped down a large mouthful of milk. "I guess we could, but it's kinda more interesting talking about your dress. When I saw you put it on, I thought it was just so you could cover yourself up because Rio was in the room."

"I don't want to talk about it. So there." Abbie gave a firm nod and dished herself some scrambled eggs.

As usual, Ina had prepared a feast. Along with the eggs, there were thick ham slabs, fried potatoes, fresh peaches, and warm tortillas with butter. Everything looked delicious. Well, everything except the extra plate set next to her at the head of the table, a place that had been unoccupied since her father's death. She hadn't even allowed guests to sit in that spot.

"Why is that there?" Abbie asked, nodding at the plate.

Victoria paused before she answered. "I asked Rio to join us. He should be here any minute. I thought since he's your husband that it's only appropriate for him to sit at the head of the table."

Abbie couldn't believe her ears—and it wasn't the head-of-the-table part that had her confused. It was the other thing Victoria mentioned. "Rio actually agreed to eat breakfast with us?"

"Well, not exactly with *us*. He agreed to eat breakfast with Gussie and me. I wasn't sure you'd be coming to the table."

"So he doesn't know I'll be here?"

Victoria shook her head. "And please don't start anything with him when he gets here."

"Me, start something with him? He's the one who's being stubborn. I've said I'm sorry, and he won't forgive me."

"Can't say I blame him," Gussie piped in. "You did tell him all those lies and all. He's got a right to be mad."

"I know." Abbie frowned and stuffed some eggs in her mouth.

Victoria lowered her voice to a near whisper when she spoke to Abbie again. "Anyway, I thought if I could talk to Rio over breakfast, that I could get him to understand why you did some of the things you did."

Gussie shook her head. "You'll need a whole bucket full of luck for that to happen."

Abbie ignored Gussie's remark and thought about what Victoria had just said. Would it be possible for her sister to talk some sense into Rio? If anyone could do it, it would be Victoria. The woman could always talk her into doing things she didn't want to do.

"Shhh," Victoria whispered even though no one said anything. "He's coming down the hall right now."

Since the hallway was behind Abbie, she couldn't see him. But she could hear his footsteps. She also heard his footsteps when they paused. And paused. Rio must have come to a complete standstill. Well, it was obvious he was trying to decide if he would eat at the same table with her.

"Rio." Victoria rose from her seat and motioned for him to enter. "You must be starving. Please join us."

Dead silence. Abbie noted he certainly didn't move closer. Probably because she was there. Her mouth tightened. "Don't worry. I won't start anything with you. Sit down and eat."

Rio walked into the room and immediately picked up the extra plate. He moved it next to Gussie. It was as far away from Abbie as he could get.

"Good morning, Victoria. Gussie." He put some eggs and tortillas on his plate. "Abbie." But he didn't say it pleasantly. He had probably uttered profanity with more endearment.

"Ya'll are still mad at each other, huh?" Gussie asked.

"Augusta Marie Burge," Victoria said in a low, warning tone.

"Awww." She wiped the milk off her mouth with the back of her hand. "Don't tell me I gotta say prayers just 'cause of that."

"No prayers. Not right now anyway." With each word, Victoria's voice dropped another notch. "And use your napkin instead of your hand."

"I suppose I'll have to say prayers for that too," Gussie mumbled. She looked at Rio. "I wouldn't mind if you stuck up for me about right now."

Rio's eyebrows flexed. "It's probably best if you mind Victoria. She just wants you to grow up right."

Abbie heard the implied comparison. *Grow up right. Not like Abbie.* She wouldn't let him know that bothered her though. He could say all the snide remarks he wanted. She'd just calmly sit there and eat her—

"And I'm sure Victoria wants you to grow up to be a truthful young woman," Rio continued, all the while keeping his slightly narrowed gaze on Abbie. "Because after all, people are only as good as their word."

Abbie crammed a forkful of eggs into her mouth. She would not let him draw her into a petty game of insults. Would not. Would not. Would not!

Rio turned to Victoria. "By the way, is there a lawyer in town?"

Victoria glanced at Abbie first. "Yes. Wilburn Starling."

"He smells like a root cellar," Gussie volunteered even though her mouth was full. "And he says 'yes indeedy' all the time. I don't like him very much, and Pig hates him. Why you wanta see him anyway, Rio?"

Abbie braced herself for his answer. *Don't say "for a divorce."*

"Because I hope he can tell me the truth about some papers that Abbie gave me." He paused to eat some of his tortilla. "I've had a hard time finding out what's truth and what's not. Basically, I've figured out if it comes from Abbie, then it's probably a lie."

Abbie clamped her teeth over her bottom lip. She wouldn't be petty. But she did scowl. Rio scowled right back. She scowled even harder, scrunching her eyebrows together. He scrunched up his eyebrows. Abbie twisted her mouth. And, blast it, he did the same thing. Abbie was about to resort to pettiness when Gussie interrupted her.

"Ya'll are still mad at each other." Gussie noisily put her glass on the table and frowned. "Why is it you get to do that, and I can't? If I stayed mad at somebody, Victoria would make me say a hundred prayers. And Abbie would fuss at me. Heck, even Harmony wouldn't let me get away with that, and she pretty much doesn't care what I do."

Gussie had a point, but Abbie wasn't about to tell her so. The situation was confusing enough. Still, it did seem stupid to stay mad at Rio even after all those ugly things he'd said. After all, this was her fault. Maybe if she took the first step, he'd take one too.

"Well," Abbie started. "I'm not mad at Rio anymore. And I'm sorry for all the things I did."

She waited. And waited. He said nothing.

Abbie waited some more. He still said nothing.

Finally, he pushed his plate aside and stood. "I'll head into town to see Wilburn Starling now. Don't know when I'll be back."

Then Rio turned and left.

Abbie couldn't believe it. Even after she'd taken the first step, he hadn't taken one. He'd just walked out as if she'd said nothing at all.

"Well, hellfire," she mumbled under her breath.

Now what was she going to do?

By the time Rio left the lawyer's office in Elliot's Grove, his mood hadn't improved much. He blamed Abbie for that. Never had he wanted to hate a woman so much, but the feelings that stirred inside him weren't cooperating.

He blamed that on lust.

That was all there was to it. Yep. How else could he explain why he still felt an attraction to the lying, scheming woman he'd married?

And she was a lying, scheming woman, despite what he learned from the lawyer.

According to Wilburn Starling, Elliot's Grove's only attorney, Abbie might have actually told him the truth about the ranch. Of course, Rio didn't want to get his hopes up, but when Starling looked over the papers, he said everything seemed to be in order. *In order* in this case meant Abbie had indeed signed the McCaine ranch over to him. Still, Rio asked the man to send a telegram to the courthouse in Fall Creek to make sure the records there matched the copies he'd gotten from the bank.

With all the lies Abbie had told him, he couldn't quite believe she'd be truthful about something as important as this. Yet that lustful yearning begged him to feel differently.

He didn't intend to do that any time soon.

Rio walked up the street of the small town. It was smaller than even Fall Creek. He spotted the saloon, The Rusty Bucket, and decided a couple of shots of whiskey would improve his rotten mood. Or at least it would make him less aware of his rotten mood. It might even make him forget the sight of his completely naked wife when she'd stepped out of that bathtub. Or the memory of her lying beneath him just before he learned of yet another lie. And maybe it wouldn't.

Maybe that was asking too much from the whiskey.

He pushed open the batwing doors and stepped into the poorly lit room, examined the well-worn floors, equally well-worn mahogany bar. There were a gleaming mirror and a billiards table. On the far wall was a picture of a woman wearing only a dreamy smile. He tried not to notice that she wasn't anywhere near as attractive as Abbie.

The half-dozen men seated at the bar and tables glanced in his direction. Long glances. Then they went back to what they had been doing. He waited a moment to see if anyone would ask him to leave. It was a white man's saloon, and Rio expected someone to remind him that he was a half-breed and therefore not welcome. He was actually looking forward to it. A good face-busting fight was exactly what he needed to get rid of some of some anger.

When no one challenged him, Rio walked to the bar and took a seat at the end near the door. Normally, he wouldn't have tolerated having his back to strangers, but the mirror made it possible for him to see everything going on behind him. His good luck with well-placed mirrors seemed to be holding up. If he could call it good luck.

"Whiskey," he ordered from the barkeeper.

The bushy-whiskered man answered with a grunt, filled a shot glass, and eased it in Rio's direction.

Picking up his beer, a tall blond man got up from a table nearby and dropped onto the seat next to Rio. "Mister, you look about as uncomfortable as a cow's rump on a branding iron."

Rio felt that way, too, but he didn't care to share that with anybody.

"I'm Wendell Calverson. My guess is you're Rio McCaine, Abbie's husband."

Rio frowned. "Wendell Calverson? The one who's been pestering Abbie?"

Well, old Wendell wasn't quite what he'd expected. No round belly, no bald head, or bad teeth. He was young, muscular, and looked like every proper lady's wet dream.

That is, if proper ladies ever had such dreams.

"Guilty." Wendell grinned and drank some beer.

"I'm supposed to make you leave Abbie alone. One

way or another." Rio hoped the man took objection to that. He really looked forward to pounding Wendell in his perfect face.

"Oh, don't worry. Your marriage took care of me pestering Abbie. I don't chase married women, even if I still think she's the finest catch in the state." He glanced at Rio. "What are you anyway, part Mexican?"

Maybe it wouldn't take long for that brawl to get started. Rio loosened his fist around his glass in case he had to put it down fast. "Comanche."

Other than a slight rise in his moon-blond eyebrow, Wendell seemed to have no reaction. "Figures Abbie would fall in love with somebody like you."

Rio choked on his drink. Abbie wasn't in love with him. She didn't even trust him. And he sure didn't like that part about *somebody like you.* "You got a problem with me?"

Wendell shook his head. "Not the way you're thinking. The only thing I hold against you is that you somehow talked Abbie Donegan into marrying you. Like I said, I can see why she'd fall in love with you." Wendell continued even though Rio choked on his drink again.

"Conventionality never really appealed to her. She was always what I like to call a free stander. I like that in a woman, and I'm also crazy in love with her."

Rio stared at the man. Nosirree, Wendell wasn't quite the way Abbie had described him. "She thinks you're only pestering her for her money."

The corner of Wendell's mouth hitched. "I own one of the biggest cattle ranches in the county, and I've got almost as much money as she does. Abbie knows that. I'm just not the right man for her."

"Glad you seem to realize that. Abbie didn't think you understood."

The barkeeper refilled Rio's glass. "Any chance you'll

be taking your wife back to your neck of the woods?" the man asked.

No chance in hell, but Rio didn't say that. He didn't like the tone in the barman's voice. "Why do you want to know?"

"Just to be asking."

"He's just hoping," Wendell provided. He ignored the barkeep's scowl and turned back to Rio. "Abbie's respected here because she's Augustus's daughter and because she's rich. But she isn't liked. Our friendly barkeeper probably wouldn't mind seeing both Abbie and you leave town. Don't worry, though. You won't get any trouble from anyone as long as you're here."

"Because of Abbie's money."

"Because you're her husband," Wendell corrected.

"I don't want any special favors because I married Abilene Donegan."

"It goes with the territory."

Rio had already opened his mouth to say it didn't when he noticed Julian and Camellia walk by the saloon. They seemed to be in a hurry, and Camellia had her arm looped through Rio's brother's.

"I guess it's no coincidence that your last name is the same as Julian's?" Wendell asked, when he saw where Rio was staring.

"No coincidence. He's my half-brother."

"Sorry to speak ill of your kin, but the man's lower to the ground than crap stuck on a rattler's ass. I hope you're planning on doing something about him."

Rio was really starting to like this Wendell. "Yep, I plan to do something about him." Though just what, he hadn't decided. It probably would involve some broken bones and blood loss.

Once the lawyer received the information from the courthouse, he could take care of Julian then. After all, it was his brother who'd somehow persuaded Abbie to go after the ranch in the first place. Abbie had even said something about blackmail, even though he hadn't let her explain that. He certainly wouldn't put it past Julian to use blackmail to get what he wanted. Still, Abbie shouldn't have gone along with it.

"If you need help to settle the score with your brother, I'll lend a hand," Wendell offered amiably.

"Don't think I'll need one, but thanks."

Wendell motioned for the barkeeper to get them another round of drinks. Then he stared Rio hard in the face. "I guess what I say next will be fighting words, but I'll say them anyway. If you plan to ride away from Kingston and from Abbie, I'd like to know about it."

"Why?"

"So I can pick up the pieces. I don't know what went on between you and Abbie back in Fall Creek, but she wouldn't have married you unless she cared about you. She's not as tough as she looks. She can carry a man's weight on her shoulders, but her heart'll break just like anybody else's. If you hurt her, I'll have to rearrange your face. Just thought you'd like to know that."

Rio gave him a cold look. "Same goes for you."

"Good, then we understand each other."

Rio wasn't sure of that at all. In fact, he was confused. Abbie hadn't married him because she cared for him. She married him—and there he had to pause—she married him to give him the ranch so Julian couldn't get his hands on it.

But there had to be more to it than that. Revenge, maybe? Yes, that's why she did it. To get revenge because Julian was blackmailing her or something.

So, there was his proof that Abbie hadn't married him because she cared.

Out of the blue her image came to him. Abbie beneath him on her bed. *I do want you Rio,* she'd said. Of course, she'd been talking about what her body wanted. Lust was something he understood. He'd heated her up a little, and that was all there was to it.

Except . . . that wasn't all she'd said.

Make me your wife. Rio tossed back his shot of whiskey, grimaced at the fire it left in his throat, and thought over what Abbie meant. Lust, again?

Maybe.

But if it'd been just plain old lust, wouldn't she have said make me your lover? Or make a woman out of me? Something other than *wife?* Wife meant a whole lot more than those other things.

Rio shook his head. He was reading too much into something a lying woman had said in the heat of passion. Hell, maybe she'd even lied about the passion part. Maybe she hadn't wanted him at all. That was easier to swallow than the alternative. That Abbie did indeed want to be his wife.

No, that couldn't be true.

Rio ordered another whiskey and mulled that over.

Chapter Seventeen

Abbie gave her mint-colored dress an adjustment and opened the door to Wilburn Starling's office. Like a soldier suddenly aware of a general's approach, the lawyer came to his feet and snapped to attention.

"Miss Donegan, er, Mrs. McCaine, how wonderful you look today. Yes, indeedy. You're wearing a dress."

Abbie frowned to let him know she didn't appreciate his compliment. She was sure she looked as troubled as she felt, and the dress certainly didn't help her appearance. She'd had no sleep to speak of. Her head felt as if someone had pounded on it with a rock. And she couldn't find Rio anywhere. The only reason she'd put on the darn dress was because Victoria had suggested it.

And because she thought Rio might like it.

He'd certainly ogled Camellia's dress. Or maybe that was just Camellia he'd ogled. At any rate, Abbie had decided to give it a try. If Rio took the time to notice the dress, then he might also take the time to listen to her.

Well, she could hope anyway.

"I'm looking for my husband," she said after a brief greeting. *Husband*. The word sounded foreign to her. Never had she thought she'd call anyone that. "Have you seen him?"

"He was here earlier. He left after I told him I'd wire the courthouse in Fall Creek—which I've already done, by the way."

Wilburn reminded her of a lapdog waiting for a pat on the head. His brown eyes were large and pleading, and he had his hands clasped like paws in front of him. "Well, thank you." *I guess.* "Why exactly did Rio want you to wire the courthouse?"

"To make sure the deed to his ranch was legal. I looked over all the papers and told him that I was almost positive it was, but he wanted me to send the wire anyway. Said he wanted to be doubly sure."

Of course he would want that. He didn't trust her even though she'd told him the truth about not cheating him out of the ranch. Julian was the one she had cheated. "Do you have any idea where Rio was going when he left here?"

"He headed down the street toward the saloon, I think."

"Thank you. You've been very helpful."

She heard him blow out a long breath when she turned to leave. Abbie hadn't quite gotten used to that reaction even though people had treated her that way even as a child. Only a few citizens of Elliot's Grove dared to show open contempt, but none of them ever seemed pleased to see her either. Money could apparently buy some measure of respect but not acceptance.

Abbie hurried down the walk toward the saloon issuing nods and greetings to the townsfolk she passed along the way. People smiled and said the right things, but it was the first time she remembered their aloofness

215

bothering her. No one looked her right in the eye. No one gave her a genuine smile.

Margaret Herrington waved when Abbie passed the woman's seamstress shop. "You're sure looking pretty, Mrs. McCaine. I see you're wearing the dress Victoria gave you for your birthday."

Abbie nodded and kept her fast pace toward the saloon. She hadn't quite figured out what she would say to Rio if he was in there, but she hoped the words would come when she needed them.

She peeked over the doors of the Rusty Bucket and whistled to get the attention of the barkeep. He looked at her but continued to wipe the glass he held in his hand.

"What can I do for you, Mrs. McCaine?"

She was about to ask for Rio when Wendell rose from the table and walked toward her. He smiled, but it was a little askew. A little like a drunk's smile. Actually a lot like a drunk's smile.

"Abbie, you're looking mighty pretty today." He tried to bow but failed miserably. "And you're wearing a dress? My, my. I thought I'd have to wait for a funeral to see that. What, did your husband put down his foot and tell you not to wear those split skirts and working jeans all the time?"

"He most certainly did not. I wear what I choose to wear." Well, most of the time she did. "Speaking of my husband, have you seen him?"

"Yep. We had a couple of drinks together."

"More than a couple, I'd guess. Where is he now?"

But as soon as Abbie asked that, her gaze drifted up the stairs. She'd heard gossip that every now and then adventurous women came down from San Antonio and plied their trade in those upstairs rooms. Women like Carlotta from the Buffalo Clover. Rio had spent time with women like that. After all, Abbie had met him while

216

he was waiting for such a woman to ply her trade on him.

Or rather he had been waiting for Carlotta to ply her mouth on him.

If Rio was upstairs with some strumpet, Abbie thought she might like to pluck out every strand of his body hair with a pair of rusty nippers. How dare he even think about doing something like that right under her nose? Their marriage might not be a real one, but that didn't mean he could cavort with strumpets while he was still married to her.

Did it?

Lord, she hoped not. She didn't think she could bear the idea of Rio being in another woman's arms.

"Don't worry. Rio didn't go up there," Wendell let her know. But he was smug about it, so Abbie gave him one of her hell-freezing looks that she'd practiced in the mirror.

"I didn't ask."

Wendell smiled. "Oh, but you wanted to know."

Since he was still smiling and smirking, obviously the hell-freezing look hadn't worked. Abbie narrowed her eyes to slits. She could barely see, but she thought Wendell might get the point. "The only thing I want to know is, where is my husband? If you have any idea, I suggest you tell me."

Wendell's smile did lessen some. "He left a little while ago. Said he was going back to Kingston."

Abbie studied Wendell's slouched posture. "Was he as drunk as you are?"

"Almost."

"Wonderful. Just wonderful." A drunk, angry man. Hopefully, he was somewhere sleeping it off. She supposed she should be thankful that he wasn't sleeping it off upstairs.

"Well, as a matter of fact, I did have a wonderful conversation with your husband," Wendell continued. "He seems a fine man. I think under different circumstances I might like him. Rio obviously has some rather unique talents, since he found the secret to taming you."

"He didn't tame me." No one could do that. Ever. She was untamable. But she silently agreed with that unique talents part. Rio could kiss the rust off an old water bucket, and that was a definite talent. However, it was something she probably wouldn't get to experience again.

"Oh, he tamed you, all right. You just don't know it yet." Wendell chuckled. "That dress says it all."

"The dress says nothing except that I'm wearing it. One more comment about it, Wendell Calverson, and you'll be eating your spurs for dinner."

She left without saying good-bye, but she heard Wendell laugh and repeat something about what a good man she had for a husband. Abbie didn't want to know what had gone on between Rio and him to make Wendell feel that way.

The carriage ride home gave her plenty of time to think. And time to worry. Instead of returning to Kingston, Rio could have headed back to Fall Creek. The lawyer had told him that everything seemed all right with the deed. If Rio believed him, then maybe he thought there was no reason for him even to say good-bye to her.

She might not see him again.

Ever.

That choked her heart as painfully as a meaty fist. Lord, she might not ever get a chance to tell him how sorry she was about lying to him. Not that he'd believe her, but she wanted to try.

While she gave that a try, she also wanted him to know how she felt about him. Not easy, that. Abbie was still mulling it over and didn't know if it was something she could put into words. But if she didn't try, he'd forever think she was a lying schemer and nothing else. She didn't want him to think that about her.

So, she'd tell him that she cared for him.

Well, unless he'd already left Kingston. If he had, she would just have to go to Fall Creek and tell him face-to-face. And while she was there, maybe the right words would come to her. Maybe she could make him understand that something inside her was different, and he was responsible for that.

Maybe she would even tell him that she thought he was someone she could love.

And maybe, just maybe, he would believe her.

"Just take a little sip of this, darling, and it'll make you feel all better," the woman's voice purred in Rio's ear.

Bitter-tasting liquid dribbled into his mouth. Because he had no choice, he swallowed some of it, but the rest slid down his cheek.

He was having one helluva dream. Or something. Maybe not a dream exactly, but Rio knew if his head would quit spinning around, he'd be able to figure it out.

"Abbie?" he moaned.

"No."

The softly spoken feminine denial had his eyes coming open. It was a dream. A strange dream. He was on a bed and there was a winged blond fairy hovering over him. The fairy smiled. But she wasn't really a fairy.

It was Camellia.

Damn it! Camellia?

It wasn't a dream but a nightmare. Rio groaned and tried to push himself away from her. He couldn't. He couldn't move at all, could hardly catch his breath. That's when he noticed she had straddled his chest, and her knees dug into his ribs. Lord, the woman weighed more than a fully loaded pack mule.

She wore some kind of costume that looked like a

gold-dusted corset with gauzy flops on the sides. There was a glass of amber liquid in her hand. The bitter-tasting drink, probably. Whiskey mixed with something else.

"Get off me, Camellia. What the hell are you doing here anyway?" he growled.

And why did his head hurt so much? He'd had three or four drinks at the Rusty Bucket, hardly enough to get drunk, and yet he felt as if he were fighting a red-eye daze from a week long of drinking.

"I found you out by the barn and brought you in here to get you out of the sun. How do you feel?" she asked.

"Like hell."

"Well, you just lie there, and I'll feed you the rest of this tonic."

"I don't want any tonic." Not from her anyway. There just might be poison in that glass, and he hoped he hadn't already swallowed too much of it. From the way he felt, he was afraid he'd swallowed a gallon.

She dramatically fluttered her eyelashes and sighed heavily. "All right, no more tonic." Camellia put the glass on the night table and took a cloth from the washbowl. "I'll just bathe you. That'll make you feel better."

He pushed away her hand when she started to press the cloth to his forehead. "You found me by the barn?"

"Yes, you'd passed out." She clicked her tongue teasingly. "Did you have a glass too many at the Rusty Bucket?"

No. Not too much to drink. Something else. But what? Rio remembered leaving the Rusty Bucket and the ride back to Kingston. He'd got off his stallion and led Smoky into the barn. When he stepped inside, something or someone hit him on the back of the head. That explained the headache and the dizziness. It didn't, however, explain what happened.

"Did you hit me with something?" he wanted to know.

"Me, hit you?" She flattened her hand against her

breasts, breasts that looked ready to fall right out of her little costume. "I wouldn't dream of such a thing. Abbie, maybe. She's very unpredictable when it comes to her moods, and I know she's upset with you right now."

Yeah, maybe, but Rio didn't think Abbie would stoop to something so cowardly. No, if she'd wanted to hurt him, she would have come right at him, the way she'd thrown that pillow in his face the night before.

"Where are we?" he asked.

"Augustus's cabin. He built it so he could have some privacy. Kingston always seems to have so many people about." Camellia pressed the cloth to his neck before he could stop her. "My, my, you do have a manly body, but I'm sure dozens of women have told you that."

He followed her gaze down to his chest. His shirtless chest. Ah, hell. He was bare to the waist, and someone had even taken off his boots. Camellia, probably. "I need to get out of here," he mumbled.

When he tried to get up, she pushed him back down. "You're much too weak to stand."

Then he'd stagger, but one way or another he wouldn't stay on this bed with her. "Come on, get off me."

"No, no. Just lie there and let me bathe you."

"I don't want you to bathe me or do anything else except get up. I want to find out who hit me on the head."

He reared up again, but Camellia caught his shoulders. This time Rio was ready for her and used the lower half of his body to flip her off him. She landed hard on the bed on her back. And giggled like a naughty school girl. Obviously she thought he was playing some kind of game with her. He wasn't. One way or another, he intended to get away from her.

Camellia rolled over and quickly pressed her lips to his. She thrust her tongue into his mouth but Rio pushed her away. She tasted of whiskey and the peppermint she

221

used to hide the smell of the liquor. Her skin was sticky from sweat and the summer heat.

"Don't do that again," he warned.

She giggled and pulled down one side of the costume to expose a lard-colored breast. Her large silver-dollar-sized nipple was brown and looked like a huge bumpy wart. "See anything you like, Rio? Oh, come on, you know what you want from me."

"I don't want that." If it fell on his face, it would probably give him a black eye. It might even knock him out cold.

The cabin door flew open.

Not good. His luck had apparently gone from bad to worse. He didn't need Abbie walking in on this. But she had. Not only had she walked in on it, she'd obviously seen everything. Him and Camellia on the bed. Camellia's huge breast right in his face.

"Mind telling me what's going on here?" Abbie snarled.

Rio had never heard her voice drop to that tone, nor had he ever seen her eyes that color—a dark pond-scum green. Her hands were on her hips, her upper lip drawn to show her teeth, and she gave him a look that would have withered a new fence post.

"I was just giving Rio a little bath." Camellia flashed a wry grin. She made a show of pulling up her costume to cover her breast.

"Oh, really?" Abbie said with deadly calm. Too calm, Rio knew. There was a mighty storm brewing inside her, and he figured she'd blow most of it at him.

"This isn't what you think, Abbie. Someone hit me on the head, and she brought me in here." But he didn't think she even heard him.

Abbie slid her venomous gaze to Camellia. "You've got about a half a second to get off that bed, or I'll cram

222

those fairy wings up one end of you and pull them out the other."

Camellia scurried off the bed, her wing slapping Rio in the jaw. She held her hands protectively over her chest. "I don't know why you're so mad at me. It was his idea for us to come here."

"It was not," Rio grumbled. He leaned off the bed, felt around on the floor, and found his shirt. Unfortunately, his arms seemed too numb to pick it up. "I didn't know anything about it. She's the one who brought me here."

"Not true." Camellia's voice went up considerably. "You're obviously not satisfying Rio, or he wouldn't have coaxed me into his bed. What's the matter, Abbie? Did you finally figure out that all the money in the world won't make a man choose you over me?"

"Maybe, but in this case the man's drunk, and men are stupid when they're drunk. If Rio still wants you and those fairy wings when he's sober, then he's more than welcome to you and them. Right now, you're leaving, and I don't just mean you're leaving this cabin. You're leaving Kingston for good."

"Your promise to your father—"

"I'm breaking it." Abbie snagged Camellia's arm. "I should have tossed you out on your butt the day after the funeral. If I had, maybe I wouldn't be in the mess that I'm in right now."

Camellia looked pleadingly back at Rio. "Can't you please do something to stop her?"

He didn't think he could stand up yet, much less stop Abbie from doing anything. Besides he didn't want to stop her. He agreed with Abbie. She should have thrown Camellia out months ago.

"Abbie?" he asked hoarsely.

She didn't say anything but glared at him over her shoulder.

"Nothing would have happened between me and Ca-

223

mellia," he assured her. "Nothing. She was here when I woke up, but I was trying to get her to leave."

"Sleep off your whiskey, Rio. I don't like talking with a drunk." And with that, dragging Camellia along, she slammed the door behind her.

Rio tried to get up to go after her, but the room started to spin, and everything went dark. Hell. What was this all about? This wasn't whiskey. This was something else. Something he couldn't fight.

He closed his eyes and let the darkness take over.

"You're ruining the costume," Camellia whined as Abbie dragged her along the grassy path.

Abbie ignored that as she had ignored the dozen other similar complaints Camellia had issued on the quarter-mile walk from the cabin to the barn.

"This costume came all the way from Paris, France, and you're ruining it. You're going to have to pay for it."

"Be thankful it's the clothes that I'm ruining and not the rest of you. I still haven't ruled out giving you a butt-whipping."

That hushed Camellia for a moment. Abbie took full advantage of the quiet and pulled her toward the barn.

"Rio is delicious, you know," Camellia gloated. "Or maybe you don't know that. I had him begging me. Really beg—"

Enough was enough. Even Victoria would have belted the woman for a comment like that. Abbie balled up her fist and slugged Camellia right in the jaw. She went down like a dropped boulder.

"Juan?" Abbie called. "I need you out here."

A few moments later, the man hurried from the smoke-house toward them. "Yes, Miss Abbie?"

She tipped her head to Camellia. "I want you to put her in the buckboard and drive her into town."

His mouth dropped open. "Dressed like that?"

"Dressed in her Parisian costume," Abbie confirmed. "Dump her ample butt in front of the Rusty Bucket or maybe at the jail. I'm sure Julian will find her. Anyway, she's his problem now."

Abbie walked to the house without even glancing in the direction of the cabin. She didn't dare look that way. If she didn't go straight home, she might be tempted to go back out there to Rio. Her mood was too dangerous for that. She'd never beaten up a drunk, and she wouldn't start now.

Even if she wanted to, badly.

When Rio finally slept off the whiskey, she hoped he remembered everything that just happened. She also hoped he had the worst headache that any man on the face of the earth had ever had. The sight of him on that bed with Camellia had certainly given her a headache.

She stomped onto the veranda where Victoria and Gussie were apparently in the middle of a reading lesson. Gussie was in the porch swing, going much too fast and high considering she was also trying to read the pages of her primer. Victoria sat in the rocker near the swing and rubbed Beans behind his ear.

"Gussie, you can go play now in the back," Victoria said after a glance at Abbie's face.

"Awww, do I gotta?" Gussie brought the swing to an abrupt stop by shoving her foot against the wall.

"Yes, you gotta," Victoria told her. "And the correct way to say that is you 'have to.'"

Gussie shrugged and dropped the book onto the swing. "Don't seem to matter too much how I say it if I still hafta go."

With that, Victoria apparently lost her patience because she put a hand on Gussie's back and walked her down the steps. Gussie continued to complain but quickly took off running when Beans started to race across the yard.

Victoria caught Abbie's arm and led her inside the house. "All right, what's wrong?"

Abbie started to tell her, but before she could get out one word, tears swelled in her eyes. "Oh, Victoria."

"You're crying?" Victoria asked, stunned. "You're actually crying?"

Abbie managed a nod and spoke through the sobs. "I found Rio in bed with Camellia."

"Camellia?" She repeated the woman's name, adding varying inflections from anger to complete disapproval. "Well, I'll venture a guess that it wasn't Rio's idea to be there."

"She had on the fairy wings."

"Oh, Abbie." Victoria put her arms around her sister and pulled her into an embrace. "I can't believe Rio would do something like that. I know he was angry, but he doesn't seem the kind of man who—"

"He was drunk," she admitted.

"I see. That was probably Camellia's doing. You can't trust her, Abbie, and you know she'd do anything to hurt you."

"Well, she hurt me all right." And so had Rio. She hadn't expected anything better from Camellia, but him . . . "How could he have climbed in the same bed with that woman?"

"I thought you said he was drunk. Maybe he didn't have a lot of choice in the matter. Besides, did anything actually happen between them?"

Abbie shook her head. "I don't know. I don't think so. He still had on his jeans."

"Buttoned?" Victoria questioned.

"Yes."

She gave a short breath of relief. "Well, there. He couldn't have done anything then. At least I don't think he could have." She patted Abbie's hand. "You can't let this get you so upset. Camellia wants you to feel this way because it's her way of getting revenge. Don't let her win, Abbie. Hold your head up high and pretend nothing's happened."

"I don't want to pretend," Abbie practically shouted. She was tired of hurting. Tired of having Rio so angry with her. "I just want Rio, all right?"

Victoria stared at her. "Are you saying you want a life with that man?"

"I don't know what I'm saying." Abbie pushed herself away from Victoria. "All I know is I've never been this miserable. I can't sleep. And I don't know what to do."

"Yes, I can see that. I can also see that your face brightens up when you're around him."

"That's because we're usually mad and yelling at each other."

Victoria shook her head. "No, it's because you care about him."

She did. She really did. Abbie couldn't say exactly when that had happened, but her feelings for him went well beyond business. "But I don't want to care about him. I want to go back to the way things were before our father died and before Julian McCaine imposed himself into our lives."

"You mean when you were in control of everything?"

"Yes!" Abbie vehemently agreed. "That's exactly what I want."

So why didn't that sound as good as it should have? Her, in control. Her, not having to answer to anyone but herself. Especially not having to feel all of this, whatever it was, about Rio. And especially going back to a time when she didn't feel she had to wear dresses.

"You'd rather have control than a husband you care about?" Victoria questioned.

"That's just it. I don't want a husband. I've never wanted a husband. Why would I possibly need some man telling me what to wear or how to act? I couldn't live like that, Victoria. I just couldn't."

Her dark eyebrows flexed. "Somehow, I don't believe Rio would put those kind of demands on you. He's not like that. I don't know him as well as you do, of course, but he seems like a decent person."

Abbie's gaze rifled to her sister. "Whose side are you on anyway?"

"Yours," Victoria answered softly. "That's why I'm telling you the truth instead of some answer you think you want to hear."

"But that's just it. I don't know what answer I want to hear."

"I believe you do. But think long and hard about this because if you want a life with Rio, then you'll probably have to leave Kingston. Could you do that?"

"I don't know." Abbie shook her head. "And it really doesn't matter because Rio doesn't want me."

Victoria made a sound of disagreement. "I think that's the problem. He wants you as much as you want him, and you're both fighting it."

"I'm not fighting anything," Abbie lied. She'd never felt so embattled in her entire life, but she wasn't ready to admit that—even to her sister.

Another sound of disagreement, and Victoria started toward the veranda. "Be careful, Abbie. If you fight too much, you just might win."

Yes, that's what scared Abbie the most.

Chapter Eighteen

Rio's first sensation was the stabbing pain that shot through his left jaw. The second sensation was somebody licking his face.

God, not Camellia and her fairy wings.

He didn't want to go through that again.

Forcing his eyes to open, all he saw was a dark brown blur. He grunted. He was probably dead and in a coffin. Abbie had probably killed him after seeing Camellia in the bed with him.

He shook his head, immediately dismissing that thought. He was in too much pain to be dead.

The bright sunlight stung his bloodshot eyes, but he still fought to get them open. That's when the brown blur got a lot clearer. It was Gussie's dog. Beans had his front paws on the bed and was licking Rio's face. Thank God it wasn't Pig. The cat would have probably tried to smother him or something. He gave the dog an obligatory pat on the head and pushed him away so he could get up.

His mouth was as dry as cotton. It was a nauseating sensation he'd felt all too often. No doubt a result of too much whiskey and too little time for the effects to wear off. He wasn't sure if he wanted to puke or take another shot just to get the taste out of his mouth.

Rio shifted his weight and bumped his head on something. A head board. He finally saw where he was— slumped in the bed at the cabin. No Camellia. Thank God. That was something at least.

But where was Abbie?

Pushing his elbow against the soft mattress, he brought himself to an upright position. His legs hit the footboard. He didn't have time to notice it. The pain swelled again, and a few curse words made it through his clenched throat.

Then he saw the blood.

There were streaky maroon splatters on his chest and jeans. The bruised knuckles of right hand throbbed. They felt good compared to his arm. His neck hurt, too. Hell, his whole body hurt. He didn't figure it did any good to identify each part.

He tried to rake his hair out of his eyes but couldn't, and it didn't take Rio long to figure out why. It was stuck to his forehead with dried blood. Probably his own, but he couldn't be sure.

Someone had obviously beaten him to a pulp, but he couldn't remember how. Or when. Or even who. He didn't remember a fight at all. The last thing he recalled was Abbie dragging Camellia out of the cabin.

"Sleep off your whiskey, Rio. I don't like talking with a drunk," she'd told him.

Then she'd slammed the door behind her. It wasn't shut now. It was open several inches. Of course, someone who would beat up an unconscious man probably wouldn't bother to shut the door. The window was open too, and the gauzy white curtain fluttered in the breeze. It looked like a ghost trying to come after him.

Beans' ears perked up, and he let out a squeaky bark. The dog trotted his way across the room, making little clicks on the hardwood floor. When he reached the door and looked outside, his tail started to wag. Since Rio didn't know if Beans was greeting friend or foe, he tried to get up from the bed. Not that he could do much to defend himself; he felt as weak as a newborn baby.

Abbie pushed the door the rest of the way open and looked inside. Rio still didn't know if Beans had greeted a friend or foe. It was hard to tell from the fierce look in Abbie's eyes.

Rio sank back onto the bed. "Don't yell at me. I think my head'll explode if you do."

"My God, what happened to you?" Abbie quickly crossed the room to the bed and looked down at him.

He tried to shake his head and failed. Rio grimaced in pain. "I thought maybe you'd beat me up."

"No," she said with a sigh. A pained expression on her face, she gently brushed her finger over his cheekbone.

Even the soft pressure was painful, and he winced. "Be honest, how bad am I hurt?"

Abbie looked him over. "You have a bruise on your jaw and cut just below your right eye. The wound's closed, but I suspect that's why there's blood on your shirt and jeans." She took a deep breath. "When did this happen?"

"I don't know that either. After you left with Camellia, I think I passed out. I don't remember anything else." He motioned toward the glass on the night table. "She gave me that to drink. I think there was something in it."

Abbie picked up the glass. She let some of the liquid touch her tongue and grimaced. "Hellfire. It's bitter. It must be valerian root mixed with Irish whiskey. My father used it when he'd get one of his bad headaches, and it would knock him out for hours. How much of this did you drink anyway?"

He shook his head and yawned. Lord, it was hard to figure out anything when all he wanted to do was sleep. "I'm not sure. When I woke up the first time, Camellia was pouring it in my mouth."

Abbie mumbled under her breath. "Well, if she gave you much of this, no wonder you passed out. That's probably what she wanted you to do. My guess is Julian was waiting nearby and came in when I left."

Another yawn. Rio settled his head back on the pillow. He recalled a vague image of Julian swinging his fist at him, a slightly less vague image of Julian connecting with that punch. Of course, he hadn't been able to fight his brother. Rio remembered a little of that too.

"Julian," he mumbled. "He beat the hell out of me when I couldn't do anything about it. Yep, that's his way of doing things, all right." He tried to keep his eyes focused on Abbie, but everything started to get blurry again. "Where's Camellia?"

"I had Juan drive her into town." She folded her arms over her chest and glanced around the room. "I'll walk back to the house and send someone for the doctor."

"No doctor." Rio could feel his eyelids start to droop, and there was nothing he could do about it. "I just need to rest."

"You might be seriously hurt."

He didn't think so. Nothing inside him seemed to be hurting anyway. He couldn't say the same for the outside though. Every inch of his skin was in pain. "Don't worry about me. I'll be fine."

"I wasn't worrying," she said.

But she was. Rio could hear it in her voice. It almost made him smile. Abbie was worried about him. She was probably still mad at him too, but right now she more concerned than mad.

She finally gave a crisp nod. "All right, if you don't want me to get the doctor, then I need to see if I can move you to the house."

"I don't want to move anywhere. Not yet. Just let me sleep. I'll be fine when I wake up." His last words came out slurred, and Rio didn't try to explain anything else. He couldn't.

He closed his eyes and slept.

Abbie stood at the edge of the bed and watched. Without touching him, she counted every bruise, every nick, and every cut on Rio's face. She hadn't thought she could feel actual physical pain at someone else's injuries, but she did now.

She desperately wanted to go after Camellia and Julian and beat them senseless. She couldn't, of course, because she didn't want to leave Rio alone. If they came back while she was gone, Rio would be helpless. Like he had been the first time.

Somehow, Julian and Camellia would pay for this. Even if she had to hunt them down, they'd pay.

Rio stirred, turned his head from side to side, and he mumbled something. He was probably still in pain, and despite what he said about not having any serious injuries, she wasn't so sure of that. She decided to check him over, and if she saw anything suspicious, she'd send Juan to get the doctor.

Rio's eyes eased open. Slowly. And he immediately squinted as if trying to focus. His eyes seemed so blue next to the bruises that had already started to darken. So blue, and so beautiful.

He turned his head slightly and looked at her. "Am I dead?"

Since his tone wasn't completely serious, Abbie sighed

in relief. "You're not dead, but it probably feels like it."

He tried to smile, but his forehead wrinkled in pain. "Worse than dead. Dead would be an improvement."

Maybe for him but not for her. Abbie couldn't bear to think of losing him. "I should clean those cuts."

She'd already poured some warm water from the cistern into the wash-bowl and placed it on the night table. She opened his shirt and looked at his chest. More bruises and some small cuts. Certainly nothing serious, but it turned her stomach to see him wounded.

Rio ran his hand through his hair to push it away from his face. "You look a little pale there, Abbie. Don't faint on me."

"Don't insult me. I don't faint at the sight of a little blood." But she did allow herself to swallow hard.

She wrung out the washcloth and moved closer. "All right. Take a deep breath and close your eyes. I'll start with your face."

"Why do I have to close my eyes?"

"Because I'm sure it'll sting some." And because she didn't want him looking at her when they were this close. It wasn't the time for her to pour out her feelings, and that's what would happen if she didn't treat this impersonally.

He didn't close his eyes. "Why are you doing this?"

"Because you're hurt, and you need some help."

"But why you? You could send Ina or Victoria to tend to me."

Abbie tilted her head and looked at him. "Do you want one of them instead of me?"

"No. I just don't want you doing anything you don't want to do."

"You know me better than that. If I didn't want to be doing this, I wouldn't be here. I would have turned around and walked right back out that door when I saw you lying on the bed." But she couldn't have done that.

It felt as if someone had crushed her heart when she saw Rio injured.

Abbie continued the bath, periodically rinsing out the cloth. When she made it to his stomach, his muscles twitched.

She pretended not to notice. While she was at it, she pretended not to notice the soft grunt that Rio made.

He grunted again when she rubbed the cloth close to the waist of his jeans. There was a narrow gap between his stomach and the pants. She hadn't really gotten a good look at him the night before. And she certainly hadn't touched him there. She wondered how it would feel to slide her hand into that gap in his jeans.

She scolded herself.

How could she possibly think about touching a man who was practically helpless? Still, this man was Rio. She'd thought about doing all sorts of carnal things with him since the night she laid eyes on him. She was obviously sick.

She still wanted to touch him.

Or at least get a good look at what made him a man.

"No one came by when I was asleep, did they?" he asked.

He meant Julian or Camellia, and Abbie hoped he understood that she wouldn't have let them set a toenail inside the cabin. The derringer in her pocket would have seen to that. Two shots. And she wouldn't have missed.

"Julian's behind this," she said softly.

Rio nodded. "How did you ever get mixed up with him in the first place?"

She stopped bathing him and put the cloth back into the bowl. "Call it a twist of fate. Bad luck. He came here not long after my father died. I think Camellia sent for him, even though she pretended to be surprised when he showed up on our doorstep to pay her a visit. Anyway, a couple of weeks later Julian said he'd heard some talk in town that the sheriff wanted to question Harmony about a raid on a ranch in another county."

"Where was Harmony then?"

"She was staying in a cabin on the far side of the Donegan property. I didn't think either Camellia or Julian knew she was there, but somehow he found out. I think he might have followed Victoria or Ina up there when they took Harmony some supplies."

"He threatened to turn Harmony in?"

"Yes, unless I helped him."

"And you did help him."

Abbie heard the bitterness still in Rio's voice and lowered her eyes. "Not the way he thought I would. He wanted me to go to Fall Creek, buy the McCaine ranch from the bank, and thereby legally steal your half from you. I left right then, before he had time to come up with a way to kidnap Harmony. I didn't really have time to think the plan through. Obviously."

"But you lied about what you did. If you'd come and told me the truth, I would have helped you."

"I know that, now. I didn't know that then." She shook her head. "Julian said you were a mean sonofabitch with a chip the size of Texas on your shoulder."

"He said that?"

She nodded. "Since I didn't know you, I figured there might be some truth to what he said. I was wrong. I know you don't believe it, but I *am* sorry."

He made a sound that could have meant anything. Or nothing.

"There's something else I'd like to tell you." So she wouldn't have to look at him, she stood and walked to the window. "I know when we got married, we said it would be just for a couple of weeks. If you still feel that way, then that's fine." It wasn't, but Abbie couldn't tell him that. She had to hold onto some pride. "We probably should think about, well, how we feel about things."

She wanted to kick herself for sounding like a limp dishrag, but there was some truth in her hesitation. They both needed time. She needed to catch her breath. Nothing had to happen right now. She should take a step back and objectively decide how she really felt about Rio. She could make a mature, informed decision.

And it wouldn't change a darn thing.

She'd still want to be with him.

She would still want to give this marriage a try.

"Hellfire." Abbie groaned. "This isn't working at all. Let me just say it outright and quit all this babbling. I want to try to be your wife. In every sense of the word."

There. Other than the fact she blushed from the top of her head to the soles of her feet, she felt better. Abbie peeked over her shoulder at him. She'd finally told Rio how she felt, and . . .

He was asleep.

The man was sound asleep!

She started to shake him, hard, to wake him up. She had poured out her heart to him, and he'd fallen asleep. Just her luck. She didn't know if she could get up the courage to tell him again.

Abbie was about to leave when she noticed a streak of blood still on his cheek. She wrung out the cloth and pressed it against the small cut, thinking the cool cloth might wake him.

It didn't.

The man didn't move a muscle.

All right.

She ran the cloth down his face to his neck. Still no reaction. He'd obviously consumed a lot of that valerian root. Abbie wondered just how much. And just how deep was his sleep? She went lower to his chest, barely skimming it with the cloth. When she made it to his stomach, she knew for certain that the man was out like a week-long drunk.

Don't even think about doing it," she said under her
breath.

But she was thinking about doing it. Or rather seeing
Knowing she was being silly, her gaze stayed on his
navel for a moment. And then went lower to that thin
strip of hair that led down his stomach. She tried hard to
talk herself out of what she was about to do, but it
seemed her head didn't plan to listen to a thing she had
to say.

With her free hand, Abbie lifted the fabric, creating a
larger gap between Rio and his jeans. No underdrawers.
Of course, Rio had said at the creek he didn't wear unmentionables.

Well.

Since there was no obstruction to her peeking, Abbie
pulled the jeans up as far as they would go. She gave up
trying to talk herself out of it, mainly because her mind
had already come up with a new argument. This might
be the only time she would get to see a naked man.

She dipped down her head and had her look. Oh. Her
eyebrows bowed, and she took a deep breath. It was just
sort of lying there to one side. And it really didn't look
that impressive. Well, not really. Except she did feel odd
to be this close to it. Not odd. Itchy. And not just itchy
either. Needy.

She swallowed noisily and eased his jeans back in
place. She probably should feel guilty for gawking at Rio
when he was helpless to do anything about it. But he had
fallen asleep when she was telling him how she felt, so
that entitled her to gawk a little. Still, she was glad he
hadn't caught her. How in the world would she explain
something like looking in his pants?

Mumbling to herself, she left the cabin and ran toward
the house to find Ivan. Despite Rio's objection about being moved, Abbie didn't think it was safe for him to stay
in the cabin alone. Maybe Julian hadn't really intended

to kill him, but it could have easily happened. That was a chance she couldn't take.

When she got to the house, she saw Juan on the porch. "Did you get Camellia into town?"

He eagerly nodded. "She was mad, but I left her in front of the Rusty Bucket just like you said."

"Good, now I need another favor. I need you to help me carry my husband. He's at the cabin."

"The cabin? But what's he doing there?"

"At the moment, sleeping. He got roughed up a little."

"Senora McCaine, you didn't!"

Abbie frowned at Juan's accusatory tone. "Not me. I think it might have been Julian, so if you see that man anywhere near Kingston, let me know. After we move Rio, I'll ride into town and have a talk with the sheriff."

"The sheriff's not there and won't be back until the morning. He's over in Floresville testifying in some trial. I know because I tried to drop Miss Camellia off there first."

Would nothing go her way today? "Then I'll have to speak to him just as soon as he returns. Come on. Let's go get my husband."

"Where are we moving him?"

"To my bedroom."

The man's mouth quirked, threatening to smile. He even clamped his teeth over his bottom lip as if trying to prevent it. "I guess it's only right that Senor McCaine be in your bedroom."

Abbie scowled to let him know she didn't appreciate the near smile. "Yes, but not for the reasons you think."

Well, maybe that was one of the reasons. But it was also the one place she knew Rio would be safe, and she could keep an eye on him.

Chapter Nineteen

Abbie was drooling on him.

It took Rio a couple of minutes to figure out what was happening, and even then he still wasn't sure he knew. He wasn't in the cabin anymore but in Abbie's bedroom. In her bed. And she was on the bed with him, drooling on his stomach.

Well, not his stomach exactly.

Slightly lower.

Rio hadn't thought he'd ever wake up to something like that.

All things considered, he didn't mind her drool or even being in bed with her, but he didn't understand how he'd gotten there. He remembered someone carrying him. Juan maybe. But he hadn't thought the man would bring him here. He hadn't thought Abbie would let him anywhere near her bedroom.

She now seemed, well, comfortable with the idea.

Abbie had snuggled herself against him, using his upper thigh as a pillow. Her hair fanned over his stomach. That alone would have probably been enough to astound him, but she also faced him, her mouth just inches away from the center of his jeans. Not the best place for her mouth to be; it felt too good. Much too good. This was the last thing he needed.

"Abbie?" he whispered.

She stirred and mumbled something incoherent. Her arm flopped against his chest, a couple of her fingers colliding with his nipple. Just as quickly she settled back onto his thigh.

All right. So, it didn't seem as if she intended to move any time soon. Abbie was no doubt completely exhausted or else she was the kind of person who could sleep under any conditions. The drool and soft snoring made him suspect the latter.

The light already seeped through the windows. He guessed it was past eight, which meant he'd slept for a long time. The rest seemed to have done him some good too. He was a little sore, but he felt healthy.

Now, he had to deal with Julian's attempted betrayal. He hadn't expected his brother to welcome him with open arms, but he also hadn't expected the man to beat the hell out of him either. They'd always fought, yes, but the fights hadn't been so dirty.

There would be a price to pay for that, and Rio would make sure Julian paid it.

Abbie shifted again. Her eyelashes fluttered but didn't open. A dream, maybe. She still seemed to be a deep sleep.

She wasn't completely dressed. Rio wondered why he hadn't noticed that right away. How could he have not noticed a half-dressed woman in bed with him? Obviously the beating had affected his mind. He'd never failed to notice something like that before. Abbie wore

241

only her camisole and her drawers. She was barefooted and had her feet dangling off the bed.

Her undergarments weren't tightly fitted, but somehow that only drew his attention to them even more. The cotton camisole barely skimmed over her breasts, and her nipples were drawn and tight. It made him wonder exactly what she was dreaming about.

Maybe the same thing he was thinking about.

Since she was still asleep, Rio caught one curl and let it wrap around his finger. Like the rest of her, her hair was peculiar—fiery red with touches of gold.

Like this, without the emotion tensing her face, she looked like a well-bred lady. Rio knew differently. He actually preferred the real Abbie to the illusion that sleep created; a well-bred lady would have bored him to death in a day or two.

There was no chance in hell he would ever be bored with Abbie.

Of course, she was entirely capable of driving him out of his mind.

She let out a deep breath, almost a dreamy sigh. Rio grimaced. Her cheek was now right against the fly of his jeans, and her breath dusted his stomach and just about everything else in his midsection. It wasn't a good idea for her to keep that up.

Abbie pursed her lips as if she'd tasted something delicious. It drew Rio's attention to her mouth. That full, lush mouth. It looked poised and ready to smile at the drop of a hat. Or poised and ready to kiss.

Kiss.

Rio was giving that a little too much thought at the moment. He certainly wasn't in any shape to kiss a woman or do anything else with one. He had been beaten black and blue. Now, if he could just get his body to listen to that complaint, then maybe he could get his mind off Abbie.

She breathed on him again. God. Her hot breath on a part of him that really wanted to feel something hot. And snug. And wet. Abbie had the answer to all his wishes.

"Mmm," she murmured.

Mmm? It was the sound a person might make when they tasted something they liked. Or when they enjoyed something. It was almost seductive. Or maybe this was all his imagination. His mind could come up with all sorts of justification for making love with her.

She exhaled another breath. Not just a soft one. This one had some punch to it. And it was hot and moist.

Rio's heart started to pound like a drum. His breathing wasn't any quieter. He ached. Throbbed. He had an erection, and it demanded that he do something about it immediately.

With the gentlest of touches, he moved his thumb across her cheekbone, tracing it along her jawline to her bottom lip.

"Abbie," he whispered.

She opened her eyes and blinked several times until her startled gaze connected with his. Her gaze didn't stay put, however. It drifted downward, to his unbuttoned shirt. To his stomach. And to the rigid obstruction that lay so close to her mouth she could have touched it with her tongue.

Rio groaned.

"Ohhhh." With her upper body somewhat limp, she lifted her head off him. Unfortunately, to keep her balance, she put her hand down.

On him.

Her soft palm landed on the hardest, meanest arousal he'd ever had. It was a prize-winner, all right. And she didn't pull her hand back right away either. She looked at it. At him. At it again.

"Oh." Then she blinked. "Another of those male reactions, huh?" she asked sleepily. She shook her head and yawned. "Do you need to do anything to take care of it, or will it go away on its own?"

Rio didn't intend to answer that. There was plenty he could do, plenty she could do also. He didn't think it was a good idea for them to do it together.

His body disagreed.

Rio decided to try to ignore it. That part of him rarely made good decisions anyway.

"What are you doing in my bed?" She rubbed her face. "I mean what am I doing in my bed?"

"Sleeping, is my guess." He couldn't say the same for himself. He was just lying there enjoying the tortures created by her breath, her undergarments, and her misplaced hand.

"But how did I get here?" she asked. "I was on a quilt on the floor."

"You must have climbed up here during the night."

Her eyes got wider. "Oh, God. Oh. God. I had my head on you. Did I hurt you?"

It took a while to understand that she meant his injuries. "You didn't hurt me."

"Thank God, because I'm a really hard sleeper."

At the moment, so was he. Hard, at least. And his condition wasn't likely to get better as long as he was on the same bed with Abbie.

He didn't want to have sex with her. All right, he did. That's exactly what he wanted. The proof of that stirred in his jeans. But what he didn't want were all the complications that came with sex. Forget that it would muddle his feelings about her. Forget that his feelings were already muddled. Sex could make a baby. Abbie didn't want a baby. And he didn't want to make a baby with her.

End of discussion.

There would be no sex.

He was still as hard as granite.

Rio wondered if he could talk her into putting her hand back on him. A little more of that, and it should take care of things. Or maybe if she just breathed on him some more. That would probably finish him off in no time.

He didn't have time to talk Abbie into anything because she scooted off the bed. "I forgot that I took off my clothes. Sorry. I thought I'd be up before you and would have a chance to dress."

"You don't have to apologize for undressing in your own bedroom."

She made a sound of indulgent agreement. "I would have undressed you, just so you could be more comfortable, but I wasn't sure if you wanted me to do that."

She could undress him any time she wanted. But Rio decided it would be a stupid thing to tell her—more muddling that he definitely didn't need.

Abbie looked down at the floor and started to pick at her fingers. "*Would* it have bothered you if I'd undressed you?"

Rio silently groaned. This conversation was not moving in the right direction. "I don't think—"

"Never mind. I asked only to relieve my guilty conscience. I have a confession to make."

This time the groan wasn't silent. "Not another lie?"

Her mouth tightened. "No. I'm trying to be truthful. I did something to you that I probably shouldn't have done."

"You've done a lot of things you shouldn't have done," he pointed out.

"Well, now you can add one more thing to that list, all right?" She threw her hands in the air. "Good Lord, Rio, I'm trying to make a confession here. Will you stop needling me long enough so I can tell you?"

That little maneuver she did with her hands distracted Rio for a moment. Everything about him that was male noticed the way her camisole stretched over her breasts when she put her hands in the air. He forced himself not to be so distracted that he couldn't try to figure out what the heck she was saying.

"Go on with your confession," he told her.

But she didn't go on with it right away. She started to pick at her fingers again. "It's a little embarrassing, but I sort of looked at something that I probably shouldn't have looked at."

"You looked at something?" Rio repeated blankly. He thought hard about it, but for the life of him couldn't figure out what she meant.

"At you," Abbie clarified.

That didn't clarify anything. "At me?"

"Not at you, exactly, but at, ah, uh, *you*."

Well, that really didn't clear anything up. Rio just stared at her.

"At you!" But her voice was angry now. "When you were asleep at the cabin, I looked in your jeans."

She said the last word so softly that it took Rio a moment to understand her.

Oh.

That's what she'd looked at.

"Why?" he asked, confused.

She scrubbed her hands over her face. "I don't know why. I guess I was just thinking how I hadn't seen you naked, and how I'd never seen any man naked. I was curious, that's all. Anyway, I'm sorry. I shouldn't have taken advantage of you that way, and you have a right to be angry if you feel violated."

Rio tried to keep a straight face. Could she honestly think he was angry because she'd looked in his jeans? He was still so hard he thought about offering her another look. For that matter, she could do some touching while she was at it.

"I'm not angry with you. About that," he quickly added.

"Well, good. I mean, we haven't exactly been on good terms, and I didn't want you to get mad at me for anything else."

She waited a moment, probably for him to say something about their lack of good terms. Or maybe to deny they were still on bad terms. When he didn't say anything, she straightened her shoulders and walked to the wardrobe. She took out a dress and hurriedly pulled it on.

"I'll finish dressing in Victoria's room," she let him know. There was a distinctive coolness to her tone that hadn't been there during her apology. "That way, you can have some privacy. If you want a bath, there should be warm water in the cistern by the tub."

He'd hurt her feelings. Rio could tell by the look in her eyes. Abbie had expected something from him, forgiveness maybe. A part of him wanted to forgive her, too, and not just the aroused part of him either. But he couldn't forgive her. Not yet. Worse, was the thought that he might not ever be able to trust her.

"Thank you," was all he said.

Her reply was as half-hearted as his had been. "You're welcome." Then she walked out, leaving him to wonder if he was the biggest fool who'd ever lived.

Rio strolled into the parlor where Ina had told him that Wilburn Starling was waiting for him. Well, Wilburn was sort of waiting. The man had a leather satchel pressed against his chest while he backed away from Pig.

"Mr. McCaine," Wilburn said shakily. He dropped back into a chair and lifted his feet high off the floor. Pig swiped at him with his claws again, and Rio noticed snags on the man's trousers. "I decided to ride out and talk to you." He eyed Pig as if the tabby were a mountain lion. "That's an ornery little creature. Yes, indeedy."

Rio stared down the cat. It stared back, green feline

eyes narrowed to slits. Fortunately, Rio's mood was more surly than the cat's could have ever been. After several moments, Pig gave an indifferent meow and sauntered out of the room.

"You have some news for me?" Rio asked the lawyer when the cat was gone.

Wilburn Starling dropped his feet back to the floor, took a deep breath and gave a bright smile. "Yes, indeedy. Just like I told you in the office, I thought the papers looked legal, and they are. The deed's been recorded in your name at the courthouse in Fall Creek."

Rio felt his heart race. He hadn't allowed himself to believe it was true. "You're sure?"

"Absolutely. The McCaine ranch is all yours, just like those papers said. Here's the telegram from the county clerk," Wilburn took it from his satchel and handed it over. "You can read it for yourself."

He did. And it verified what Wilburn had just said. So, Abbie hadn't lied to him. About that. But one truth couldn't discount all the other lies she'd told.

"Is there anything else I can do for you, Mr. Mc-Caine?"

Rio shook his head. "Thank you."

"Well, I'm always eager to please anyone in the Donegan family." He stood and took more papers from his satchel. "Will you be so kind to give these papers to your wife?"

Rio glanced at them. It occurred to him that Abbie might have already started the process for a divorce. "What kind of papers?"

"Huh?" Wilburn was busy closing the hasp on his satchel. "Uh, oh yes. They're for the Donegan shipping business. Mrs. McCaine hired a man to oversee the daily operations, but she's still responsible for the bulk of the records. I need her to look those over and sign them."

"Oh." Not divorce papers. He took them and tucked

them under his arm. "Has Abbie said anything to you about our marriage?"

Wilburn twisted his face as if giving the question some thought. "Not as I recall. What would she have said to me about it?"

"Nothing."

"Well, you are entitled to half of the estate if that's what you're wondering. Mr. Donegan put that in his will."

"I don't want any part of the Donegan estate."

Wilburn shrugged in a gesture that said *suit yourself* and gathered his things. "You'll make sure Mrs. McCaine gets those papers?"

"I'll make sure."

In fact, he would make sure right away. He'd find her. Give her those papers. And maybe even talk to her.

About what though?

Rio scowled. A man didn't have to have anything specific in mind to talk to his wife. They could discuss anything. The weather. Julian. The deed to his ranch. Maybe he could even apologize for not believing her about that.

Maybe.

And while he was at it, he could thank her for everything she'd done. Surely he could forget the lies and mistrust for a couple of minutes while they had a civil conversation?

"Well, my my, if it isn't Abilene Donegan McCaine."

Abbie stopped a couple of feet away from the sheriff's office and glared at the man who had a shoulder propped against the doorjamb. "Go away, Wendell. I'm a married woman now, and you can't pester me anymore."

He grinned around the cheroot dangling out of his mouth. "Oh, I can still pester you. I just can't pester you about marrying me." He gave her an exaggerated, gentlemanly bow. "Probably didn't pick a good day to wear that outfit. It looks like rain. You'll likely get that pretty dress all wet."

Abbie glanced up at the sky. Not just rain, it looked more like a storm brewing. Odd, she'd been so occupied with her own thoughts, she hadn't even noticed it.

"By the way, I met your husband," Wendell admitted.

"I know that already, and I also know that you got him drunk." She went inside the sheriff's office, but Wendell followed her inside.

"I didn't get him drunk. I'm the one who got drunk, to console myself over your marriage. As I recall, your husband was sober as a Sister of Mercy when he left the Rusty Bucket."

Abbie ignored him and turned her attention to Sheriff Clayton Knight. "I want you to arrest Julian McCaine and Camellia Barnwell immediately."

The lawman didn't seem surprise by her abrupt demand. "I'd like nothing better. Tell me what they did."

"I have reason to believe they attacked my husband."

"Reason or proof?" the sheriff questioned.

"Both. Julian McCaine's the only person in Elliot's Grove who would want to harm Rio."

"Well, that's probably true," Wendell added. "But you shouldn't have to worry about Julian McCaine or Miz Barnwell any longer. They left on the train late yesterday afternoon."

Abbie turned to him. "You saw them?"

"Me and about a dozen other people. Men mostly. I guess they wanted to see if Camellia would wear those fairy wings again. We were all a mite disappointed when she didn't have them on."

The sheriff mumbled an agreement. "I can send out a few telegrams if you like, and see if they've shown up anywhere close to here."

"Thank you. I'd appreciate that."

"My guess is they know they're in trouble, and they've

moved on. I don't think they'd be stupid enough to show their faces around here when they know you'll be looking for them."

Abbie could only hope. Of course, she'd been hoping that for months, so she wouldn't let her guard down any time soon.

"I do have some news about your half-sister, Harmony," the sheriff added.

"What?" Abbie asked cautiously.

"I got a telegram in this morning. The Rangers arrested the group of Apaches responsible for the raids. Not Gray Wolf's men."

Abbie held her breath. She didn't want to celebrate just yet. "These men confessed?"

"No, but there's evidence. This bunch even had some of the items with them they'd taken during the attacks. So, if you see your half-sister, tell her I no longer want to question her."

Abbie nodded.

Well, things seemed to be working out. Finally. Camellia and Julian were gone, possibly out of her life forever. And Harmony had been cleared of all charges. Everything was fine—except for two things.

Rio was barely speaking to her.

And she was utterly miserable.

She didn't expect her mood to improve any time soon either. She didn't know where Rio was, and even if she did, she wasn't sure she actually wanted to see him. Even worse, she was fairly sure he didn't want to see her.

That morning he'd all but brushed her off like a fleck of dirt from his boots. There she was, lying half naked in the bed with him, he was aroused . . . and yet he'd done nothing about it.

Hellfire. What kind of man was he anyway? She could understand him not liking her after all the lies, but what kind of man turned away from a woman in bed with him?

Delores Fossen

Obviously an uninterested man.

One who wasn't interested in her.

Well, she was tired of barking her head off at tree knots. It was time to face facts—her marriage to Rio McCaine was over. Over, and it hadn't even had a chance to get started.

Hellfire and damnation! She'd lost him.

Chapter Twenty

Rio finally found her.

It hadn't been easy; he'd looked for Abbie for over an hour before he finally located her in front of her father's cabin. She was alone, beneath a peach tree and she looked angry. She'd pushed up the sleeves of her dress, and her hair was loose, falling wildly around her face and shoulders.

He watched from behind as she picked up a peach and hurled it. It smacked into the tree, sending juicy pulp flying everywhere. There were already several bird-nibbled peaches lying on the ground, and he spotted more smashed ones, probably others that she'd thrown.

There was a distant rumble of thunder, and Rio glanced overhead at the dark sky. The storm was close, but he didn't think any storm would compare to the one brewing in Abbie. He was the cause of that anger, no doubt. He hadn't trusted her about the deed, and it seemed to be one of the few times she'd actually told him the truth.

Abbie plucked a ripe peach off a low-hanging branch and sank onto the narrow limestone steps. Rio let her take a few bites before he walked closer, hoping she would calm down a little. He didn't want one of those peaches aimed at him.

He glanced around. It was the first time he'd gotten a good look at the cabin, since the other time he'd been brought here, he had been unconscious. Unlike Kingston, the building was simple clapboard, aged by time and the weather to a soft dove gray. Two nine-paned windows flanked each side of the door. Both windows and the door were wide open.

Abbie looked up, saw him approaching, and looked away just as quickly. "It's fixing to rain. What are you doing down here, anyway?"

"I brought you some papers your lawyer left for you."

She made an unfriendly sound. "What are they, divorce papers?"

He momentarily was taken aback. "No, something to do with your business."

"Oh." She accepted the papers and laid them on the floor inside the cabin. "You didn't have to go to all the bother of bringing them out here."

"It wasn't any bother."

She took a large bite off the peach, some of the juice running down her arm. She kept her attention focused on the ground and poked at a rock with her toe. That's when Rio realized she was barefooted. Her dainty low-cut shoes lay haphazardly beneath the peach tree.

"Something else I can do for you?" she asked none too pleasantly.

Yes, she could listen to him while he ate some crow. And there was no mistake about it; He had some to eat.

"Remember I told you that Wilburn Starling checked on the deed for me?"

Abbie nodded, bit off another chunk of the peach.

He felt a first raindrop spatter on his shoulder but didn't think it would be a good idea to ask Abbie to take this conversation inside. She didn't look ready to budge yet. "Well, the deed was legal."

She shrugged. "I told you it was. I've done a lot of rotten things, but I didn't cheat you out of your ranch."

Rio was about to apologize for not believing her, but Abbie stood and threw the rest of her peach against the tree. "Look, I'm just going to say this outright, and you can laugh if you want." She swiped away a drop of rain that had fallen on her cheek, but the action ended up smearing peach juice across her face.

"And what would you be telling me that's so funny?"

She scowled. "Well, maybe you can't laugh, because I don't think I could handle that right now. Hellfire, do whatever you feel like doing, just hear me out. Laugh until you're rolling on the ground. I don't care."

Confused, Rio nodded. "I'm listening."

She swore and pushed her hand through her hair. "Since practically the moment I laid eyes on you, I've had this fire in my body."

He hadn't expected her to say that, but Rio knew exactly how she felt. He'd lived with that same fire for so many days now, it seemed as if he'd invented it. "Go on."

"Well, that fire heats up when you kiss me, and it got especially hot when you had me on the bed and put yourself inside me. I thought since it hurt some that this fire would go away. I mean, why would I want to do that again with you when it hurts?"

"It only hurts the first time," Rio assured her after swallowing the lump in his throat.

"That's what I figured. After all, no one would be so

eager to do it if it hurt like that every time." She folded her arms over her chest and started to pace. The rain began to fall in earnest now, but Abbie didn't seem to notice. "All I want to know is if there is something you can do to make this fire go away. Because I'll tell you now, I don't know how much longer I can stand feeling like this."

Rio stepped forward, stopping only a few inches from her. He tried to steady his racing heart, tried to rein in the fire in his own body, but it was impossible to control his responses after a remark like that.

"What exactly are you asking me to do, Abbie?"

He knew. At least Rio thought he did. But so many things had gone wrong between them that he wanted to make sure before he did something they would both regret. Or enjoy. It could go either way at this point.

Abbie tossed her hand into the air. "How should I know? That's what I'd hoped you could tell me."

Oh, he could tell her all right . . . Could show her. His body leaned more toward the showing.

"You're getting wet," he said, hearing the texture of his voice change. Along with his voice, the rest of him began to change too. Preparing itself for something it wanted. "We should go inside until the storm passes."

Looking over her shoulder at him, she stepped into the cabin, and Rio followed. A moment later, a gust of wind blew the door shut behind them.

"Are you still mad at me?" she asked.

"Not at the moment." He reached out and skimmed his finger along her shoulder. "Are you mad at me?"

She shook her head but didn't look at him. "No."

"Good." He didn't want anger to have any part in this. Anger could make for good sex, but that wasn't what he had in mind right now. He wanted sex all right. But he wanted to take it slow, and he wanted it to mean something.

The room was cool and damp, the rainy breeze spilling through the windows to play with the curtains. The white gauzy fabric fluttered and brushed over the unmade bed. Outside, a rumble of thunder announced a full-fledged storm.

Overcome, he stepped toward her and lowered his head, intending to kiss the back of her neck. Unfortunately, at that exact moment Abbie whirled around to face him. Her shoulder caught him right in the nose.

"My God, are you all right? Did I break it?" She reached for him. He went to put his hand over his nose. Their hands collided, jamming his thumb.

He winced in pain but tried to keep his profanity to himself. It would certainly spoil what remained of the moment. "I'm fine, I think," he finally managed to say. He touched his nose and was relieved when he saw he wasn't bleeding.

"Sorry. I didn't know you were right behind me."

Rio intended to assure her that it was all right, but the words didn't make it out of his mouth. As their gazes locked, his heart slammed against his chest. And it just kept right on slamming.

Maybe he was still in a lather about that talk she'd just given him, or maybe he'd been in a lather since the night he met her. Rio suddenly didn't care.

She was here.

He was here.

They were alone.

And he wanted her mouth for supper.

While he was at it, he wanted the rest of her for dessert. Before he could talk himself out of it, he leaned over and put his mouth right next to hers.

"I guess this will muddy the waters." Rio brushed his lips against her earlobe. Abbie shivered, a tiny sound coming from deep within her throat, an invitation for him to give her more.

It was the only invitation he needed.

"It doesn't feel like you're muddying the waters," she pointed out. "It feels like you're kissing my ear."

"That, too."

She grabbed his shirt with both hands and locked him in a fierce grip—to stop him, was Rio's first thought, but she didn't push him away. She just grabbed him.

He nuzzled the little area just below her ear, dampening it slightly with the tip of his tongue and then whispering a hot, soft breath over the same spot.

Abbie whimpered.

The seductive dance with his mouth continued. Rio moved from her ear to her cheek, making the journey one long, slow kiss.

"Oh," she whispered. "No matter what part of me you kiss, I feel it in all the other parts."

That's what he had hoped for.

And that sort of information took a real bite out of his self-control.

He was suddenly desperate to taste her, so he dipped his head and took. She was all peaches and rain. He needed that taste in his mouth. This felt like something beyond need, something only she could give. Only she would satisfy. Like the warm air feeding the storm clouds, she would give him exactly what he needed.

Her eyelids fluttered downward. "Yes," she whispered.

"Here?" Rio said.

"Here," Abbie agreed.

"Now?" He reached for her again, gripped her waist in his hands.

"Now."

Thank God. Rio didn't want to wait. Couldn't wait. Their mouths met again, and desire overwhelmed him in a splintering wash of heat. It overtook all sense of anything but her and the way she felt against him.

She pressed herself nearer. Encouraged by her response, he shoved his knee between hers, pushing his hard thigh up against a place he thought would please her. It must have, because she started to make little squeaky noises. Rio kept up the pressure until the squeaky noises turned to throaty moans, and she was bearing down as hard as he was.

"I like this as much as the kisses," she gasped. "Maybe better."

He smiled. "I thought so."

"How could you tell?" She looked a bit embarrassed.

Easy. The way you're rubbing yourself against me. "By the look on your face," he answered, so that he wouldn't have to say something vulgar.

She smiled. "I'm all hot and wet where we're touching. Is that supposed to happen?"

Oh, yes. That's exactly what was supposed to happen. "It'll feel better when we take our clothes off."

"Really?" she asked with a fair amount of disbelief. "Better than this?"

"Much, much better," he assured her.

Apparently she took his word as gospel because she began to pull at his clothes. Actually she did more than pull. Abbie ripped open his shirt and shoved it off him. They knocked into each other a couple of times, and she bumped his nose again. Rio didn't let that stop him. He got her dress off, pleased that underneath he found only a camisole, pantalets and warm feminine skin.

"Hurry," she demanded.

He moved as fast as he could. Rio pulled off her camisole while she went after his boots. She yelped when his knee bumped her head. At this rate, they would injure themselves, but there was no way to slow down—and Abbie didn't look anymore desirous of a leisurely pace. Pushing restlessly against him, she caressed his neck, his collarbone, his shoulders. With her mouth she retraced the path her hands had taken. Rio grimaced and managed a strangled groan.

"Your jeans," she hissed. "I want them off. You said it would be better with no clothes."

Heck, he wanted them off too, and he would have doffed them immediately if Abbie hadn't taken it on herself to remove them. Unfortunately, she wasn't very good at unbuttoning a man's jeans. A part of him was greatly appreciative of that, but one specific part wasn't. She pulled and yanked at the buttons and wasn't especially careful about what else she pulled and yanked.

A groan clawed its way past his throat. If she did much more of that, he would go off like a Fourth of July firecracker. "Let me do it."

He managed to get his jeans unbuttoned, but before he could push them down, he noticed what Abbie was doing. Undressing. She slid off her pantalets. Good Lord, there was no way that wouldn't distract him. She looked like sex. She smelled like sex. And when confronted with her naked beauty, Rio had to pause and do some sampling.

He dropped to his knees, pressed his mouth to her stomach, and circled her navel with his tongue.

"Is this . . . allowed," she asked, panting.

"Absolutely. There are no rules here, Abbie."

Rio sucked. Bit. Nibbled.

"Yes." Abbie fisted her hand in his hair, froze. "Oh, yes, yes, yes. I like the part about no rules. Aunt Dorrie didn't mention that. Exactly where do the rules start?"

He moved slightly lower. Kissed, tasted, lingered. "At the bottom of your feet, I think."

"There a lot of room in between."

There was. Rio thought it would be fun to explore. He sank even lower, leaving kisses along the way. He stopped at her triangle of nether curls and looked up at her.

"Th-this is allowed, too?" she asked.

He grinned. "Yeah."

Rio paused to savor the look on her face. He wanted to do some other savoring, too. When his mouth touched her, her back bowed and her eyes glazed. She slid her knee onto his shoulder. Pushed her body closer. And closer.

"Definitely, yes," she mumbled, shoving her hands deeper into his hair. "Aunt Dorrie didn't say anything about this either."

That didn't surprise him. He suspected they'd do a lot of things today that Dorrie couldn't possibly imagine.

Her grip tightened in his hair. "Oh, yesssss."

Those repeated yeses of hers were making him hotter than El Paso in August. Rio considered finishing her off right then, right there. He could put his mouth to good use and give her the kind of kiss she'd never forget. What would it be like to see her shatter? To taste her when she did? He didn't think he could wait to find out.

He apparently thought about it too long because Abbie latched onto his shoulders. "Now," she demanded. "I've got to have something, and I don't think your mouth's going to do it."

He could have quickly proven her wrong, if she hadn't started to drag him toward the bed. They fell in a heap onto the soft mattress.

"Ah, hell," he hissed.

"What?"

"Jeans."

She tried to help him again, but it was no easy job since there was more of him now than there had been when the jeans first went on. Rio also noticed she didn't pay nearly as much attention to his jeans as what was underneath. When he finally managed to get the pants off, Abbie took a long look down and then up at his face.

"It's different," she announced.

"From what?" He couldn't imagine that she'd had much experience looking at men's private parts. After all, until very recently she'd been a virgin.

"From the time I saw it before."

"Oh, that. I wasn't aroused then."

"But it was soft, like a big brown caterpillar."

Rio didn't appreciated the comparison, but he sure wasn't soft now. He was huge. Hard. And ready. "This is the way I get when I want to—oh, God."

Before he'd realized her intentions, Abbie had gripped him and run her fingers the entire length of his shaft. "Why does it get like this?"

Rio ground his teeth together. "To give you more pleasure. Trust me, it wouldn't be nearly as much fun if I stayed soft."

She smiled. And licked her lips. "You mean all of this is for me? Just so I'll enjoy it more?"

He didn't want to take the time to explain that in this case her pleasure would also be his. All at once it seemed too complicated to put into words.

"Aunt Dorrie forgot to mention a lot of things." She continued to slide her fingers, gently, slowly, lightly over his rigid flesh. Her voice stayed level, but Rio saw her eyes ripen with the same slow, eating hunger that gnawed at him. "Dorrie made it sound like this wouldn't be much fun. Like churning butter, she said."

"Churning butter." Well, that was a different way of putting it. Since she seemed to enjoy touching him, Rio slid his hand down her stomach. Because he was so close, he saw the pulse hammer at her throat. "But I can see why she'd call it that."

"Oh*hhh?*" The word became a moan as he moved his hand lower to cover her.

"Think about it. All that churning. The long, hard part inside all that soft, creamy, warm, um, stuff. In and out. In and out."

262

Abbie pressed her forehead against his cheek and moaned. "How about we try that now?"

She didn't have to ask him twice. He pushed Abbie back on the bed and lay atop her. He slid his hands to her bottom, lifted her and opened her legs so he could force his hips between them.

"Oh, I like the way this feels," she said. "I like your weight on me."

It was mutual; he liked having her beneath him. Rio caught one of her legs and wrapped it around his waist. "I can make it nice and slow later, but right now I have to have you."

"Who said I wanted nice and slow? Fast and hard sounds good."

And that's what he gave her. Intimately, possessively, but without a shred of patience, he slid his hand between them and covered her. His fingertips dipped inside and found her wetness, and he touched the tiny bud of her feminine passion. Abbie arched her neck and shoved the back of her head against the mattress.

"Ohmygod, yes," she muttered. "Oh. My. God. Yes."

The ohmygods were just getting started as far as he was concerned. Within moments he had her starved for him. He knew she wanted more, and she wanted it now. Abbie pushed herself against his fingers, trying to relieve the desperate hunger he was creating.

"Yes," she managed. "Yes. Just like that. How do you know?"

"Know what?"

"Where to touch me?"

It wasn't as easy to answer as it seemed. Fearing it could open a long conversation, he just answered, "I guessed."

He didn't stop touching her. Despite his own obvious need, he had to see her like this, had to know she was his. His fingers continued to torment her, to heighten the sensation. She thrashed against him and dug her nails into his shoulders.

"Take me now, Rio, or I'll have to hurt you."

Oh, he very much intended to. He took her hands and their fingers laced. Their eyes met, their breath froze. The tip of him touched her. It was just the slightest graze, a brush of hard against soft, but it jangled his already raw nerves and sent a primal rush through him. She was his mate, and he would take her. Now.

Capturing her mouth in a deep, wet kiss that was almost brutal, he positioned the blunt tip of his arousal against her, intending to move very slowly. Abbie obviously had other plans. Using her heels for leverage, she pushed herself up and completed the union in one forced stroke.

She cursed, then called out in a prayer.

Her body quickly adjusted, gripping him, taking him in a way meant for no other. She was tight, wet, and apparently just as eager as he was. Rio withdrew, then drove into her until he was seated as deeply as he could go. And God help him, it was perfect.

Abbie made a sound, a whimper, which almost brought Rio back to his senses. Almost, but before it could completely do that, she twisted her hands in her hair and rocked against him. Rio realized then she wasn't in pain. Far from it. She shoved her body forward. A delicious little smile flickered across her lips.

"Ohmygod, yes," she declared.

Rio cursed. Her hot slick heat might kill him. Or at least make all of this end much, much too soon. Of course, a month would have been too soon for him. He didn't think he would ever get his fill of her.

He withdrew almost completely, then thrust into her again, burying himself utterly. He wasn't gentle, but it wasn't the time for that. And Abbie apparently didn't want gentle, because she pushed as hard against him as he drove into her.

There was nothing graceful about the rhythm they found, but Rio was driven by hunger—his own and Abbie's body writhing against him.

"Don't stop," she warned.

"No plans for that," he quickly assured her. Every part of them was creating friction, every part was slick with sweat.

"You have to *do* something," she said frantically. "You know how. Please tell me you know how."

He understood. Completion; it was a need as old as time. He would supply it to her, too. Grasping her hips, Rio shifted their positions and gave her what she wanted. He didn't bother to hold back the sound that rushed out of his mouth, the sound of conquest. Ecstasy. Fulfillment. She matched it.

While her eyes struggled to focus, he pressed his hands to her face and made her look at him. "You're mine, understand?"

Rio wasn't even sure she heard him. It didn't matter. He would tell her later. Later, when the fireworks stopped shooting off inside his head.

Chapter Twenty-one

The rain hadn't stopped, nor had time. For a while after she returned to earth, Abbie thought those things possible. It didn't seem as if such mundane occurrences could go on while something so wonderful happened to her.

"This is nice," she whispered as her fingertips idly strummed the muscles of Rio's back.

Her body still glowed from their shared passion, and she didn't plan to move unless it was absolutely necessary. It made her wonder why people weren't doing this all the time. Maybe they were. Maybe people were doing exactly this in houses all over the world. Still, it didn't diminish what had gone on between Rio and her. Those other people probably didn't enjoy it nearly as much as she had. No one could have had that much fun.

It had been perfect.

And it hadn't just been sex, but love. There was no doubt in her mind that she was in love with Rio. The

266

notion didn't frighten her as much as she'd thought it would. She loved him.

Truly, madly, completely.

But how did he feel about her?

He'd never said that he was in love with her. Never even hinted at it. Was it possible for a man to make love to a woman the way Rio had and not be in love with her? Abbie didn't think so. His whole heart had seemed in it. Still, she'd heard that everything was different for a man.

Maybe all of this would mean nothing to him.

She refused to think about it. This moment was too perfect to ruin with doubts. Later, there would be time for those, and maybe regrets. Even though Abbie didn't think she could regret this at all.

No, not this.

She didn't think Rio would regret it either, but the activity certainly seemed to have taken a lot out of him. At first, she thought she'd killed him. In those last moments of passion, Rio had grunted some fairly creative profanity and collapsed in a dead heap on top of her. But he wasn't dead. Every now and then she felt a special kind of stirring. It was slight but in an area that indicated he was not only alive but might soon be ready to do it all over again.

"Rio?" she whispered.

He grunted.

"Rio, that was wonderful. *You* were wonderful. I've never felt anything so wonderful in my entire life."

Another grunt.

"I can't believe this finally happened," she continued. Abbie smiled at another of those special stirrings. It was in just the right spot. "I mean, I've wanted this to happen since I first saw you, but I was beginning to think it never would. And you made it just perfect for me."

He added a short groan to the grunt.

She smiled again at the adorable masculine sounds he made. So this was what happened after a man and woman made love? They stayed joined for a while. With him still on top of her.

Earlier Rio's weight had felt good on her, but she was starting to get a cramp in her leg. Abbie didn't know how they'd managed it, but somehow she had her right knee under his arm pit, and her other leg was slung high over his back. There was a lump in the mattress, and it poked against her shoulder blade.

"Uh, Rio?"

He only grunted again. Abbie decided she'd move him just a little so that she could get more comfortable. She soon learned it was easier said than done. He still had a firm grip on her hands and had them pinned to the bed. Her legs had fully cramped up now and she couldn't use them to get leverage. Her hips still worked though. She pushed up. And up.

He groaned and lazily nuzzled her neck. "Not yet, Abbie. Let me catch my breath."

The thought of making love with him again greatly appealed to her, but Rio was really heavy. He grunted again, but this time it didn't sound so adorable.

"Uh, Rio. I'm having a hard time breathing. You'll have to get off of me."

He did. Without saying anything, he rolled off her and disjoined them. Like a landed trout, he fell on his back on the mattress. And grunted.

Abbie smiled. Much better. Well, except she'd liked the way it felt when he was inside her. Still, it was easier to breathe this way. She sucked in some heavy gulps of air before she snuggled against him.

"I hope I didn't hurt you," she whispered.

He managed a husky laugh and sleepily rubbed his

mouth over her forehead. "That's what I'm supposed to say to you."

"Why?"

Rio yawned and stretched his legs out. "Because it was your first time. Well, almost your first time. We didn't get very far the other night when we were in your bedroom. Did I hurt you?"

"No. I was worried about your cuts and bruises."

"Didn't even feel them. Sex has a way of numbing pain."

Yes, she supposed it did. She felt a little sore now, but she hadn't even noticed it when they were in the throes of passion.

She pressed her nose against his neck and inhaled deeply. "I like the way you smell. And the way you feel. I've lusted in my heart for you for so long, Rio. It's good to finally lust in the flesh. This is so much better, don't you think?"

"It's the best way I know."

She liked it best too. She also liked the way he looked at her. There was a glow in his eyes that she hadn't seen before. A warmth that seemed to go all the way to his heart. Abbie didn't want to get up her hopes, but it seemed there was love in his eyes. Maybe he would tell her how he felt about her if she prompted him a little.

"What are you thinking?" she asked.

He smiled. "This." Rio pressed his palm over her left breast and closed his fingers over her nipple.

"Oh." So, he hadn't been thinking about how much he loved her.

"And this." His hand went lower—much lower—and pressed against a different part of her body.

All right. So he hadn't had feelings on his mind at all. Well, not the kind of feelings she'd been thinking about. But maybe this wasn't so bad if it led to other things.

"You're a beautiful woman." Lazily, he slipped his

finger inside her. "I could never get enough of you."

Abbie sucked in her breath. It was hard to think about anything when he did that. His finger wasn't quite as nice as that other part of him, but that part didn't look ready for activity yet. It looked like a big brown caterpillar again.

She let him gently push her back onto the bed. The mattress was so soft it swelled around her, cocooning her in the cover. Something else was swelling too; she could feel it. Abbie put the heel of her hand against Rio's chest to give herself room to look.

"You're getting hard again," she said in amazement. "Just like that. I thought it would take a long time for that to happen again, and here it is happening right before my eyes."

"Being next to you has a way of encouraging it."

Yes, Abbie could see that. She started to roll Rio over so she could see even more of him, but he turned over instead, causing her to sprawl on top of him. She gave a little grunt. The sprawling position had certainly put her more in contact with those special stirrings—and with the part of him doing the actual stirring. And it felt—she grinned like an idiot—really, really nice. So nice, she decided to move a little.

"It'll feel even better when I'm inside you." Rio leaned forward and nudged her nipple with his lips. He circled the erect bud with his tongue and drew it into his mouth.

Abbie's body arched. Her fingers fastened into Rio's hair, twisted and knotted the silky strands. "It's time for fast again," she ground out. "Quick, get on top." She started to climb off him, but he stopped her.

"Wait. Let's try this." Pulling her against him, Rio slipped himself inside. He was huge and hard, and Abbie winced at the invasion, but soon it didn't seem like an invasion at all. It was exactly what she and her body wanted. She pushed down a little. Oh yes, this was exactly what she wanted.

She looked at him—at where they were joined, and then at Rio again. "What now?" she asked.

"It's like riding a horse. I've seen you do that, and you're darn good."

Yes, but she'd never ridden with her body on fire like this, and she'd never ridden a man. Still, how hard could it be?

"This is like being saddled, huh?" She wiggled a little. "Except I'm the saddler, and you're the one being saddled." Abbie grinned. "I think I like that."

"I figured you would."

Her grin widened when she rocked back and forth. Heavens, this was fun in addition to feeling awfully good. She slid her hand down his chest and touched him where their bodies met. "And exactly what part of the saddle would this be?"

He groaned, almost in agony, but Abbie didn't believe for one minute he was in pain.

"Not the pommel." She chuckled softly and gave him another nudge. "Not the swell either, even though I think we could say there's some definite swelling going on here."

"You're trying to kill me," Rio gasped.

"No. Just trying to figure out what part of your saddle you have inside me." She leaned down and ran her tongue over his mouth—not quite a kiss, but Abbie liked the glazed look that went through Rio's eyes. "I got it. This part I'm touching—"

"Squeezing," he corrected, adding another tortured groan.

"All right, the part I'm squeezing is your horn neck." Using her knees, she levered herself up, momentarily disjoining them so she could run her thumb over the tip of his erection. Rio cursed her and called her a dirty name that made her laugh. "And there's no doubt about what this is. This is your horn. A rather nice one, too. A lot bigger than you'd normally see on a saddle, but I think I can figure out what to do with—"

Rio growled, caught her hips and thrust himself into her. Abbie felt her eyes roll back in her head.

"Show me what you can do," he challenged.

It took her a moment just to catch her breath, then she started to move. Little nudges, followed by a few sways. And bumps. Rio gripped her hips tighter to add some guidance to her somewhat awkward movements. The right guidance, it seemed.

"What happens if I go faster?" she asked. Her grin faded some, and she was pretty sure she had a stupid look on her face. She couldn't help it. This had a way of making her feel mindless.

"I'll start to beg."

The idea intrigued her. She couldn't imagine Rio begging for anything. "And what'll happen if I stop?"

"Same thing. More begging."

Power. This was the in-charge kind of power that Abbie loved. She pushed his hands off her hips and took control. She soon learned that Rio had told her the truth. When she went faster, he begged. He also said things she'd never heard a man say before. She thought she'd heard everything. But Rio came up with a whole repertoire of combinations of fascinating expressions. And everything she did would elicit something new.

When she squeezed her knees around his hips, he begged and grunted. And he didn't seem to like it at all when she stopped, but then that wasn't much fun for her either.

No, fast, hard, and frantic was the way it felt best. She pretended she was riding a wild mustang through hilly terrain. Then she took her wild mustang through a valley. Then back up the hill again. She bucked. Raced. And rode hard. Once she even yelled out a yippee.

"I want you with me," Rio gasped under her.

She wanted to assure him that she was most certainly with him, but Abbie soon learned that wasn't what he meant at all. He slipped his finger against the spot where they were joined. But not exactly that spot. A little place above it. It was obviously a little bullet ready to fire, and Rio seemed to know exactly how to make it do that. He rubbed, stroked, caressed, and gently pinched.

Suddenly Abbie couldn't stop bucking. It suddenly seemed as necessary as drawing her next breath, and it no longer seemed that she had control of what was happening.

His finger moved faster.

She bucked faster.

His caresses got harder.

She rode harder.

His finger slid over that spot in one rough slippery stroke after another.

The little bullet fired.

Sure she'd just experienced a freaking miracle, Abbie gave a wail of completion. Nothing less than a miracle could have felt that good. Sin, redemption, and paradise all rolled into one, and Rio had made it happen.

He stiffened beneath her, the muscles in his body corded. He latched on to her with his hands and pulled her tightly to him. His hips bucked in one final surge. His bullet was fired, too, and Abbie couldn't help thinking how much bigger his was than hers.

"I love you, Rio," she mumbled. "I love you."

Her words had almost no sound, but she heard them as clearly as if she had shouted. Speaking them, Abbie also knew they were true. And it had nothing to do with the way he'd just made her feel.

Well, maybe something.

But something bigger had happened. Something more

273

monumental than just exploding bullets. And Abbie thought it was the best thing that had could have ever happened.

She was in love with her husband.

Somewhere deep below the ground, Satan was probably in search of some firewood. Hell had no doubt just frozen over.

Chapter Twenty-two

Abbie picked wildflowers on the walk home. She hummed. And smiled. Actually she grinned. Anyone who saw her now would think she'd pretty much lost her mind.

Maybe she had.

Maybe that's exactly what had happened to her.

She certainly wasn't the same person she had been just a couple of weeks earlier. To the best of her knowledge, she'd never picked wildflowers and she'd never worn dresses two days in a row. She'd never smiled this much. And most certainly she'd never felt so happy.

The rain had stopped, and now everything smelled fresh and new. Just the way she felt. She hoped, Rio felt the same. She didn't know because she had left him asleep in the cabin. She found it odd that he'd fallen asleep so easily after they made love—Abbie didn't think she could have slept under threat of death—but she hadn't wanted to disturb him.

She wanted to jump for joy. To celebrate. To tell someone. She didn't think she could hold all of this joy inside her much longer.

Before Abbie even reached the house, she saw Victoria standing on the front veranda. Her sister looked concerned, but Abbie only smiled and waved.

"Where have you been?" Victoria asked. "I've been worried about . . ." But her words faded when Abbie walked closer.

Abbie didn't have to guess why. She was fairly certain that even Victoria could tell where she had been and what she'd been doing. "I was with Rio."

Victoria walked down the steps and cautiously studied Abbie's face. "You've got little marks all over your neck."

That wasn't the only place she had them. When she'd dressed, Abbie had found them on her breasts and stomach, too. She figured she had some in places she wouldn't be able to see without use of mirrors.

"Are you all right?" Victoria asked.

Abbie gave a breathy laugh and handed her sister the bouquet of flowers. "Yes, I'm all right. Better than all right. Oh, Victoria, something wonderful happened. Something better than wonderful. I can't wait to tell you all about it." She took the woman's hands and had her sit on the steps.

"You don't have to tell me," Victoria calmly explained. "I think I can pretty much figure it out for myself. You consummated your marriage."

Abbie laughed. "I did at that, though I don't like the word consummated. It doesn't come close to describing what we did in that cabin." She fanned her hands into the air. "Maybe bullets firing. Or stars exploding. Fire. Heat. Para—"

"Spare me the details, please. What I want to know is if you're sure this is what you want?"

276

Yes, she was absolutely positive that she wanted Rio, and Abbie didn't want to think beyond that. She wanted to enjoy her giddiness a little longer before she had to deal with reality.

"So, I guess you're really in love with Rio, or you wouldn't have made love with him." Victoria concluded.

"Oh, I'm so much in love with him. I mean, I didn't think it was possible to feel this for another person. It's like my heart has grown twice the size it should be."

Victoria gave Abbie's hand a squeeze. "Well, I don't know whether to be happy for you or not."

"Be happy, definitely."

"All right, I'll be happy for you. For now. When the dust settles, you might see things differently."

"I won't. I'll love him just as much as I do right now."

Victoria shrugged. "Did you tell Rio?"

"Not yet." She'd whispered it to him, but he likely hadn't heard her. She would have to tell him, of course, or else he might just head off to Fall Creek without knowing how she felt. Abbie frowned. He might just head off anyway. In her giddy state, she hadn't considered that. "What do you think he'll do when I tell him that I love him? I mean, this will change everything. Won't it?"

"It will complicate everything certainly. I don't know what to say. Rio's ranch is miles from here, and you can't expect him to stay at Kingston. This isn't his home."

No, it wasn't. But it was hers. "Then we'll just have to work out something." Abbie wasn't ready to give up their lovemaking, not so soon after she had just discovered how good it could be. Nor was she ready to give up Rio. They would have to come up with a solution. But could they? Could they work out something?

Abbie's frown deepened.

Reality started to set in, and she didn't like it at all. She wished she could climb back in bed with Rio and have him make love to her again. That would stop all these doubts that were beginning to creep back—doubts about how he felt about her, about any future they might have together.

Victoria cleared her throat. "I almost hate to ask this, but did Rio use one of those male preventatives?"

Lord, she'd forgotten all about that. It'd been the last thing on her mind when she was in bed with him. Well, that was one more worry she could add to her ever-growing list. "No. I didn't order them, and I forgot to look through Father's things for one." She shook her head. "It's not like I went out to the cabin with the intention of making love to Rio. I went out there to throw peaches."

"So, you were with him, and you didn't do anything to prevent becoming pregnant?"

Abbie didn't care much for the blunt way her sister had put that, but that's exactly what had happened. "Does prayer count?"

Victoria's stern expression softened, but she shook her head. "No."

"Wishful thinking?"

"No!"

Abbie was afraid of that. How could she have forgotten something so important? Two generations of women in her family had died in childbirth. Yet she'd made love without giving it any thought whatsoever.

"Well, there's nothing I can do about it now." Abbie pushed out a deep breath. "What's done is done."

"It's one thing to say that but another to understand exactly what it means. What if you're carrying a child?"

Abbie shrugged. This was one of those times when people said it was no use crying over spilled milk or such nonsense. And it was true. She couldn't go back and undo the afternoon she'd spent with Rio. She didn't want to undo it, though she didn't want to be pregnant either.

"Well?" Victoria questioned. "What if you're carrying his child?"

"Then I'll have a child, won't I?" Abbie tried to sound unconcerned, but she didn't fool Victoria. She didn't fool herself either. Giving birth terrified her, and there might be nothing she could do about it.

But—and this was a very big but—it wouldn't be just any child. It would be Rio's child. He would be part of her life forever if she gave birth to his child.

Forever.

Funny, that part didn't sound so bad.

But Rio might not think so. Never once had he said anything about having children. Maybe he didn't even want them. Maybe the prospect of fatherhood frightened him as much as giving birth did her. Maybe he'd just been caught up in the moment as well.

Victoria patted her hand again. "I'm sure it'll be all right. I've heard you can't even get pregnant the first time anyway."

But there hadn't just been a first. There'd been a second too. Abbie didn't think it mattered that they were less than a half hour apart. She also didn't think it mattered that she had been on top the second time.

"You know, you don't really have to be at Kingston to run the Donegan shipping business," Victoria commented. "You could do that from almost anywhere. Fall Creek, for instance."

But Abbie's mind was already awhirl with other thoughts. A pregnancy. Her feelings for Rio. His feelings for her. Their future, or even if they had one.

"Ladies," a man drawled. "Good afternoon."

Abbie shot up from her seat on the porch step and reached for her pocket derringer, but it was too late. The man raised his revolver and aimed it right at Victoria.

"No, no," Julian scolded. "Don't go for your gun, Abbie. I don't want to hurt your sister, but I will if you don't cooperate."

"What do you think you're doing, Julian?" Abbie demanded.

"I think it's called paying you back. You shouldn't have swindled me out of what was rightfully mine."

"Yours! The ranch wasn't rightfully yours. You ran it into the ground, and then tried to get me to steal it from Rio."

"And did you steal it from him the way I asked you to? No. That's why I'm here." He turned his head slightly and spoke over his shoulder. "Camellia, you can come out now."

"Camellia," Abbie growled. "I should have known you'd be in on this too."

The woman stepped out from the side of the veranda. She also had a gun, and like Julian she grinned from ear to ear. "What can I say? This is what happens when you go back on a deathbed promise."

"No, this is what happens when I didn't shove those blasted fairy wings up your behind."

Camellia only gave a smug "humph."

Julian stepped between the two of them. "Camellia will stay here with Victoria and Ina. We've already tied Ina up inside," he added. "Juan, too, so there's no use looking around for him. There's no one here to save you."

"What do you want?" Abbie tried to keep her voice level, but she didn't think she could do that for long. Because her head had been in the clouds, she hadn't even seen this coming. Now she'd placed Victoria and the others in danger.

"What I want is simple," Julian explained. "I want you to take a little ride with me into town. We have just enough time to get there before the bank closes."

"And why would I want to go to the bank?"

"To take out money, of course. Lots and lots of money.

If you do as you're told, then Camellia won't hurt Victoria. However, if you give me any trouble . . . well, let's just say you won't see your sister alive again."

Abbie didn't dare ask about Rio or Gussie, even though she was sure Julian hadn't forgotten them. Maybe they were safe somewhere. Maybe Rio was still sleeping off the effects of their lovemaking. Well, that was one good thing at least. Julian hadn't barged in when Rio and she were in bed.

He grabbed her arm and started toward the carriage, the one Abbie had used to go into town earlier. Shoving her onto the seat and sitting beside her, he snapped the reins to get the horse moving. Abbie glanced behind her. Camellia was already leading Victoria into the house at gun point.

"Where's that good-for-nothing brother of mine? You better hope for your sake that Rio's too hurt to come looking for you," Julian warned.

Rio wasn't too hurt, and he would most certainly come after her. When he woke up, that was. Abbie kept quiet about that. She had to think of a way to get away from Julian so she could help Victoria.

"I bet you're wondering why I didn't shoot Rio," Julian continued. "Well, I have something much more interesting in mind for him."

That sent a shiver down her spine. "What do you mean?"

"As we speak, a friend is sending a wire to the sheriff, detailing my half-brother's involvement with those Indian raids."

"Rio had nothing to do with those."

"I know, but the sheriff doesn't. I suspect he'll go straight out to the cabin since the wire will say that's where Rio is. He'll arrest Rio, and when my brother is behind bars trying to defend himself, I'll just ride back to the McCaine ranch Of course, I'll have the deed.

281

Well, *a* deed. The people of Fall Creek will certainly take my word over that of my half-breed brother."

But surely Sheriff Knight would see right through that telegram. He couldn't possibly believe that Rio would do something like that. Could he? Abbie wasn't so sure. After all, Sheriff Knight didn't know her husband. Worse, Rio might try to defend himself if the sheriff held a gun on him.

"If anything happens to Rio," Abbie warned, "you won't make it back to the McCaine ranch alive."

Julian pretended to cower in fear, then he snarled. "Threats are so unbecoming, especially when you've got nothing to back them up. For once in your life, Abbie, be a good girl and do as you're told.

Pigs would fly before that happened. One way or another she would come up with a plan to stop him.

Rio stood in the doorway of the cabin and bit into a peach. Abbie had been gone for nearly an hour, but her scent was still with him. So was the memory of their lovemaking. It made him smile.

He'd had his share of other women, though nothing beyond sex really. Quick and dirty romps in the sack with women he hardly knew. He hadn't thought much about it until now, but Abbie certainly had a way of shedding a new light on things. And he'd never seen so much enthusiasm when it came to lovemaking.

Now, he had to figure out what to do about her.

He could leave, of course, and pretend it'd just been sex this time too. Or he could be honest with himself and try to work out something with her.

But work out what exactly?

Rio didn't know, but they were still married, and there was no reason for that to change. They couldn't get an annulment now even if they wanted one. They'd consummated their marriage—twice.

Maybe Abbie wouldn't leave Kingston, and maybe he had no choice but to return to his ranch, but that didn't mean they couldn't get together every now and then. They just wouldn't be together all the time like most married couples. But when they did, it would be special. Heck, he could live with that.

Couldn't he?

He didn't have time to answer his own question because he heard Beans's squeaky bark several moments before he saw Gussie traipsing through the woods toward him.

"Don't shoot," she called out. "It's just me."

"I can see that. What brings you out here?"

"Things." She picked up a peach from the ground, wiped it on her overalls, and stuffed it into her pocket.

"What kind of things?"

Gussie stopped and stared at him. "I'm gonna do something Victoria said I couldn't ever do."

That didn't sound good, not at all. "Then are you sure you want to do it? I wouldn't want you to get in trouble with Victoria."

"I'm pretty sure I want to. Pretty sure I hafta do it. I'll just get into trouble later, I guess."

"What is it exactly that you think you have to do?" he asked hesitantly.

She frowned. "I'm gonna tattle."

Rio wasn't about to breathe easier yet. This could cover a lot of territory. Maybe more lies that Abbie had told. Maybe something worse. He hated that his good mood would probably soon be spoiled. "What are you going to tattle about?"

"Well, I was listening to Abbie talk to Victoria about you."

"What about me?"

"About how much she loves you and all."

She had talked about loving him? Rio leaned against

the cabin and let it support him. Just in time. His legs nearly gave way. "You're sure she said that?"

"Sure I'm sure. I was real close. Close enough I could see the twinkle in her eye. That's what Miss Ina calls it anyway. She said you put a twinkle in Abbie's eye. What exactly is a twinkle, anyway?"

Something better than he could have ever hoped for.

Something that changed everything.

Rio didn't know whether to climb on the roof and shout for joy or pound his head against the wall. Right now, he leaned more toward shouting for joy. Abbie was in love with him! He'd deal with the other side of that coin later.

"There's more," Gussie said, tugging on his sleeve. "And you're not gonna like this part at all."

"What?"

"When Abbie finished her talk with Victoria, guess what? That man, Julian, stepped out, and he grabbed her real hard and made her get in the buggy with him. I heard him say he was gonna take her to the bank where's she's gonna have to get him lots and lots of money. He had a gun."

That hit Rio like a punch. "A gun?"

Gussie nodded. "I was gonna help Abbie then, but Victoria saw me hiding in the bushes, and she shook her head real meanlike. I think she was saying she didn't want me to help her or anything. I was gonna tell Ina, but then I peeked in through the window of her bedroom, and I saw Camellia holding a gun on her. That's when I decided I'd better come and talk to you. I'll probably get in trouble for listening to stuff I shouldn'ta been listening to."

Rio didn't even take the time to assure her that she'd done the right thing. He grabbed his revolver. "Where's Juan?"

"He's tied to a chair. Camellia's holding a gun on him,

too. I don't think she could hit a bull's backside with a handful of banjos, but you never can tell. She might get lucky."

God, he hoped not. For once, he needed luck on his side. Abbie's life might depend on it. "Stay here, and don't leave this cabin." Rio bolted out of the door and started up the path.

"Where you going?" Gussie called out.

"To find Abbie." He hoped.

Hell. How could he have let something like this happen? He should have expected Julian would do something this low-down and dirty. He should have been protecting Abbie instead of standing around and thinking about her.

Now, he not only had her to worry about but Victoria and Ina as well. He hoped Camellia didn't do anything stupid. If he could just get Abbie away from Julian, then he could come back and take care of Camellia. That was a lot of if.

Rio prayed it wasn't too late.

Chapter Twenty-three

Abbie supposed that anyone watching them wouldn't even see the derringer that Julian had jammed against her ribs. The gun was so small, and the shawl he'd draped around her pretty much hid it and his hand.

Still, she could hope that someone would be suspicious that her brother-in-law had his arm around her.

"Mrs. McCaine is here to make a withdrawal," Julian told the bank teller.

The teller, Ben Weimer, smiled, revealing a spacious gap between his front teeth. "Well, good afternoon, Mrs. McCaine. Always good to see you. I don't recall you wearing a dress in the middle of the week before. Is this some kind of special occasion? Nobody died, did they?"

Abbie nearly groaned. Julian was holding a gun on her, and the only thing Ben could notice was her clothes? She tried to give an odd arch to her eyebrow. Then she tried tipping her head toward Julian. Ben didn't seem to notice either gesture. He just kept that silly grin on his face.

"Mrs. McCaine and my brother are about to leave on their wedding trip," Julian calmly provided.

Ben's grin grew even wider. "A wedding trip. That'll be nice. The wife and me went to Houston right after we wed."

Julian cleared his throat to interrupt. "Mrs. McCaine would love to stay and chat, but she's in a bit of a hurry. Her husband is anxiously awaiting her return to Kingston."

"Oh, sure. How much would you like to withdraw?"

Julian spoke for her. And ground the derringer harder against her ribs. "Well, you see my sister-in-law needs a rather large sum for traveling expenses because the wedding trip will be a long one. She'd like to withdraw as much as you have in the safe."

Suddenly there was some concern on Ben's face. He swallowed, sending his Adam's apple into a bobble. "As much as we have?"

Ben glanced around as if seeking someone else's advice, but he was the only one in the bank. That didn't surprise Abbie. The bank was within fifteen minutes of closing, and she was sure Julian had planned it that way.

Ben scratched his head and walked toward the safe. "Well, I can give you two thousand, I guess. Any more than that, and I'd have to get Mr. Peterson, the bank manager, back down here. He's already left for the day, and he wouldn't be none too happy about coming back. Of course, he probably wouldn't get that mad since it's you, Mrs. McCaine."

"The two thousand will be fine," Julian assured him. "You can put it in this." He handed the teller a tapestry bag.

Ben took it and soon returned with money. "You have a nice wedding trip, Mrs. McCaine. All of us in town are looking forward to meeting your husband."

Abbie only nodded, but Julian even cut that short. He said a farewell to Ben and hurried her out of there. Wasting no time, he forced her into the buggy and pulled away from the bank.

As they made their way down the street, Abbie looked around to see if she could alert anyone to her predicament. The two people that she did see just waved at her and called out hello. One commented on her pretty dress.

She very much wanted to shoot that person in the foot.

All right. Since it seemed as if Julian might actually get away with robbing her blind, Abbie came up with a plan. It wasn't a good one, but nonetheless it was a plan.

The bag of money that she'd just withdrawn from the bank was underneath the buggy seat. Julian had it anchored between his feet. If she were to kick the bag, it might just throw him off enough so she could wrestle that derringer away from him. She might could even push him out of the buggy.

He might just shoot her, too. But that was a chance she had to take.

Camellia was holding a gun on Victoria. Abbie could pretty much figure out what would happen once they all got back to Kingston. Julian and Camellia would try to leave with the money, but they might not want to keep any witnesses. That meant Victoria and the others were in danger. If she could somehow stop Julian now, then maybe only he would get hurt. And Camellia, of course.

Abbie was looking forward to hurting her.

"Don't even think about it," Julian said confidently.

Abbie scowled at him and at his satisfied expression. He'd had that smirk since they left the bank with her two thousand dollars, and Abbie wanted to wipe it off his face. "Don't think about what?"

"Doing something stupid."

"Too late. I've already done something stupid. I didn't shoot you weeks ago when you stepped foot inside Kingston. That's the biggest mistake I've ever made."

He smiled and snapped the reins to get the buggy horse

moving faster. Abbie didn't know how the horse could possibly go faster on the muddy gravel road. If Julian kept this up, he just might send them into a ditch.

"You didn't shoot me because underneath all that rattle and horns, you're a very trusting person," Julian explained.

"Trust had nothing to do with it. I thought maybe you'd marry Camellia and take her off my hands."

He laughed. And since her remark seemed to have amused him, Abbie decided it was time to try her luck at kicking that money bag. Lord, why had she worn a dress today of all days? Slowly and trying to be inconspicuous, Abbie began to gather up the dress fabric so she could free her foot.

Julian shook his head and slapped a hand onto her knee. "Remember what I told you about doing something stupid? If we're not back at Kingston with the money in half an hour, then Camellia will set the place on fire."

Abbie's mouth dropped open. "What? You're going to burn the place down?"

"A man does what a man must, and I'd prefer to leave Kingston standing. But I won't if you don't cooperate. I shouldn't have to remind you that Victoria's in the house as well as Ina and Juan."

But not Rio or Gussie. God, where were they?

She hoped Gussie was hiding and would stay hidden until it was safe. Maybe the sheriff had already come to arrest Rio. And maybe he'd managed to escape. Maybe Rio had already made it to the house to rescue Victoria and the rest.

Abbie tried to hold on to that notion. She hadn't been able to protect them, but maybe Rio already had everything under control. For once she wouldn't care if someone else's plan worked. After all, hers had failed, and she'd put the people she loved in danger.

Now, she just wanted everyone safe.

*   *   *

Rio positioned himself behind a cluster of cedars just off the road that led to Kingston. When Julian rode by with Abbie, he fully intended to shoot his brother right out of the carriage. How dare that sonofabitch take her!

Julian didn't know it yet, but it was the biggest mistake he'd ever made, even bigger than trying to steal the ranch from him. Rio didn't intend to let this go unpunished. He'd get Abbie back, and Julian better not have harmed one red hair on her head. He wouldn't let himself think beyond that. Abbie would be all right. She just had to be all right.

"Drop that gun, McCaine."

At the gruffly shouted command, Rio stiffened and slowly turned around. He'd been so occupied with his thoughts, he hadn't heard anyone come up behind him. Stupid. Really stupid. He'd never be able to save Abbie if he kept doing such stupid things.

It wasn't Julian, and Rio didn't recognize the man. "Who are you?"

"Sheriff Clayton Knight." He walked closer, his Peacemaker revolver aimed right at Rio's chest. "Drop your gun and put your hands up in the air."

Rio wasn't about to drop anything, especially his gun. Any minute now he would need it to stop Julian. "What do you want?"

"You. You're wanted for questioning about some Apache raids over near Rocksprings."

"Raids? You've made a mistake. Until a couple of weeks ago, I was a negotiator with the Department of the Interior. I was trying to stop those raids, and I damn sure didn't take part in them. Hell, I'm not even Apache."

"I got a telegram that says different."

"And who sent this telegram?" Rio demanded.

"The sheriff over in Rocksprings."

Rio cursed under his breath. He'd bet his last dollar

that no lawman had sent the telegram. This was probably another part of Julian's plan to get him out of the way while he robbed Abbie. "You're making a mistake. You have the wrong man."

"So you say. If you're telling the truth, we'll soon have it all cleared up. Just drop the gun and come with me."

"I don't have time for you to clear it up. Julian's taken Abbie, and Camellia's holding a gun on Victoria back at Kingston. Instead of arresting me, you should be trying to save them."

The lawman only shook his head and motioned for Rio to drop his gun. "That's not true. Your brother and Miss Barnwell left town yesterday afternoon."

Every muscle in Rio's jaw tightened. "Well, they obviously came back, and I don't have time to stand around and convince you otherwise. My wife, her sister, Ina, and Juan are in danger."

There was some movement in the bushes behind the sheriff. Wendell Calverson stepped out, and before Rio could say anything, the man had clubbed Sheriff Knight over the head. The lawman crumpled into a heap on the grass.

"I didn't figure you had time to stand around discussing things with a man hell bent on not listening," Wendell said confidently. "Your brother's buggy's about to come over that rise."

"He has Abbie."

"I know. I saw her riding out of town with him. I knew Abbie wouldn't get in the same buggy with Julian unless he had a gun on her. I would have taken out Julian then, but he rode away before I could do anything. I figured I'd ride out here and cut them off . . . then I saw you and the sheriff."

"I had the same idea." And time was running out. Even though Rio couldn't see the buggy yet, he could hear its horse picking his way through the mud. He needed to get back in position so he could take aim at Julian. "Let me take care of my brother, and you go back to Kingston to see what you can do about Camellia. She's holding on a gun on Victoria and the others."

Wendell scratched his head and made a sound as if he was giving that some thought. "I'll tell you what. I'll help you on one condition. You'll have to give up Abbie."

Rio was sure he'd misunderstood. "What?"

"All you have to do is agree to ride out of here when this is over, and I'll give you all the help you need."

Rio nearly punched the man out right there. "Go to hell."

Wendell shrugged. "I was just checking."

"Just checking on what?" Rio snarled. "How short my temper is right now?"

"Nope. Just checking to make sure you're really in love with Abbie."

"What! What the hell are you talking—"

Wendell cut him off in mid-howl. "You're in love with her, all right, and it won't do any good to deny it. I just don't know whether to pity you or congratulate you. Guess I'll have to decide later. At least I'm not losing her to someone who doesn't care for her. Now, get on over there so you can stop Julian. It should really get Abbie's goat when you have to save her. She hates it when she can't do something for herself."

She did. But Rio didn't intend to let that stop him. When that buggy came over the rise, he would do whatever it took to save her.

Abbie could just get mad about it later.

Abbie was so mad she could hardly see straight. She decided she'd punch Julian and then bite him as hard as she could.

In her opinion, biting wasn't really a fair way to fight, but this wasn't a fair situation, and she'd already wasted enough time. Here they were, practically at Kingston, and she hadn't figured out how to get away from him.

Julian had told her if they didn't arrive at Kingston with the money in a half hour, then Camellia would burn down the place. Abbie didn't know if Camellia would actually do that or not, but it was a risk she couldn't take. Not with the others inside. When she managed to overpower Julian, she'd have to hurry back to Kingston. Then she'd somehow overpower Camellia before the woman could do anyone any harm.

That seemed like a lot of overpowering, but she didn't have a choice.

"You might want to keep your urges in check just a little while longer," Julian mumbled.

"And what urges are you talking about?"

"The urges to escape. It won't do your bastard sister any good if you don't cooperate."

"My bastard sister?" That was the wrong thing to say, the *wrong* thing to say.

Abbie balled up her fist and drew back her hand, fully intending to wallop Julian into another county. She swung at him and connected with his jaw just as he grabbed her arm.

A loud cracking noise tore past her head.

For one stunned moment, Abbie thought Julian had shot her. He hadn't, but someone had fired.

Julian latched onto her hair, pulling excruciatingly hard, and roughly twisted her body until she was between him and the shooter. "Quit fighting me, or I'll shoot you myself," he warned.

Abbie called him a name, one that questioned his paternity and sexual habits in the same breath.

Julian shoved his gun against her chest and shouted. "Rio, if that's you, then you'd better back off. I've already got the money so I have no real need to keep your bride alive."

293

Abbie didn't know whether to hope it was Rio or not. She didn't want him in danger, but she didn't want to die either.

"Step out where I can see you, Rio. Now!" Julian ordered.

Abbie didn't expect Rio to do that, so it surprised her greatly when he did. Actually, what he did stunned her. She saw his rifle fall to the ground only moments before she saw him step out from behind the cluster of cedars. Taking careful, silent steps he walked closer, his hands tucked behind his head.

Surrendering.

Damn it. He's surrendering?

For some reason she'd thought Rio might be able to save her, to save them both. Or she hoped he could at least buy them some time so she could figure out what to do. But he hadn't even done that. Instead, Rio had surrendered to a man who had a gun against her chest.

"I want you to let Abbie go," Rio said calmly.

Julian chuckled, his chest shaking against her back. "Save your breath, little brother. Here's what we're going to do. You'll walk ahead of the buggy until we get to Kingston. I'll tie you two up, and Camellia and I can get away. By now, she should have collected enough valuables to make our journey easier."

"Valuables?" Abbie repeated. "You're ransacking the place?" Julian only poked her harder with the gun.

Abbie's gaze connected with Rio's. There was a slight lift in his right eyebrow. The corner of his mouth was slightly askew. For the first time, she recognized something in his eyes. Exactly *what,* she couldn't say, but he was definitely trying to communicate with those subtle gestures.

In a move that seemed at a speed not humanly possible, Rio's left hand came from behind his head. He whipped out another gun he'd hidden. Something small.

The sunlight licked the silvery metal and sent a flash across Abbie's face. And he aimed it directly at her.

Abbie had no time to think, no time to react. She briefly, very briefly, considered that Rio and his gun would be the last things she would ever see. He pulled the trigger, the shot cracking like an enormous firecracker. Abbie waited for the pain or numbness to follow what was certainly a fatal head wound.

That didn't happen.

Instead, Julian howled in pain and clutched his right shoulder where Rio had shot him. His derringer clattered to the floor of the buggy. Abbie quickly retrieved the gun and jumped down. She kept her eyes on Rio, afraid to blink for fear he'd disappear before she could get to him. Reaching him, she soon learned, wasn't even necessary. He made it to her in one step. She grabbed him and held on for dear life.

"You came," she managed to say.

"Of course I did." He kept his gun aimed at his brother but curved his other arm around her. "And don't give me an argument about rescuing you."

"I won't." It hadn't even crossed her mind. What had was how close that bullet had come to hitting her. "I was afraid you'd shoot me."

Rio slightly rearranged his expression, apparently insulted with her lack of faith in his marksmanship. "Those were instinct shots. I wouldn't have missed. Not ever."

Abbie didn't know what instinct shots were but prayed she would never have to put him to the test again to see if they were always as accurate as he claimed.

"We'll tie up Julian," Rio explained. "But we have to get back to Kingston. Camellia's holding Victoria."

"I know."

"With any luck Wendell will have things under control before we get there."

"Wendell?"

Rio didn't answer her. He climbed into the buggy, yanked off Julian's coat, and removed his suspenders. "Get up here and get this buggy moving," he told Abbie.

She quickly did as he said while Rio tied up Julian.

"Did you see Victoria?" Abbie asked. "Is she all right?"

"I don't know. Gussie's the one who came out to the cabin and told me. I told her to stay put, then I came after you."

And thank God he had. "You don't think we'll be too late, do you?"

"I don't . . . hell."

"What's wrong now?"

Rio pointed to the black coil of smoke rising in the sky. Abbie didn't give herself time to say anything. She snapped the reins and raced toward Kingston.

Chapter Twenty-four

Rio didn't like the looks of that fire. By the time he stopped the buggy in front of Kingston, orangy flames lapped from the boathouse's windows, and worse, no one was in sight. He didn't even see Wendell, though the man should have had plenty of time to get there.

"Victoria!" Abbie called out.

But Rio knew if anyone was in that house, their chances for survival were decreasing by the minute. He had to go in and get them out. "Wait here."

She didn't, of course. Abbie was right behind him as he ran toward the veranda. He stopped on the steps and looked down at her. "You have to wait here," he insisted. "You can't go in there. It's too dangerous."

"I have to go. Victoria—"

"I'll get her. And the others." Well, he'd try anyway. Something had to go his way today, and it just might as well be this. He knew how important Abbie's family was to her. Heck, they were important to him too.

Rio picked one of the doors where there seemed to be less smoke and kicked it open. No actual flames, but there was plenty of heat. Pig shot out between his legs and ran into the yard.

"One down. Four to go."

When Rio took a step inside, he realized Abbie was right on his heels. He reeled toward her and forced her back onto the porch. "Listen, I don't have time to argue with you, but you aren't going in there. You could be killed."

"So could you," she pointed out.

True. But he wasn't about to risk her life. He had to come up with something to keep her away from those flames. One glance at the buggy, and he thought he had the perfect solution. "Go back to the buggy and keep an eye on Julian. I don't want him to escape."

"But—"

"No buts. If he escapes, he'll hold us all hostage when we come out of the house."

She nodded. Finally. But he could tell she wasn't delighted with the order. She turned and started toward the buggy. "Please, be careful. I love you, Rio."

The woman had certainly picked a lousy time to tell him that. He didn't answer. He could tell her how he felt later—if there was a later. He'd never thought of himself as crazy, never thought of himself as overly devoted to anyone, but here he was ready to run into a burning house to save people he hardly knew.

He was about to call out Victoria's name again when he heard her calling out his. And she hadn't called out from inside the house.

"Don't go in there!" Victoria shouted. "We're over here."

Rio batted away the smoke and finally saw her. Victoria was quickly making her way across the side yard.

Ina and Juan were behind her, and they were holding on to each other.

Abbie left the buggy and ran toward her sister and the others. "You're safe. You're all safe." She gave frantic hugs to everyone. "We thought you were all still inside. How did you get out?"

Victoria tore herself out of Abbie's fierce grip. Rio figured it was probably so she could draw some breath. Abbie had seemed to be squeezing the life out of her sister. "We got out as soon as the fire started. Camellia hadn't tied me up, so when she ran, I freed Juan and Ina. We hid in the smokehouse."

"Are you all right?" Rio asked Victoria. He wiped a big smear of soot off her cheek.

"I think so. But Camellia got away."

Lord. If Camellia got away that meant she could double back and help Julian escape.

Victoria glanced around the yard. "I've been worried sick about Gussie. Is she with you?"

"She's at the cabin." But the moment Rio said that he realized it was probably the first place Camellia would go. She would just exchange one set of hostages for another. And this time she'd have a child.

Abbie caught his arm, and he could see the alarm in her eyes. "Are you thinking what I'm thinking?"

"I'll go after her," he assured her. "Stay here, and use the gun if Julian tries anything."

"Nobody has to go after me."

Rio looked around at the sound of Gussie's voice, and he finally saw the little girl hurry up the path behind the barn. And she wasn't alone. She had Camellia and Wendell with her.

Abbie ran to her immediately. "My God, Gussie, what happened?"

Gussie shrugged. "Camellia thought she was gonna take me. But I took care of it all on my own without anybody's help. Mr. Calverson didn't even get there until it was all over."

Rio looked at Camellia. She didn't look as if she'd had an easy time of it. There was a huge knot in the middle of her forehead, and her blond hair hung in strings around her face. Some of the ends were singed. Someone, Wendell probably, had a rope tied securely around the woman's hands.

"How did you capture her?" Victoria asked frantically. Like Abbie, she checked Gussie for any signs of injury. The little girl seemed completely unharmed.

"Easy. I beaned her right between the eyes with a peach I had in my pocket. Abbie taught me how to throw 'em. And that peach was green and real, real hard."

"I thought she hit me with a rock. Felt like it anyway." Camellia gave them all hell-freezing looks. "Where's Julian?" she snarled. "He was supposed to help me."

Nearby, Julian groaned, and even though he was still trussed with his suspenders, he lifted his head so Camellia could see him. "Rio shot me."

"Oh, poor baby," Camellia said caustically. "As if I care. That brat knocked me upside the head. I'm still seeing double."

Julian returned her caustic tone and added some venom of his own. "Why the hell did you set the place on fire?"

"I didn't set it on fire. That damn cat clawed me, and I accidentally knocked over the lamp. I hate that thing."

Rio didn't care much for Pig either, but he wanted to reward the cat for attacking Camellia. Though that scratch had caused the fire. Abbie and the others would certainly lose their home, and there was nothing he could do to stop it.

Wendell caught Camellia's arm. "Juan, why don't you ride with me into town? The sheriff should have come to by now, and I think I can help him clear all of this up. The jail's empty so there should be plenty of room for these two."

With Juan on one side of her and Wendell on the other, they hauled Camellia to the buggy. She didn't go easily, but Wendell finally dumped her unceremoniously onto the floor next to Julian.

Gussie tugged on Rio's sleeve as the buggy pulled away. "Will Camellia go to jail?"

"Absolutely."

"Good. I hope they lock her up and throw away the key. I swallowed a key once. A little bitty one. It was for the desk where Mr. Donegan kept all his important papers. Maybe I could swallow the one for the jail, too."

"No!" Victoria, Abbie, and Ina all said in unison.

Obviously that hadn't been a pleasant experience, so Rio didn't ask about it.

Gussie pulled a cloth bag out from her overalls. "I took this from Camellia when she was out cold. It's Abbie's mother's jewelry. Camellia was gonna steal it and sell it."

Abbie and Victoria hugged the child again, and Gussie beamed from the attention. When the hugs finally seemed to be over, Gussie looked up at Rio again. "Did you have time to ask Abbie about what put that twinkle in her eye?" she asked, then winked. Or tried to. It took Rio a moment to figure out what the girl was trying to do.

"Not yet." But Abbie had told him that she loved him. Of course, she'd said that because she thought he was about to go into the fire. Maybe she'd said that without thinking it through. Maybe she didn't--

Before he knew what was happening, Abbie launched herself into his arms. She pressed a flurry of kisses over his face. "Oh, Rio. You saved my life. You rescued me from Julian."

"And you let him?" Victoria asked hesitantly.

Abbie slanted her a scolding look. "Of course, I let

301

him. There's nothing wrong with Rio saving my life every now and then. After all, he is my husband. If the opportunity ever arises, I will save him."

Victoria shook her head. "Well, let's pray the time won't come anytime soon."

"Awwww," Gussie complained. "We gotta pray now? I thought we wouldn't have to. I mean, I got Camellia, and Rio saved Abbie, and the house is burning down anyway. Praying's not gonna do anything to stop that."

Rio had almost forgotten about the fire. The house would certainly be destroyed.

He tightened his grip on Abbie. Rio only hoped she didn't start crying.

Abbie stared at the heap of cinders and ash, all that was left of Kingston. Coils of smoke were still rising, but the flames were quickly dying out. When they did die out, there would be nothing left except the barn and the smokehouse.

Rio gently kissed her cheek. "I'm sorry about your home."

She shrugged and pushed out a hard breath. "Oh, well. It couldn't be helped, I suppose. I really didn't like that house anyway."

"Neither did I," Gussie readily agreed. "People aren't supposed to live in boats. Maybe now we can get a real house. One without red walls all over the place."

Victoria wiped away some soot from her face and nodded in agreement. "Maybe one that doesn't feel like you're living in a hotel."

Rio looked at them. "But your home—"

"It was just a place," Abbie interrupted. "Some wood and glass. And not very pretty wood and glass either. Besides, now I really don't have to worry about keeping my promise to our father. Even after Camellia gets out of jail, she couldn't possibly stay at Kingston because it no longer exists. And she burned it down. I don't know why I didn't think of that sooner. If I'd just burned the place to the ground, I wouldn't have had to do all that scheming."

"And you wouldn't have married Rio," Victoria quickly pointed out.

"Well, that's one good thing that came out of the scheming."

Rio made a sound of agreement. "But that doesn't mean I want any more schemes or lies."

She thought about it, then nodded. "No more."

Gussie obviously didn't put much faith in Abbie's promise. "Make her swear on a Bible or something."

Abbie frowned at Gussie's suggestion, and because she wanted some privacy, she took Rio by the arm and led him away from the others. "I am sorry, you know, for saddling you with this whole mess."

He gave her an odd look, a twinkle in his eye. "Well, I'm only sorry about parts of it. There are some parts that I'm actually glad about." He paused and took a deep breath, suddenly somber. "But I do have to apologize to you."

"About what?" Abbie couldn't think of a thing. He had saved her life, he'd stopped Julian, and most importantly, he was here with her. She didn't know how things could be more perfect.

"I might have made you pregnant. Have you thought of that?"

"Oh, that. Yes, I have."

He swore under his breath. "I can't believe I didn't do anything to protect you. I should have remembered."

"Don't beat yourself up. I didn't even remember my name when we were in that cabin, so I certainly don't blame you for forgetting the preventative. Besides, I lied about ordering them. There probably wasn't one of those things anywhere around here."

"But a baby——"

"It'll be all right. Don't you see?" Her expression brightened. "I love you, so everything will be all right."

Rio shook his head. "No, I don't see. I love you too, but that doesn't change the fact you could be pregnant. You——"

Her hand whipped out to stop him from finishing. "Wait a minute. Go back to that part before you said it doesn't change the fact I could be pregnant."

"You mean the part about loving you?"

She nodded. Definitely that part. She wanted to hear him say that a thousand times. "Do you really love me?"

He looked at her and smiled. Abbie saw a twinkle in his eye. "I really, really love you."

Abbie smiled too. But she wanted to verify something before she got too happy. "Do you think it might be the forever kind of love, or is this just the kind where you want to see me every now and then?"

"It's the forever kind." He ran his thumb over her bottom lip. "Now you go back to the part where you said you love me."

"I do love you," she quickly assured him. "I love you. I love you. I love you. And it's definitely the forever kind."

She stood up on her toes and kissed him. She'd meant it to be short and sweet so they could talk some more about how much they loved each other, however, her mouth had a different idea. So did her hands. She clamped on to Rio and drew him against her.

Apparently his mouth had the same idea as hers, since the kiss soon got out of hand. Breathless, she pulled away from him though she didn't want to. It felt so good to be in his arms, to touch him.

"Would you consider coming to the McCaine ranch with me?" he asked.

She smiled. She'd more than considered it. She would

leave right now if that's what he wanted her to do. Still, she wanted to make sure they were on the same buggy seat here. "Exactly what would be your intentions if I do that?"

"My intentions?" He grinned. The expression was naughty and slightly crude. He started to play with a lock of her hair that had fallen over her breast, and he didn't confine his touch to her hair. "To strip off all your clothes and kiss every inch of you. To have you in my bed every night."

As intentions went, those were pretty good ones. She wouldn't mind returning those intentions. And she thought she wouldn't mind returning them right now. "Are you sure you want me at your ranch?"

"I'm sure I don't want you anywhere but with me. Same goes for your sisters, and for Ina and Juan. We can all go to the ranch, and you can run your father's business from there. I already checked with that lawyer, and he said you could do it that way."

The intentions got better and better. And his grin got more and more naughty. She worked her fingers into the little gap between his shirt buttons so she could touch his chest. "You think we could go to the cabin and, well, celebrate?"

"Now?" The grin faded, and he glanced back at the others. "But what about them?"

She cupped her hands around her mouth. "Rio and I have something to discuss. All of you go into town and check into the hotel. We'll meet you there after we've finished, uh, talking."

"Hotel?" Gussie questioned. "I don't wanta go to no stinkin' hotel. I thought we'd go back with Rio to his ranch."

"You will," Rio assured her. "We'll leave first thing in the morning."

Gussie started to jump up and down, and she clapped

her hands. Abbie didn't want to stay around and celebrate with her sisters, not yet anyway. There'd be plenty of time for that later.

She grabbed Rio by the arm and started down the path toward the cabin. They made it about halfway before they started kissing again. All in all, that slowed down the journey considerably. Rio's mouth on hers had a way of bringing all other activities to a complete halt.

Abbie finally gave up and just concentrated on the kissing. And unbuttoning his shirt. She finally gave up on that, too, and tore it off him. When she felt his warm male skin, she knew she was lost. She wanted more, and she wanted it right away.

"We'll never make it to the cabin," she let him know.

He nodded, keeping his eyes on hers, and while they were still face to face, he picked her up. Abbie did what felt natural and wrapped her legs around him. It surprised her a little when Rio backed her against a tree. It surprised her even more when he bunched up her skirt and started to free himself from his jeans.

"We can do it like this?" she asked, stunned.

"We can do it any way we want. Like I said, there are no rules."

Abbie wrapped her legs even tighter around him and kissed his neck. "I like this lovemaking stuff. No rules. Finally, something in life that makes sense."

He tore the center seam of her pantalets. She liked the frenzy. The hurried touches, and the equally hurried kisses. She also liked that if she tilted her hips forward, she could feel the aroused part of him touch the aroused part of her. And he was ready to go.

Rio stopped and looked at her. "This probably isn't a good time to mention that we still don't have those preventatives."

"No, it isn't a good time." She thrust her hips against his and took him inside her. "Don't worry, Rio. Weren't you listening? We're in love. Nothing bad can come from that." But there was certainly a lot of good that could come from it. "Do that touching thing with your fingers so my bullet fires."

Thankfully, he seemed to know exactly what she meant. Abbie didn't know if she could explain it any better. Especially now. She started to push against him pretty hard, and Rio pushed right back.

"Maybe I won't have to use my fingers this time." He adjusted his position and pressed against the spot, not with his finger, but with him.

"Oh. Yes."

Rio was right. And so was she. They were in love, and nothing bad come could from that.

Epilogue

"Rio, is Abbie gonna die?" Gussie asked.

"Gussie!" Victoria snapped. "Will you stop asking that?"

Harmony echoed her. Ina scolded the child in Spanish. Dorrie only frowned at the child.

The little girl rolled her eyes. "I know. I gotta go say my prayers. But I just want to know if Abbie's gonna die, that's all. Nobody ever tells me anything around here. That's why I have to keep asking. 'Cause I really want to know if Abbie's gonna die."

Rio wanted to know the same thing. He also wanted to shoot himself. How the hell had he let this happen? One by one, he looked at the faces of the Donegan women—Victoria, Gussie, Harmony, and Dorrie. Their gazes weren't condemning, not even Ina's, but they sure as hell should have been. After all, he was responsible for putting Abbie in danger.

Dorrie patted Gussie on the head and gave Rio a reassuring smile. "Everything will be fine. This is in the Lord's hands now."

Dorrie was right: He damn sure couldn't do anything to save Abbie now. But nine months ago, if he'd just kept on his jeans . . . if he'd just waited until they had those preventatives. If he hadn't taken her against that tree.

"When do you think Chey will be here?" Gussie asked no one in particular.

"Soon," Victoria replied.

Rio wasn't sure he could face his brother-in-law. Chey and he had become friends since Abbie's move to the ranch, but he didn't think Chey would be pleased that he'd endangered his sister.

"It might take Juan a while to find him," Harmony explained to Gussie.

"But will he make it here before Abbie . . ." the child wanted to know.

The women all started to scold Gussie again.

There was a kittenish wail, and everyone in the room suddenly went silent. The wail stopped just as quickly as it'd started. Moments passed. Slowly. Rio pressed his hands to the sides of his head and squeezed.

"Hellfire, I can't take anymore of this." He stormed toward the bedroom door and threw it open. Unfortunately, he nearly smacked the doctor right in the face.

"Don't know why you called me out here for this," the man growled. "It's freezing cold outside, and you got me up in the middle of the night for nothing."

"Is Abbie dead?" Gussie asked.

The doctor twisted his face into a grumpy scowl. "Dead? No. Why would you think something like that? This was the easiest delivery I've ever done. The baby was out before I even got my gloves off. There wasn't any need for me to be here."

Rio looked over the doctor's shoulder to see for himself. Abbie looked worn out, even a little frazzled, but very much alive. She was sitting up and holding a bundle in her arms. "But the baby quit crying," he said to the doctor.

"Not because anything's wrong. Because Abilene's nursing."

Rio stepped around the doctor and cautiously walked to the bed. Abbie looked up at him and smiled. "Oh, Rio, come see. We have a little girl."

Rio couldn't look at the baby yet. His hands shook, and his eyes wouldn't focus. "You scared me to death. I thought you were going to die."

She shrugged. "It did hurt. A lot. But the pain went away as soon as I saw her."

Rio didn't think the pain would ever go away for him. He'd certainly never forget it. "I swear I'll never touch you again. We won't even sleep in the same bed. I swear it. No kiss—"

She caught his hand and pulled him closer to her. "What are you talking about? Of course, we'll sleep in the same bed. Where else would you sleep?" Abbie babbled several nonsensical sounds to the baby. "Isn't she beautiful?"

The baby needed absolutely no encouragement to latch onto Abbie's nipple and suckle. Her tiny mouth made slurping, smacking sounds.

Abbie laughed.

Rio looked at her as if she'd lost her mind. How could she laugh after everything that had happened? She might have died. She should be crying and screaming at him for risking her life.

The baby abruptly stopped to listen to her mother's laughter but quickly returned to eating. Abbie continued to fight back soft giggles. "It tickles," she finally said when she noticed him looking at her.

"It tickles?" he flatly repeated. "You mean you aren't

mad at me for putting you through all of this?"

"Mad?" She smiled dreamily and kissed him. "Why would I be mad? You've given me the most wonderful gifts. You. Our baby. We're a family, Rio."

Yes, he could see that side of it. He was happier than he'd even been in his life. Still . . . "You could have died."

Abbie smiled again. "But I didn't."

True, she hadn't. Abbie was very much alive and holding the baby—*their daughter.* Rio moved himself, boots and all, onto the bed next to her. He caressed the damp thin mat of dark brown hair that covered the baby's head.

"She's so little." Rio figured every father before him had said the same thing. Now, he knew it for himself, and it still amazed him that this tiny baby could immediately mean so much to him. So, this was love. Unconditional love. He'd felt it before, of course. For his own mother. For Abbie. And even for Gussie. But somehow, this was stronger, different. It stirred something he hadn't even known was inside him.

The others started to come in, and Rio realized he was the only male in the entire room. The group converged toward the bed, all of them cooing and making baby talk.

"She's kinda ugly," Gussie said.

The others promptly disagreed.

"She's a lovely baby," Victoria declared. "An angel sent straight from heaven."

Dorrie nodded. "And except for the color of her hair, she looks exactly like Abbie's mother, God rest her soul."

"And such a sweet little face," Ina chimed in.

Harmony agreed. "She's a Donegan all right. Look at her eyes. They'll be just like Abbie's."

"Rio's hair though," Victoria added after further inspection. "I think she'll have his mouth too."

He didn't know how he felt about everyone attributing Abbie's and his looks to that tiny face. What he saw when he looked at his daughter was that she was certainly the most beautiful baby that had ever been born.

Apparently unimpressed, Gussie wrinkled her forehead. "She's pink and crinkly if you ask me." She eased closer to the baby and touched her cheek. "But I guess I can still love her a lot no matter how she looks. Will she be my sister?"

"Your niece," Victoria corrected.

"My niece. You mean she'll call me Aunt Gussie like we call Aunt Dorrie?"

Abbie nodded.

"I didn't think I'd even be something as big as an aunt. I think I'll say my prayers tonight without anybody havin' to tell me."

Victoria gave Gussie a nudge toward the door. "That's a wonderful idea. Why don't we all get out of here so Rio and Abbie can spend some time alone with their daughter?"

Rio didn't stop them from leaving. He did want some time alone with his wife and daughter.

When the last of them had filed out of the room, he kissed the baby's cheek. Then he gave Abbie a proper kiss, one fit for a woman who'd just given birth. He kissed her again, this one fit for the wife he knew he'd never be able to resist. All that talk about separate beds didn't make a lot of sense when he was this close to her.

Abbie kissed him and smiled. "She's our first child, but there'll be others."

No doubt. They'd probably have a house full of daughters. Maybe a dozen of them, stubborn, hardheaded Donegan-McCaine women. Troublemakers all. And he would be saddled with taking care of the lot.

Rio grinned.

He was certainly looking forward to it.

KATHLEEN NANCE

THE WARRIOR

Callie Gabriel, a fiercely independent vegetarian chef, manages her own restaurant and stars in a cooking show with a devoted following. Though she knows men only lead to heartache, she can't help wanting to break through Armond Marceux's veneer of casual elegance to the primal desires that lurk beneath.

Armond returns from an undercover FBI assignment a broken man, his memories stolen by the criminal he sought to bring in. His mind can't remember Callie or their night of wild lovemaking, but his body can never forget the feel of her curves against him. And even though Callie insists she doesn't need him, Armond needs her—for she is the key to stirring not only his memories, but also his passions.

___52417-1 $5.99 US/$6.99 CAN

THE PLEASURE MASTER

✦NINA BANGS✦

Stranded by the side of a New York highway on Christmas Eve, hairdresser Kathy Bartlett wishes herself somewhere warm and peaceful with a subservient male at her side. She finds herself transported all right, but to Scotland in 1542 with the last man she would have chosen.

With the face of a dark god or a fallen angel, and the reputation of being able to seduce any woman, Ian Ross is the kind of sexual expert Kathy avoids like the plague. So when she learns that the men in his family are competing to prove their prowess, she sprays hair mousse on his brothers' "love guns" and swears she will never succumb to the explosive attraction she feels for Ian. But as the competition heats up, neither Kathy nor Ian reckon the most powerful aphrodisiac of all: love.

___52445-7 $5.50 US/$6.50 CAN

A Passionate Magic

FLORA SPEER

Sent as an offering of peace between two feuding families, Lady Emma is prepared to perform her wifely duties. But when she first lifts her gaze to the turquoise eyes of her lord, she senses that he is the man she has seen in her most intimate visions. Dain of Penruan has lived an austere life in his Cornish castle on the cliffs, and he doesn't intend to cease doing so, regardless of this arranged marriage to the daughter of his father's hated rival. But though he attempts to disdain Lady Emma, the lusty lord can not ignore her lush curves, or the strange amethyst light sparkling from the depths of her chestnut eyes. Perched upon the precipice of a feeling as mysterious and poignant as silvery moonlight on the sea, Lady and Lord plunge into a love that can only have been conjured by . . . a passionate magic.

___52439-2 $5.50 US/$6.50 CAN

Dorchester Publishing Co., Inc.
P.O. Box 6640
Wayne, PA 19087-8640

Please add $1.75 for shipping and handling for the first book and $.50 for each book thereafter. NY, NYC, and PA residents, please add appropriate sales tax. No cash, stamps, or C.O.D.s. All orders shipped within 6 weeks via postal service book rate. Canadian orders require $2.00 extra postage and must be paid in U.S. dollars through a U.S. banking facility.

Name_____
Address_____
City_____State_____Zip_____
I have enclosed $_____ in payment for the checked book(s).
Payment <u>must</u> accompany all orders. ❑ Please send a free catalog.
CHECK OUT OUR WEBSITE! www.dorchesterpub.com

Aphrodite's Kiss

Julie Kenner

Crazy as it sounds, on her twenty-fifth birthday Zoe has the chance to become a superhero. But x-ray vision and the ability to fly are only two things to consider. There is also her newfound heightened sensitivity. If she can hardly eat a chocolate bar without convulsing in ecstasy, how is she to give herself the birthday gift she's really set her heart on—George Taylor? The handsome P.I.'s dark exterior hides a truly sweet center, and Zoe feels certain that his mere touch will send her spiraling into oblivion. But the man is looking for an average Jane no matter what he claims. He can never love a superhero-to-be—can he? Zoe has to know. With her super powers, she can only see through his clothing; to strip bare the workings of his heart, she'll have to rely on something a little more potent.

___52438-4 $5.99 US/$6.99 CAN

⚜the Mermaid of Penperro
LISA CACH

Konstanze never imagined that singing could land someone in such trouble. The disrepute of the stage is nothing compared to the danger of playing a seductress of the sea— or the reckless abandon she feels while doing so. She has come to Penperro to escape her past, to find anonymity among the people of Cornwall, and her inhibitions melt away as she does. But the Cornish are less simple than she expected, and the role she is forced to play is harder. For one thing, her siren song lures to her not only the agent of the crown she's been paid to perplex, but the smuggler who hired her. And in his strong arms she finds everything she's been missing. Suddenly, Konstanze sees the true peril of her situation—not that of losing her honor, but her heart.

___52437-6 $5.50 US/$6.50 CAN

Alicia's Song
Susan Plunkett

For Alicia James, something is missing. Her childhood romance hadn't ended the way she dreamed, and she is wary of trying again. Still, she finds solace in her sisters and in the fact that her career is inspiring. And together with those sisters, Alicia finds a magic in song that seems almost able to carry away her woes.

In fact, singing carries Alicia away—from her home in modern-day Wyoming to Alaska, a century before her own. There she finds a sexy, dark-haired gentleman with an angelic child just crying out for guidance. And Alicia is everything this pair desperately needs. Suddenly it seems as if life is reaching out and giving Alicia the chance to create a beautiful music she's never been able to make with her sisters—all she needs is the courage to sing her part.

___52434-1 $4.99 US/$5.99 CAN